ON THE BRIGHT ROAD

**Other novels by Paddy Figgis
published by Marion Boyars
as Helen Wykham**

Ribstone Pippins
Cavan
Ottoline Atlantica

as N.P. Figgis

The Fourth Mode

ON THE BRIGHT ROAD

A novel by
Paddy Figgis

Marion Boyars
London ❖ New York

First published in Great Britain and the United States in 1999
by Marion Boyars Publishers
24 Lacy Road, London SW15 1NL
237 East 39th Street, New York NY 10016

Printed 1999
10 9 8 7 6 5 4 3 2 1

Distributed in Australia and New Zealand by Peribo Pty Ltd,
58 Beamount Road, Kuring-gai, NSW 2080

The author acknowledges the award of a bursary from the Arts Council
of Wales.

A CIP catalogue record for this book is available from the British
Library.
A CIP catalog record for this book is available from the Library of
Congress.

ISBN 0-7145-3057-3

Typeset in 11/13pt Garamond by Ann Buchan (Typesetters), Shepperton.
Printed and bound in Great Britain by
WBC Book Manufacturers, Bridgend, Mid Glamorgan.

For Dickon, Ailinor and Thomas who lived with me
on the road from Castlegate to Hengardd

I would like to thank Helen for the weeks of careful and courteous editing

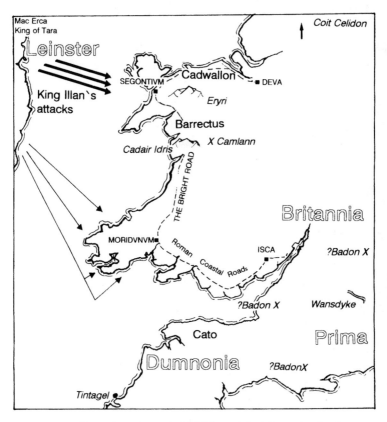

Western Britain circa AD 500, with historical places
and spheres of war-leader influence.

A glossary of names, terms and places can be found
at the back of this book.

Say now little children:
Sweet Jill of our hill hear us
bring slow bones safe at the lode-ford
keep lupa's bite without our wattles
make her bark keep children good
save us all from dux of far folk
save us from the men who plan.
Now sleep on, little children, sleep on now, while I tell
out the greater suffrages, not yet for young heads to understand.

David Jones, 'The Tutelar of the Place'

FIRST

Dangerous to men is the wood of Broceliande.
but those fewer, now as then, who enter
come rarely again with brain unravished
by the power of the place —

— *Charles Williams*, 'The Calling of Taliessin'

Pwyll, Prince of Dyfed . . . sounded the horn and began the chase . . .
and whilst he listened to the hounds he heard the cry of other hounds,
a very different cry from his own and coming in the opposite
direction . . . and of all the hounds that he had seen in the world, he
had never seen any that were like unto those . . . and a horseman
coming towards him . . . with a hunting horn about his neck . . .
'O chieftain,' said he, 'if I have done ill, I will redeem thy friendship . . . but I know not who thou art?' 'Arawn, a King of Annwvyn am
I.' 'Lord,' said he, 'How may I gain thy friendship?' 'There is a man who
is ever warring against me . . . One year from this night,' he answered,
'is the time fixed between him and me, that we should meet at the
Ford; be thou there in my likeness.'

— *'Pwyll, Prince of Dyfed'*, The Mabinogion.

that Grace come
and that the world pass away

—*Fragment of prayer, early Church*

. . . he raised his shaking arm to put his hand on the trunk of the Central Tree. Drips of rain ran in the rills of the bark, curved, twisted, dropped on to lichen and old scars. Not like tears, more like time going on. Just running down the bark of the tree in unstraight courses.

He stood still; alone, as he now perceived it. Close to, the tree was immense. From further off, coming towards it through the wood, it had seemed to be of ordinary size. A tree, tree-sized. But now, now that he was up against it and under its canopy it was beyond all degree or measure. Its great, lyre-shaped branches were the sky, its root-system the ground. Its ancient tap-root had shrunk over the last decades and left a long, dripping tunnel between the natural slabs of the slate bedrock where the tread of his feet on the surface had rung as a distant echo. Heaven and earth and the waters under the earth . . . From where he stood, that made it the Tree of Life: the Central Tree. Because it stood in a small clearing, made for itself in its youth by crowding out younger and weaker saplings and now kept open by the rabbits and the occasional runaway sheep who came to the clearing for the grass, rare in the unmanaged wood, and thus encouraged it to grow — so the great ash tree had gained a visual singularity; a centrality which was vegetative as well as metaphoric.

Its presence awed him. Above, below, before him the tree enveloped him, had its being all around him. He was nothing to the tree, but the tree was everywhere to him. The tree negated him, undid him into a transient shadow, a marginal effect in time which was of no consequence. He was indeed alone. He took his left hand from the bark and held it out into the dim light under the tree's canopy as if to touch a palm with his palm, but there was no other hand to touch his. *Ocha, ocha —*

He put it over his mouth. Against the palm he could feel the curve of his own lips; the warmth of his animal skin; the moistures of his own flesh. It would be quite possible to move his hand and touch the tree, instead. Would he? Would he be any closer to the tree that way? With his hand on it? The thing about his hand, where it was, was that he could also, through his lips and cheeks, feel the hand. If he put the same sensate palm on the tree, what would he feel?

He put his right hand on the trunk. Then the palm that had been against his mouth. He could feel only the tree. Only one thing. Only the bark. Is this all there is? Because the tree did not feel him. He stood there, not giving, not receiving.

Yet he had a sense of immanence; of latent potency. There was a towardness here, somewhere between the skin and the tree bark. The two substances were apressed, no space between them. None whatever. But between them there was a space and across it he said,

'Come closer. Come. I am sick for your coming —'

He had entered the wood looking for giants, for spirits or numinous materialisations. He did not know what it was that he sought except that it would only be found somewhere beyond and far from the City. The ravening mouth of the lion and the horn of the unicorn, the circling of the dog packs and the white bulls were realities which had been expelled from the City with all the mythic men, the croaking, raggy ravens and the horns dimly blowing. If they had been exiled anywhere, it was here that he would he find them.

He had no carnal fears. This business (was he dying?) was not frightening him. Maybe it would, later; but now his model of it was suffused with images picked up from disparate and irrelevant sources. He saw himself beset by counsellors and doctors who were not obliged to tell the truth; who were committed to life and to the evasion of death by the living. He found it, oddly, uninteresting. If the muscular deterioration in his arm was really the onset of some terminal disease, to whom did he want to talk to about it? Himself. Beyond himself, nobody. All around would be bright hope and encouragement and the deceit of optimism. Who would believe that he did not, actually, care that he might be beginning to die, and was not yet frightened of anything except missing out on it?

Death by Natural Causes was a little passé, he thought. Natural Causes were outmoded, no longer 'done'. Hence the giants, the dog-packs and the carrion fowl. Vast and awesome, un-human and therefore uninvolved, dangerous in the most final way. Did he want to take Gemma by the hand and drag her into the forest (what forest?), have his wife torn by thorns, whiplashed and bruised by branches and undergrowth, exhaust her and present her with a Mythic Man in the heart of the wood? He did. He did want to do that. But there was no Mythic Man in the heart of the wood, probably never had been. If he, Cathal, saw the Man he would be hallucinating or fantasizing — the Mythic Man would not be there and so, even if he were there in some way for Cathal, he would not be available as a tutor for Gemma since his very existence would be created out of the language of fiction. And it was out of the fiction of the City and into the verifiable forest that he wanted to drag her. ('I don't think you know the Williams' of Abergavenny, Gemma, or the Realities of Death?' 'How interesting to meet you —')

Not that he would be able to make her come into the wood anyway, let alone awe her. It was the essence of Gemma that he could not awe her, could not even frighten her. It was what she was for; what she had always been for — to close the City gate and keep him in. And to keep out those who live in forests. But now he had contracted gaol-fever, and his left arm shook, and like any captive creature he had come back to the forest to die. He thought, Metaphorically that is right. But Gemma was not a metaphor, she was his wife. She did not behave as a metaphor, or a symbol, and had no names or titles under which he could address her metaphorically or symbolically. They could only converse on an agreed plane of carnality — the one in which his arm was palsied and her salary was almost as much as his.

He had often wondered about frightening her; by saying for example — and only for example — that he wanted to take time out and spend a year on his own in Wales, in their weekend cottage. Or that he wanted to divorce her or talk to a Mythic Man or experience loss. He had wondered, too, about hurting her to the extent of an injury, making her aware of fear — aware of the presence of Death even within the confines of the agreed carnality. It was the stain of old affection, as well as the hangover of twenty-three years of marriage, which had produced that little impulse to share, to bring her along with him.

An impulse of fear. A weakening. Not generosity or affection at all. No. Where Gemma was there would be, if not the actuality, at least the possibility of safety. For twenty-three years she had kept him safe — that was the contract of carnality. There would be no loosing from the flesh in wild flights of nightmare, imagination or bitter discontent; and in return for this promise of stability, as the world saw it, she would provide his mind with weights to hold it down in the 'real world' as the world saw it — inclose him in the safe custody of *civitas populi*. But now that he had the gaol-fever, his 'palsy', he could not keep the contract. One way or another he was loosing or being loosed from his flesh, and in one way Gemma was falling from him like a shed carapace. In that way he was raw, as naked as finger-ends from which the nails have shrivelled. In another way he was coming towards. Adventing. Could Advent presage death or must there be a life between? That was his fear: how, if he were loosed from the flesh, would living kill him? In what other way?

He was aware that he was feeling giddy again. That it had suddenly become cold. That his boot had a leak in it. That an icy fog was there amongst the branches where it had been clear air and gilded, October sunlight. That it might be a good thing to cry and that he would not cry.

He put his hands back on the trunk of the Central Tree, gripped it with his fingers;

'I am sick for your coming —' he shouted.

But the ash tree was old. It had grown here for sixteen and a half decades, fruit of a long line of ash trees which had seeded and rooted and grown and fallen when the time came. Around them alders and wild apples, saplings seeded from wings blown from other parts of the wood, other forests. Hazels, hollies and rowans had grown and fallen, replaced each other, displaced each other, succeeded each other. Sibling ash and incoming ash had, by coincidence, never rooted at a time when the competition was fair; the dynasty had its young on site when the great ashes crashed on to the forest floor and left them air and light in which to grow for another sixteen and a half decades. In a sense, then, it was a tree central to the wood as its ancestors had been central to the forest. Now it was old and the icy mist in its branches sifted through dying limbs. Only the heart of the tree was truly alive, reserved in the core of the great trunk as interlocked chains of cells which had still the exhausted remnants of life in them, should spring come again. It would not seed any more, it was too far gone for that and its final fruits lay in the litter under its creaking boughs, but it had it in its power to put out another season of leaf — small perhaps, and close to the trunk, but fully shaped nonetheless, and green. Should spring come . . . For the man who dug his fingers into its wrinkled bark, it had nothing to spare. It was, itself, *in extremis*.

Cathal, who might also be dying, felt the chill of the river mist in the crown of the Central Tree as if the tree itself were withdrawing from the wood. As if, were he to leave his hands on it for long enough, it would fade out of the wood and of the forest and if he were still gripping it by the bark, that it would take him with it. Not his physicality, but the cold, lonely part of his mind that was shouting at the tree as if it were concealing the Mythic Man from him, although there was no Mythic Man in his thoughts. The feeling that he wanted to cry was strong in him, but he had not wept for many years and neither knew how to make it happen nor why he wanted to do it. He only knew that he was lonely and that he did not want to die so alone; but there was no one in his secular world who would come towards his death with him. He had gone out into the wood in a mood to wrest from it some vital vision or even a bunch of berries to nail to his door in the City as a sign to whoever might be seeking him out, lest they miss each other in the narrow streets — a dark romance to which he had not admitted, even to himself.

Because he could not bear to see her make that tidy, dispossessed emptiness with which she liked to leave the cottage after a weekend, he had told Gemma that he wanted a breath of fresh air before closing himself up in a car for the long drive back. But the air was not fresh; it was dank and odorous with the stink of fungi and fallen leaves and minute, bloated life-forms drowned in the autumn rains. He had been visited by the idea that the car would crash and he be killed and never come back to the wood; that the forest which was the wood's genesis and which was, he felt, there in the wood in some way, was also his genesis and his destination in a way that the flat in St.John's Wood was not; and that if he died in a ruck of searing metal on the M40 he would be cut adrift from both his death and his life. He did not know what he meant by this thought when he articulated it in his mind, but he had come to take

15

something from the wood to hold close as a talisman, should the car kill him tonight.

He had come upon the Central Tree by accident. In all the twelve years since they had bought Castlegate, he had never diverged from the worn trail at this particular place; but now the rains had loosened the soil under a young sycamore and brought it down across the uphill path from the road. He had turned aside to avoid scrambling through its wet foliage and springy branches and caught sight of the great ash through a gap between an alder and a holly. It was so large, so grey, so old a thing — he had hesitated before pushing his way through to come close to it. The sun had been out then, high and golden, striking through the ancient, bare crown, bejewelling the ground with prisms caught in raindrops and silver filigrees spun by spiders from fern fronds to ivy trails. He thought he had come to the forest to where one would be who, shoulder-pommel to shoulder-pommel, would march with him to his death. He had put his hands on the aged bark and said,

'Come, I am sick for your coming.'

He told Gemma when she had her back to him, one hand stretched out to lift the door latch. She stood very still while he spoke. Then she finished the movement and pulled at the door. Caught on a minute pebble, it gave a sickening cry as it scraped on the flagstones. Cathal shrank from the tone in which she would say, 'Don't be ridiculous . . .'

She said, 'Don't be ridiculous,' dragging the screaming door open. 'If you own a flat and a house, and have two cars and a wife with an effective salary, they're not going to give you the dole.'

Cathal tried a laugh. 'I didn't know — I thought you just went to a Job Centre when you were out of work. They give you Social Security, don't they? But if you know more, maybe you could pay me an allowance, then? For housekeeping and upkeep. I could buy food for you at the weekends and call a plumber when the taps leak.'

'For Christ's sake, Cathal, I want to leave now. I don't want all that long drive in the dark.'

'Leave, then. You're ready, aren't you?'

Gemma: 'I've been ready for half an hour. I've been waiting for you for half an hour.'

I said: 'I'm not coming. I'm staying here. If you don't want to drive in the dark, you'll have to go now.'

'Just like that?'

There was a silence.

Then he said, 'Just like that.'

The silence again.

He said, 'I have been trying to tell you for a month. If you chose to disbelieve me, that's made it your problem. I have taken all the holiday due to me in advance, and I'll be paid until around the end of November. After that I will have unpaid leave. There will be no money coming in. I am going to live here at Castlegate.'

She was staring, not at him, but at the vacated room around him. She looked, he thought, rather like a child who has broken something and does not know whether it was precious. Then she said, 'But you can't. You can't stay here.'

He half put out a hand and let it fall again. 'You'll be all right. You'll manage. You know you will. And there's my Life Assurance — you'll be all right, Gemma.'

'What? O, yes. Me. No, it's you, Cathal. It's you that won't be able to manage. You never have. You've never managed anything — not even your daydreams. Half my life is spent trying to fit your — your dopiness — into the realities of life.' And while his mind shouted wildly about the Realities of Death, she grew indomitable and rather beautiful, and at the same time more important than she had seemed to be when he stood in the wood. Important in a diurnal, secular way.

Sick with fear that she would face him directly, he

shouted, 'Gemma, go to London. Go back. I'm not coming. I'm not coming back to London. That's for you, now — all of it. Life, flat — life. I have to stay here. I have to —'

'For what? To dream? To let everything go, so that you can sit around staring at the wall and talking to yourself? How will it feel, Cathal, when there's no one to pull you out of it? No one to put dinner in front of you and explain for the umpteenth time that you're "here" because your parents gave birth to you, and that's the sum of it for you as for everyone else? You've brought no books — not even those ridiculous things about peculiar religions, shamans and Welsh fairy stories or whatever, that you've been brooding over since — come to think of it, since we bought this place. I suppose I ought not to be surprised that it's here that you want to sit and bloody rot. Or are you going to make an attempt to come to terms with the world as it is? As if you and I were ordinary people. Hope would be a fine thing!'

And still they stood, he by the empty grate, she with her hand on the door latch. As if nothing extraordinary had happened; as if at any moment she might say, 'Wake up, dear, the stroganoff's on the table', or slide an invitation to a wedding on top of the page he was reading ('How much should we spend on a present for these two, do you think?'). She did not see that it was time to break her side of the contract. Did not see that its validity was passed. But she had used the word 'ridiculous' and given him the anger of the scorned. Out of a pulse of this familiar, bitter strength he said coldly, 'Come back on Friday, as usual. I'll be here. We'll talk about it then.' And, remembering some of the words he had imagined himself as saying, said them: 'In the meantime, you'll find the correspondence about my leave and all that in the second long drawer of the bureau. I put it there for you to read. That's one of the virtues of the Civil Service — they have a dictum for every contingency.'

'Are you leaving me?'

Now the inside of his head went cold and bright, as if a

New Year's dawn had broken in it. His legs were cold, too, and watery. Now the extraordinary had happened. And it was she who had articulated it. In a moment of terrifying, empty exaltation he felt himself thinking, Is she going to countenance it? Is she going to think of allowing me to leave her? Is she? . . .

Very afraid of how his voice might sound, he said carefully, 'I've left the Records Office and I've left London.'

'Cathal, if I were you —' And she turned to face him.

For the first time ever, he screamed at her, 'But you're not me —'

And for the first time ever, she looked at him with surprise.

'Fuck off, Gemma. Just get in the car and fuck off.' He had never heard his own voice sound so tired.

Then he had been convinced that the car would not start. Gemma had turned the key several times before the engine fired. He had almost thrown up on the side of the road there, waiting for the engine to kick. Unable to face the fiasco of his leaving her and having to call up the AA on a Sunday afternoon to tow his marriage away.

It could easily have turned out like that. However tired he might be now, he would have crumpled under the contempt of a machine which would not work. But Gemma had gone. By now, five hours later, was riding in her (his) car through the outskirts of London. Was skimming along the throughways of Cash-and-Nooky Land, along the streets to the Civitas. Her eyes would have lost their swollen redness already, her voice its unaccustomed shrill. She would have become less beautiful and less important again. He stood in the cottage living room with no cash and no inclination for nooky, all alone.

'Salutations, dream-world,' he said, possibly only to hear

the sound of his voice. It was dark outside. It was very dark inside. If he had not thought that he was dying he might have lit candles and the paraffin lamp, stoked up the fire Gemma had carefully raked out, and buried himself in a drink, solitude and soft music. Parts of him wanted to do all that, but another part had no heart for it, and anyway she had taken the radio with her. He switched on the overhead tungsten light instead, and stooped to relight the fire.

He had not expected anyone to be in the room, so why was the room so empty? Who had he hoped would be there? If he made a home for them, would they come? Nonetheless, he moved the armchairs around so that the full heat of the fire reflected on one seat only — blocked it from the memory, expectation, of Gemma on the other side of the hearth. She would have all the lights on in the London flat by now, the heating murmuring softly, the fridge open, offering the neat slices of chicken pie wrapped in cling film which always greeted their return from the weekend in the country. Would she eat both slices? Was it important? Would he ever know? If she did, would it indicate that she appreciated what had happened to them? Symbolically consuming his share, because he would never be there again to claim it — had left — had slipped off the juggernaut of habit, broken the contract. Or because she was hungry after all that crying and shouting at him. He would never know.

Voids. The room was full of voids. He did not fill it. He would learn to fill it. He wrote, 'Fill the room,' on the back of an envelope and put it on the mantelpiece. His writing was small and dense, and he could not read it from the chair. Coffee. His was the generation that had smoked heavily, drunk cheap wine and coffee and married each other. In the kitchen — a lean-to affair that he had so far evaded 'doing-up' as requested — there was a smart percolator on the Calor gas ring. He set it aside and made instant coffee with the kettle and milk out of a bottle. It was hot and foody, as it used to be, or still was on picnics. Only. Gemma's coffee was not sustaining.

What was this — nostalgia induced by chicory and over-tasty milk? Nostalgia for what? For that which should be crowding out the voids and was absent. He stared around the room, standing in the centre and moving slowly so that he saw every space there was. It must be years now since he had first been consciously aware of the shoving and jostling and tapping around him; of being crowded and pressed around and called to. And now suddenly, when he could answer, there was silence and voids. In all that time had he, in some way, killed the Mythic Man? In some way that had not been accessible to Gawaine? If he had, then his sin was indeed, and in itself, awful.

He saw himself; him, sitting on the side of the bath while Gemma did her face cream: *'Mea culpa, mea culpa* — I have slain the Mythic Man in the Woods.' He would be put away in a pastel-painted room with blinds over the windows and muted soft furnishings while someone, somewhere, would tell Awe not to trouble to come back.

Had Awe already left? Where are you? Where is who? He wanted to say, 'Where are you?' aloud, but did not have the courage to make the sounds into that silence. Like first words in a foreign language: they can be heard in the head, but the tongue will not risk it yet. Perhaps he should write, 'Learn to talk,' on the back of an envelope. In his head he said again, 'I am sick for your coming —'

Shit.

Outside the cottage, the trees rustled in the rain and the light wind. It was late before he heard them, hours after the tinned game soup and fruit cake in sealed silver foil which he found to eat. Gemma only ever brought exactly enough down from London for the weekends. He listened to the trees for a while, just rustling and stirring, as they would have done if he had gone back to Cash-and-Nooky Land, and there were no light in the cottage. It was nothing to them. He was nothing to them. They were only trees and nothing to him. But he could hear them. Was it important?

THE BOOK OF PANIC

Then Arthur fought against them in those days, together with the kings of the British; but he was the Dux Bellorum, the leader in battle.

The first battle was at the mouth of the river called Glein. The second, the third, the fourth and the fifth were on another river, called the Dubglas . . . The sixth . . . the seventh was in Celyddon Forest, that is Cat Coit Celyddon . . . the ninth battle was fought in the City of the Legion. The tenth battle was fought on the banks of the river called Tribruit . . . The twelfth battle was on Badon Hill and in it nine hundred and sixty men fell in one day, from a single charge of Arthur's, and no one laid them low save he alone; and he was victorious in all his campaigns.

Nennius, Historia Brittonum

The historical evidence is that Arthur was not himself the ruler or war-leader of a single kingdom, but that he was the leader of battles, *dux bellorum,* on behalf of several kingdoms.

Leslie Alcock, By South Cadbury is that Camelot...

[A] tradition preserves the highland view of Arthur, a tyrant who came to conquer, and came from foreign parts, east of the Usk, outside Wales and the west. The tradition of an alien Arthur, an enemy who ruled the lands that became England . . .

John Morris, The Age of Arthur

1

He listened carefully to the young trees to his left. They stirred and creaked in the light wind that had come up from the south-east and blown the evening's cold mist away. Ahead of him the hill reared up, angry, as if the Romans' old road had been flung across the river valley and brought up hard against a wicked curb. Just visible in the starlight, the track twisted up from the street — an aged serpent too tired to strike, lying on the breast of the hill and yearning for the fires and warm lights from the thatched huts cooped up and around the king's hall on the summit.

The moonless sky was quick with fast clouds lit dimly by the stars and into it the forest edge cut a hard, still blackness. He crouched among the stones, spine curved round; a silhouette indistinguishable from any other boulder in the cooking enclosure into which he was curled. From here he could see across the emptied fields to where the river came out below the coppiced hazels to his left, while in front of him, due west across a narrow strip of open pasture, the old street ran like a pallid memorial to itself and the First Cohort Sunici; a ghost-line along the foot of the hill and away to the south between the fields. Once the street had emerged from between the top of the hazel copse and the forest it had no cover, running flat and unguarded down to the point where, away to his right, the river bent towards it and the forest was homing in again, ragged and uneven across abandoned grazing lands. An army could have moved through there tonight, with the sound of the cascade between the rocks booming and pounding over any noise it might make, and saplings growing in to the road, almost closing it in places.

The stones into which he was curled stank of burning and cow-fat and dogs' piss, but the breeze brought the smell of the forest to him, and he could find it by raising his head. There was no sound and no scent on it to threaten him. He ran his tongue over his gums the way he did when he was uneasy. Inside the enclosure, which was made of discarded fire-cracked stones, the current fire-pits were still warm and odorous. When he had arrived there had been a fox in there, scavenging off such skin and hair-tufts as had been left after last night's deer-roast, and licking the bloody earth; but it had bolted out of the open, riverside end when he hissed at it, and since then only a weasel had come nosing and crunching amongst the carrion insects and snails.

Across the river, a heron dreamed on one leg in a still pool, haze-grey and silver in the dim starlight.

Nothing had moved on the street since dusk. Far off, beyond the hazels and the street and behind the hill, the wild land rose bleakly into summer pasture, winter snowfields, raven and kestrel skied. The cattle were all back now, and the mountains deserted. The wolf-pack which always wintered there in a recess under a cliff had been calling tonight for the first time this year. At the eerie sound, the Tracker had heard the horses neighing and a bullock bellowing in the inner corrals up in the ill-defended settlement on the hill. But the pack would not come close for a long time — not until after mid-winter when the hunger closed in with the blizzards and the north wind. He touched his flanks lightly with the nerves outside his fingertips, thinking winter. Thinking hunger. Thinking danger.

Immediately to his left three young ash trees had been left to grow together as a wind-break or shade cover. It was to them that he was listening. The largest of them had a creak in it this year, which had begun after the great gales last spring. It seemed that every year now the winds were wilder, the snows stayed later, the rivers ran fuller and faster. It was a sign that the times were in spate. The crying in the ash tree was a voice of the times . . .

Long ago, as children, he and Carac had made a mark for his mother on the child-tree's bark; and now the tree was making its mark in his hearing. His mother had died in very great pain, ripped up by dogs. He had not seen it, but he had heard . . . The settlement had been a rich dinas then: part fort, part royal stronghold for the king's fighting men and his close kin. Then one high spring day, the Leinster men had swept down the old great-road from the Irish colonies in the north, and the king's sons had been unready. The old men, the maimed and the smallest children had held each other's helpless hands while the Irishmen bolted the slave chains around the necks and ankles of the king's sons and the king's warriors. In her terror, the Tracker's mother had been thrown into undue birth pangs, and her screams and the smell of blood had excited the dog pack. There had been a grey bitch among them with a white star on her forehead and a white left paw. The Leinster men, loaded with the king's saddles and the king's luxuries, had waited for her, laughing, while she coupled with the dogs. The bitch had squealed high, as the Tracker's mother had, and as the sapling had under Carac's knife the next day. Now the grown tree was passing these pains back to him through its crying.

He was not ready to go up to the old dinas with its clogged ditches, leaking water-towers and scuffed, unpainted houses. A sense of incompleteness held him back among the burned stones and the crying tree. He had been far out in the forest for some time now, one animal among many — scenting, listening and watching every sign of movement amongst the king's enemies and the king's prey. He had much to tell — but, still largely an animal, was vulnerable to the noise and stench and distresses of the fires and the torches. Behind him the river suckled and lipped at its stony bed and its rootwoven banks. Further down it started to speed and then to leap and roar as it crashed into the gorge and boomed into the frothing white chaos of the cataract but here, sidling past the open end of the three-sided pit enclosure, it ran wide and slow.

He raised his head again, watching the water over the top of the stone pile. Silver and niello, the heron in the still pool.

He waited a long time while shapes changed and merged and reformed as the clouds shifted and ran across the night and the stars gleamed and were shut and flung wide and closed again. Then with a momentary ripple, the heron put down his foot, stood erect and stirred his great wings. Once he stood firm, staring across the water, head up, the Tracker moved out from the stones towards the serpent track up to the dinas.

In the llys there would be warmth and beer. It would be better to be in there, in the smoky aisled hall where the men gathered, talked and drank, than alone with the taste of blood on his gums. In there, the ancient ceremonial chariot cloths hung on the walls, the insignia of gods and heroes which had been paraded in the fathers' fathers' times, even before the enemy was Rome. There, too, were painted shields which had been displayed at the hostings of the fathers before the battles on the Dubglas, before the Battle of the City of the Legions, before the siege of Badon. The salt taste of his own blood was from lesser times, and the sights and sounds that rose in his mind were of small defeats and secret pain. They had to stay outside, clean and terrible, or they would soften like green flesh and kill him. The smell of a man dying of green flesh was the worst smell there was, and the eyes of a man whose dream had rotted were like the eyes of a man whose flesh was green. That was his understanding of life.

In the hall of the llys, which served as a sort of men's house, they were talking about the red poppies that grew around the deserted Roman forts and the once cultivated lands outside their walls. He found that he did not say that poppies were the colour of bright blood.

Carac, melancholy from chewing on his dream-mushroom, his eyes full and round like a pregnant mare's, was saying,

27

'The Bear wears a red cloak, they say, that colour.'

Echw said, 'Makes a good target of himself, too. It's one thing to be a rallying point, quite another to be the hit point of every enemy in the field.' A big man, he was the king's eldest foster-son, and because he was the most skilled fighting man in the dinas he commanded attention whenever he spoke in the hall. He went on, 'But there are quite a few of those old Roman cloaks around now — his horse-master wears red, I'm told. You go looking for red cloaks, Carac, and you'll find your Bear one day!'

Carac said tonelessly, 'He's out there, somewhere. I'll reach him, wherever he is. My grandfather the king hates me for wanting to leave the dinas — but the king is no war-lord. Not like the Bear. Wherever he is, down there in the south . . . He'll have me in his vanguard when I get to him . . .' He spoke as if he could see through walls and forests and hills, through the dark to where the Bear was, secretly. Biding. His voice vibrated like black gut, running through them from bowel to bowel, fixing them to each other and each to the Bear. For a brilliant instant the Bear was there, was with them and then not, and Echw said quietly, as if he were afraid of his own words: 'He may come to you, Carac. The king your grandfather is in danger. We are all in peril now. The king cannot face the Leinster men alone if Cadwallon does not hold them this season. It's my belief that the Bear will come north to stand with Cadwallon, and the king your grandfather will raise the battle-cry here and everywhere around. He will call the Och Mor, and you and I, shoulder to shoulder with whoever goes against the Leinster host —'

The old men sat very still. The young men looked down. Behind them the battle cloths proper to each fighting man — father-to-sons, uncle-to-nephew gifts of pride and rank and epic — hung faded and cracked, all unused except in ritual at festivals. No fighting-man now went to battle painted like a gibbering Pict.

After a while the Tracker sighed heavily and took some beer from Echw. When he had been young he had come here and joked of drinking and fighting and fucking and death. The young men of today joked too little. They knew there was no blood on their gums, as there was on his and Carac's and Echw's, and they were content to be ashamed of it. The little, cold scorn he had for them was like a spot on his mind which might go green. He blamed them for it. Feared them for it, if he was honest. He said:

> 'The three red strands of the dinas;
> The flower, the blood and the tyrant's cloak;
> The Bear wore them all on his back at the ford.'

'Terrible rhyme,' the Smith, a Son of the yew trees, said acidly.

'But better than no rhyme?' the Tracker hinted.

Echw: 'Not much . . .'

At last they laughed. The Tracker had never been able to rhyme.

Carac shouted across their noise, 'Not on his back — the man from Badon will wear his blood at the front —'

Echw: 'And where will we wear it? In the end all that matters is whether we all wear his blood, or he alone. In the end, it is going to be our blood he wears.'

'O, yes.' Carac's whisper was so small and tight that it raised the hairs on the Tracker's neck. 'O, yes. Mine. O, mine —' . . . his eyes black with love.

Watching him, Echw said, 'He's an ageing man, now, and his arm's not as strong as it once was. You know what is done to dead bears, Carac. Cut the paws off and hang them from the trees as trophies. That is what the king your grandfather knows.'

'The dinas does not stand alone,' the Smith said, cautiously. 'The Bear has a mighty army; his own men, mounted, paid, armed. And I make your jewels and your ornaments out of his coin, his glass, his gold and bronzes —'

Echw: 'For which he takes our horses to mount his band. Don't talk to me about that. Look at them now — fat, beautiful, well-trained. The Bear's horse-master will be up here in no time to take them. You know he will. He wants them down south for the winter — he has better fodder there. And when the mares foal, they'll all be his.'

The Smith: 'We are still bound together — he needs the horses —'

Echw: 'So do I. But for what war? It's a long time since Badon. There are more Saxons now in the east than were dreamed of then, and they're land-hungry, crushing against the Bear's Great Dyke like stampeding cattle against a fence.' He looked at them carefully, as if judging their ability. 'So I need our horses, too. For this dinas. And what about Barrectus, just over the pass? He comes across here from the east with a host . . . Where is he going to get enough horses or grass for them? He's starving up there by Cadair Idris — and I have no trust in a starving man, however he may declare himself against the Leinster king. After a winter on the mountain —'

'After will see to after,' Carac said, rising to his feet and standing with his back to Echw, his face closed against any after that followed so great a love as his. He stood facing the woven cloths which swung against the painted walls of the chamber. The patterns had come down from the fathers of the fathers, from the time when the dinas had been a great power and the reeking brand of Rome was smouldering in the flesh of the land; when the First Cohort Sunici had driven the street across the foot of the dinas. So many men might die in a morning, then, that only the patterns on the limbs might be left to show who the wife, who the widow: 'A forearm with part of a dog's head, running, found in the second ditch; a flap of belly-skin with a double triskele found by the inner gate; a shield with an open circle expanding to the left, the fingers still in the grip, found by the ford . . .' and so on and on through the triple circles and the boar's manes, the extending gyres, the limb-shapes and trumpet-shapes and leaf-shapes, and every line and every curve a fighting-man's elegy.

So Carac stared at the woven cloths and the painted shields, on which the sinuous coiled spiral around the thin-beaked bird-head was in some way himself; seeing out beyond them, beyond the forest and the furthest known milestone, to a bloody hillside and a reddened river and a pattern woven in blood into the long scarlet cloak of a demi-god.

He said, 'The Bear will wear my blood. After will come after . . .'

Like a prophecy? Carac's eyes had been white around, his lips stiff. The Tracker leaned against the rotten gate of the dinas knowing that Carac would leave the dinas soon now and go and search for the Bear; find him, in the old way, join his warband, drink, sing and adore and then die in front of him. In the old way. Carac knew something special, something the rest of them had largely forgotten. But not altogether forgotten, or the Tracker would not recognize what was happening to Carac. The king of the dinas knew, and the old men knew; knew, and did not want to know, that the ancient thing had brushed Carac lightly while they slept their old man's sleep.

But for the Tracker himself? I, he said, maybe to the planks of the gate, or whatever tree the planks had once been; I, whose hands are hare's feet and whose ears are owl's; whose eyes see what the cat sees and whose feet scent the running slots: I live deep in there where gods are among the waters and the odorous leaves and the sound of sunset. Do I, too, want this god of Carac's? If he comes for me after Carac's gone, who then will run downhill beside me, shoulder-pommel to shoulder-pommel on to the spears? There is none come who would run with me. I am the breath of the hart, he said, maybe to the once-tree; I am the furled, thin tongue of the wolf and the wind in the buzzard's mail; I am the pulse in a running man's thigh. Am I? Am I?

The man's hands of the Tracker were warm on the planks, but not warm enough or big enough for the immensity that the tree and its numberless, vital cells had once been. Nearly nothing to the wood of the gate, the man's hands: just a place on the outermost, weathered surface, just a movement with neither grace nor finity. No sign whether, in his need, the gate would stand to, for the man.

Now, when there is no man's hand to touch it, is there still nothing?

That night there was dancing and music. On the undersides of the grain stores and water-towers the drums bounced back beat, and the reddened torches leaped on limed hair dressings high over the fires. Another level of sound and light, there was: that dance brought into being above the beaten earth where the feet of mortals stamped and thudded the names of maybe gods or maybe not; and maybe someone was there in the air above the smoke, and maybe not — as was the habit of the kind. But never ask, for it is not our business whether someone comes or not, unless called — as Carac tried to call up the Bear. Too unlearned to bring him in from wherever he was, Carac went on and on and on stamping and calling him and calling him in by every name, every rhyme and sound, every *och*, even the *och mor*, by red even, like the Bear's own cloak; snatching up an old she-goat's tether and lashing red blood out of his own breast to bring the Bear in to his own colour in the red, red firelight. Belonging. That was the name of the night. The night of Belonging. The red cloak belongs to the Bear; the red blood to Carac. Red belongs to red.

Bring him in, man, and give him the dinas over our heads

— hiss, willingly, hiss, hiss. The mushroom drink, the dream-drink, passes from hand to hand — not to all, but to those who know how to dream; for dreaming is hard and dangerous and can open the road to Annwn. For the others, mead will do, with its stink of sweetened horse piss — the wage due to a king's fighting-man; and for the bondmen there is night-cooled beer and scrapping and the wet thighs of women.

But Carac has drunk deeply of the dream-drink — dreams rising in steam off his sweat. Dreams from the drink, those dreams of his own with which he was in love, his love affair with the Bear-dream and the rumours of the Bear had become all song and leaping skin and bright ornament. But if there were no Bear for him? Carac would shrivel and die, dessicate in the frost like an old crow hung upon a spike to scare other dreamers away. And if the Bear were real? Then Carac will blaze up like a king's brooch, brilliant, and knowing his brilliance. To become such a thing — so coloured, so shapely, so enviably wrought . . . Carac, now in the flame light, shaking like a beast on fire but not burning, the colours of his body paint caught in the glitter of his sweat and streaked with his blood, his hair stiff but not whitened, his eyes red like a fox behind embers — a thing begun but not complete; an idea of Carac, this. Whose idea? The Bear's? A trick of Carac's own desire? A feint in the Tracker's mind? No certainty. Nowhere certainty but the ululation of the old women and the soft hiss, hiss, hiss of the old men and the wb! wb! of the calf skin drum and the thing that was going around. Around and around like the stars or winter or the things that circle by night. Like a mare in a corral; a woman's girdle; the belly within the girdle; the womb within the belly, the child —

Rush of a javelin sent south east straight out into the sky —

Carac, striking the night in its black belly-pit, creating a new star.

2

He did not want to sleep any longer in the bed he shared with Gemma. Indeed, could not sleep in it. Not being able to had him awake at half past four, wanting to be else-where, on his own in a way that he was not alone there. Two people could not own the same bed without loss. It would be cold to get out, hump duvet and pillows on to the unused mattress on the spare bed. It would possibly be damp. He had learned about the horrors of damp bedding by being married. He still had some childhood recollection of the feel of damp cotton sheets and the smell of must in walls, and could not assess his desire to experience them again. They might even be restful, in the way that the lousy coffee he had taken to making was restful. Somewhere out there in the dark, there was an omniscient 'They'-being who would watch to see if he dropped what they would call his 'standards'. He fancied that at half past four They might be presumed to be asleep, and that if ever he were going to move into the little room with the damp single bed, he would be safest to do it now.

He crawled out of bed, looking for socks, and turned on the gas heater. Then he ambled about, in a coat, turning on all the lights in the cottage and filling the kettle and taking an electric bar into the back room. He had never done this room up, either. Now he was glad. It had thin, yellow curtains on a plastic string, a bitten-looking brown carpet and a big, unsteady table with a lamp made out of a wine bottle and Woolworth's fittings. The bed was wide and flat, with a skinny, dark headboard and a smaller, similar, footboard. He pushed it against the wall, heaving, because it had no modern rollers on its plain legs. With its passage, it rucked the carpet into a long wave. He went downstairs and made a mug of coffee, turned off the lights and returned to the little, must-smelling room. With his clothes on the table and his cigarettes and coffee mug beside them, it looked like . . . but he could not remember. Somewhere appropriate to some course of action whose direction he had not yet discovered.

He lay on a woolly blanket with the duvet, still warm from his earlier effort at the night, hugged around him. He remembered now how steamily hot a slightly damp mattress became, and found himself grinning naughtily as if there were someone there to be scored over. Outside, the 'They'-being slept unconsciously on, unaware of his victory. A little, bright thing — he wanted to call it Delight, but that was a word he was unused to — flicked on the edge of his mind.

Curiously, although he was comfortable, in his sleep near dawn he dreamed of feral dogs resting under the three young ash trees which whispered and creaked beside the cottage.

The morning was brazen with autumn and shouting wind; very positive and self-aware. Cathal leaned against the doorpost and stared at it, feeling invisible. The colours and the shouting in the high branches were nothing to do with him, ignored him as if he were not there. They would be exactly the same if he had gone back with Gemma. Whereas, if he had gone back, he would now, at twenty past nine, be affecting other people. Opening letters, receiving communications, initiating further communications, fugging up the office window pane, polluting the air with his cigarette smoke, jostling his kind in narrow passageways and therefore existing. Yet not existing, because all the time there were sheets of virgin paper; there were leaves on trees which he could see through glass and neither smell nor feel. If he had gone back with Gemma he would be shutting himself into the men's lavatory now, just for the solitude. At the end of today he would have gone back to the flat, frantic to be there before her; to have moments at the window, staring at a sky without stars and stained by street-lighting, aching to exist. So many early evenings, so many 3 ams, standing by windows, searching sullied skies for his self.

There was nothing here that made him exist. The little garden ran down from in front of the cottage to the road, but there was no one on the road. The trees swayed and cried out and whistled in their thin twigs along the side of the road and the garden beside the cottage, but they did not in any way know that he heard him. If he cried back — what? 'Come — I am sick for your coming' ? — they would not in any way be touched. He was less self-aware, less positive than the morning. He was without, he thought academically, any confirmation of himself. So much for Descartes. Had the man lived alone in a threshing wood? He could not remember, but doubted it.

There were dogs among the trees. Not really, but there had been last night. These were the trees he had been dreaming about: ash trees with curving boughs and sinewy extremities. So where were the dogs? In some way they were still there, simply because they had once been there. What sort of once? In time? Doubtless. For thousands of years there had been dog-packs here among the woods, and they must have rested, tongues lolling, on the roots of trees even then, dead and forgotten. Last night, in another sort of 'once', they had been there again, resting. The crux question: were they the same dogs? In any way the same? He shifted uneasily. This was not why he was here. But it was the hell of a question. He moved, needing contact with his body, feeling the door jamb against his spine, the slates under his feet. That was him: the one with the palsied left arm, that was becoming increasingly unmanageable; the one that was here because he was afraid to eat out in public, let anyone see that there was disfunction, be interfered with. Hiding? Or seeking? That was him; the hide-and-seeker. So who cared who the dogs were?

It was, he understood, not who but where the dogs were

that mattered. And now there is a red post-van on the road, audible, visible, scurrying round the curve at the edge of the long wood, past the telephone kiosk perched so ambiguously close to nowhere that it was equidistant from everywhere (a feat of great imagination, he had always felt), out of sight for a moment in the dip and now here at the gate. He waved in a spasm of contact but the van went on, red, unresponsive, under the wall and away, sound fading, and his arm fell back, as if unused. His arm fell back, unused. The truth lay somewhere.

He felt a little sick. And cold. He bumped his back against the door jamb again, as if he were pushing himself into independent stance, and turned into the cottage. The sun made merry for myriads of dust flecks dancing in his room. He felt reluctant to push through them, or at least inclined to apologize as he made his way to the kitchen, brushing the great pot of cardinal beech branches which he had stood on the floor, somewhat in the way. They rustled. The motes spun.

Damn them. And damn him.

The smile that was on his lips was an insult to the motes and the leaves. His self had jiggered the dust-dance; his self had made the leaves speak as he passed. They had confirmed him to himself by being other than himself, and so he had smiled. The postman in the red van had not confirmed him, therefore he had felt un-used.

On the shelf over the fireplace the envelope said, 'Fill the room.' But he had to empty it first, and he had not even the skill for that, no idea how to begin to acquire it . . .

He made himself coffee and brought pen and paper to his place at the old, polished table. He would have to start from the very beginning. Like a child. With do's and don't's. Self-consciously he wrote a 1 at the top of the page and drew a ring around it.

Discipline, he wrote slowly in large letters.

Eat, Sleep, Explore area.

Exercise arm, Measure success. (How, for God's sake?)
Measure failure. (Like dropping the coffee mug?)
Discover:Why am I here?
Who am I?
Who/what/why Gemma?
Death. DEATH.

Letter by letter he wrote *Structure* further down the page and underlined it. The only thing it could apply to was *DEATH* — scarcely an easily structured activity, he thought crossly. The longer he looked at the two words, the closer they seemed to draw together on the paper, until he realized that he had in fact written, 'Structure death.' There was no other way his eye would read it.

To distract his treacherous eye he inked the two words out with a huge black circle which covered them both and then found that wherever he was in the room the huge black circle remained on the periphery of his vision. He knew that circle as a device which he had learned about as a younger man. Then it had stood in for visual entrance, through the body, to the mind and the vision-tunnel . . .

Now that he had unconsciously recreated it, he could not efface it. He could, of course, if he burned it or threw it into the messy rubbish bin — would he do that?

After an hour he had written 'Eat, Sleep and Walk' on a new sheet of paper and put the earlier one in the bread bin, which proved to be empty. As a master plan for the rest of his life, it was not rivetting. He had also written 'Think', put a line through it and replaced it with 'Daydream', which he had crossed out as well. He realized that he was profoundly nervous. Of himself? He added, 'Something to Do' to the scattered injunctions. Was he not also a bit hungry? Yes. definitely hungry. Perhaps that was why 'Eat' had come top of the list. He pushed back the chair and stretched. It was still high and noisy outside; he could see the three ash trees flailing about and the grass crouching and ducking. He would walk to the post office and buy some food. That would be Something to Do and when he came back he would cook it, eat it and climb to the top of the wooded hill behind the cottage. He saw himself sitting in the sun on the summit, making a sketch map of the places where he would take his walks in his structured approach to death. The Roads of Death, he would call them, as on nautical charts. The pun would perhaps amuse him later. It did not amuse him much now.

He thought that the labels he chose, the words he selected to define his activities were going to be of generative significance and that one of the things he should do first was to decide on a vocabulary. The difference between 'Think' and 'Daydream', for instance, could turn out to be critical. Once a word was committed in writing, he knew that he would be in some way committed to it. 'Daydream' had a fictional ring about it, and the vocabulary of fiction was not appropriate to the understanding of his own incipient death (if it was incipient — how could he tell?). It would be best to have something definite in mind before he had accumulated any more pieces of paper in, for example, the bread bin.

In the meantime he should put on his coat. He ran his hands through his hair again and realized that he had not shaved this morning. Did it matter? Should he grow a beard? Did he want to grow a beard? He never had. He would organize his desires. First he would shave, then he would buy a great deal of food from the post office so that if he did decide to grow a beard he would not have to stamp around looking like a a recidivist hippie with designer stubble. Not, he thought, that the lady in the post office would know about designer stubble, she would just think he was grubby. Then, with the left side of his chin shaven and the right still rough, he wondered why he did not want her to think he was grubby. He had never even met her. Was it his effect on her he was concerned about, or the repercussions of that effect on himself? At any rate, he was not going to grow half a beard. He finished shaving, rinsed the razor and put his coat back on again.

Money. Gemma *(Gemma . . .)* had taken most of the loose change with her, sweeping it up automatically into her blue leather purse as she always did, and driving away with the purse on the seat beside her. He scrabbled around in his pockets, on the mantelpiece, in the kitchen and down the back of the chair, and netted six pounds ninety two. A little shaken, he paused for long enough to write 'Gemma' on a third piece of paper which he laid beside the second on the table. As he let himself out of the front door the wind whipped in and flung both sheets into the corner of the room, but he did not notice it.

It was a mile and a half to the post office from Castlegate Cottage. He turned right out of the narrow garden gate on to the road, walking in the direction that Gemma had taken on her way back to Cash-and-Nooky Land. This made it, suddenly, a dangerous road and a dangerous direction. It ran, straight as a Roman road, between the cottage and the river, crossing a bridge immediately above a wide shallow ford. Here the water was clear and thin, the pebbles brightly coloured under the quick ripples. Tractor marks ran down to it and up the other side to rejoin the road, for the bridge was narrow. Drystone walls, lichened, mossed, bracken-spilling, ran on either side and bounded the fields on both sides of the valley, thorn and holly bushes striking up dark and savage lines above the rounded stones. The valley was narrow and enclosed by the hills on either side, the small, rough fields steeply sloped with thin ridges like ribs running across them where sheep had filed to and fro for generations and the thin topsoil had slipped into multiple creases. There were scarlet berries on the thorn trees already, like Christmas so early that it might be left over, shrivelled, from last year.

Entering the post office was jarring. He was aware that his coat was big and loose and likely to flip little packets of sweets off the counter. That his boots were muddy. That he was relieved that he had, indeed, shaved. That he had no idea what to buy.

'Can I help you?'

God, I hope so . . .

She had wiry grey hair and a stern nose below spectacles that were round in the fashion of the last time spectacles were round, not this time. Her bosom was big and uncontrolled under the flowery overall. She was immensely clean and smelled of hotel soap. He had an urge to say: no, I shouldn't think so for a moment, but found he had said good morning, yes, quite competently instead. That amused him, so he grinned as well.

'Stamps, is it?'

'No. Hunger.'

She looked expectant. Probably used to amateur hikers dropping in for bars of chocolate fudge or Alternative biscuits like mouse-bait.

'I want to buy food.'

She made a very small pointing motion at the shelves around them both. He could see that gestures were not part of her vocabulary. He turned. Baked beans, of course, and sardines. And the oddest looking wriggly things in orange liquid — yes, he'd seen them in the advertisements that interrupted his programmes on the television. No slices of chicken pie or plates of mashed potatoes.

'Potatoes,' he said desperately. 'I want potatoes.' It sounded rude. 'Please.'

'How many?'

'O, enough for three meals or so.' He had no idea how many potatoes that would be. Lots.

'Five pounds?'

Just before he emitted the squawk of protest rising in his

throat, she picked up a plastic bag with potatoes in it. Five pounds' weight . . . He let his breath out rawly.

'I'm on my own for a bit in the cottage — Castlegate Cottage. Not used to buying for one,' he said quickly.

'On holiday, then?'

He was prepared for that one and said yes, his wife had to go back to London, but he had been able to stay on for a while. He praised himself for having thought that up in advance. He spotted some tinned beans and some real onions and eggs. He bought a jar of powder which said it was coffee. He put a tin of baked beans and one of tuna fish on the counter and stood back to indicate that he was through.

'You'll be Mr Kerr, then?' Not checking, he thought: creating. Naming names — making a Mr Kerr that could be contained by the perimeters of postage, shopping and an alimentary tract. He crushed an impulse to claim a new, strange identity in which he could hide.

He said hurriedly, 'Yes, Cathal Kerr. I know my wife's been in here a few times.' He had not foreseen that he might still have use for Gemma in this way but was unable to take the words back.

'I don't always have what she wants,' he was told, accusingly. He felt the grin again, but it called up no response.

'How much?' he said, hurrying her on from speculating about Gemma.

'Five pound seventy two, thank you,' She had no till? No calculator? She had done it in her head? She was right? As much as that? He paid up smartly and watched his multiple coins vanish into a heavy drawer under the counter.

She gave him a bright Safeway's polythene carrier bag to put his food in, since he had brought nothing with him, folded her arms and watched him leave. On his way out he passed a dumpy man in a cap who said 'Mournin,' but did not look at him.

The road home seemed very clear and peaceful. It would

be nice to walk along it in the wind.

It was evident that the post-lady wanted no Cathal Kerrs lurking about in her village, even married ones with up-stage wives. Whilst this was excellent in terms of his freedom from being wanted, it was a little chilling in terms of his humanity. After all, he had smiled twice . . .

Smiled twice, mentioned Gemma, implied that he was alone and helpless. Not a very commendable beginning. But since the exchange had not been witnessed he could erase the entire event from existence. Mrs Post Office would certainly disremember the episode with alacrity, far preferring him to be distanced and untroublesome. Which left him with no way of finding out how to cook potatoes. Because he and Gemma had had no children (had he really agreed to the importance of her career or had he given in to a conflict he could not face? O, too late to trouble with that one now. He should have tried dying years ago, if he was going to think about being childless) and because it fed Gemma to excel in everything — in her office, in the flat, in the kitchen, at the party, at the cartographer's seminars, on water-skis — he had been more than content to sit silently reading when another man of his generation might have learned how to share in a domestic life. He had never had a domestic life, he thought; just well-organized domestic affairs. That had been the contract between them. He would make way for all her excellences, a background to her brightness. It was from the history books, some new, some second-hand, with which he overloaded their book-cases, that she had picked on the idea of becoming a collector of antique maps — a hobby which so elegantly contacted both his obsessions and her own work in Cultural Vacations for the rich. In return for this symbolic public coupling she would protect him from his secret dreams; stand between him and nightmare; wake him, recall him. It

43

had worked well until the time when palsy came, and with it the loneliness. The I-Have-To-Go-Home-Now time.

Still, it was quite funny, this middle-aged man with his bright polybag, sauntering down the middle of the road with five pounds of raw and filthy potatoes to turn into dinner, and not an idea how to do it. Why had he not bought bread?

He had solved the problem of *Something to Do* all right. He spread the potatoes out on the draining board and looked at them. There was soil on them; he should wash them. He scrubbed them with the nail-brush. Bristles came upon the pink, naked looking skins. He picked them off, needing his glasses to find them all. He would boil his potatoes. He put four of them in a saucepan and lit the gas. After a long time a ceiling of ivory scum rose to the top of the pan, obscuring the potatoes beneath. He had never seen scum in his dinner. He ladled it off with a knife edge, but it kept coming back. He became nervous. He was here to die of the palsy in his left arm, not of ptomaine poisoning. Or salmonella. From what he had heard, with salmonella you just screamed your way to the hospital, throwing up until you kicked it in hideous agony with no chance to sit down and find out who or what you were before you very suddenly weren't. He became agitated at the thought of a quick, inaccurate death.

Picture: Cathal, feet first, with a luggage label on his toe and two pieces of paper left lying on his sitting-room table, indecently exposed to the perusal of the local coroner. Would they bother to dissect his left arm — had Mrs Post Office noticed it, even? — and if they did, would they realize that he had died by mistake? Did Death by Incompetence and Death by Misadventure carry the same connotations?

Flakes were coming off the parts of the potatoes that he could see under the remains of the scum. He poked them with a fork. Soft. Cooked? He spooned them out on to a

plate and sniffed at them. They smelled familiar, like potatoes. He felt like laughing. He felt hungry. He put some
butter on them, mashed them up with a fork and ate them,
using his right hand only and forgetting about the luggage
label lying in wait for his big toe.

In the afternoon — he supposed it was the afternoon
because he had eaten potatoes thus having made a 'dinner'
time — he went out again, this time in the opposite
direction, past the telephone kiosk (from which he would
not, or would, make contact with Gemma in Cash-and-
Nooky Land) and along the road to the bend where he had
seen the red post-van in the morning. There the road made
a sharp turn to the right, but the track through the wood
turned backwards and ran up from the road to the left as if,
in antiquity, they had been one, laid straight through the
wood and across the foot of the hill. A crotchety gate
divided the curve of the modern road from the overgrown,
ruler-straight path which drove in among the trees and
passed behind Cathal Kerr's cottage. There was a hand-
painted notice-board by the gate forbidding the lighting of
fires and overnight camping and requesting that the gate be
kept closed at all times. He obeyed this strictly, climbing
carefully over the wobbly barrier at the hinge end and, after
a stride or two along the track, was immersed in the wood.
    It was not cold; the trees shut out the wind. Shut out the
sun, too, but it eked its way between spreads of canopy
and through lacunae in the pale of trunks. He was not
alone; he knew that from the start, but did not know who
was with him. Animals, probably — little ones whose
names he knew but which he had never seen: voles,
shrews, wood mice and things. And dozens of different
insects, with long appellations in Latin. He would recognize
few of those and probably would not like any of them. It
would be rather a waste of time to learn about them and try

45

and come to terms with their no doubt fascinating, if not endearing, qualities. Spiders, he supposed, and earwigs and those etiolated life-forms with too many legs for aesthetic status, living under bark and stones and sod. They must all be there, all round him, but he could not see them, hear them, smell them. In fact, he could hear practically nothing, just the shifting of air in the trees and the internal sense of his own breath. As if the wood were deliberately exclusive of sound other than its own — which at the moment it was withholding.

As soon as he had thought this, he realized that he was making of the wood something proper, in the old sense. Attributing to it an existence outside his own experience of it. Estranging it from his physical participation in it. When he was almost at a level with the cottage, he peered down through the trees, but there was nothing there — only the wood. The cottage had become invisible. To his right a smaller, winding path led steeply uphill from the straight track. It must go to the summit, winding, zig-zag and overgrown between the hollies and ash saplings. It was darker here, dim as if it were not quite outdoors; a sense of a place Within. This side path was trappy with ground-ivy laid like snares across it and viper-ridden with bramble shoots; fern boles and root systems heaved and bulked under the thin leaf litter. Fallen tree fruits rotted, blackened and unfertilized.

He stopped. There were no earwigs, voles. Light meandered without consequence. Air drifted, wappe and wan. Stones harboured their forms. Would, could a leaf fall? No leaf fell to tell him. The leaf would fall only when it would. Unless he, as an autonomous body, caused it to do so. He was standing so still that breathing was significant, almost a distraction. The potatoes were still present in his stomach. How could he — what? Think? Be? With air in his lungs and potatoes in his stomach? His own physicality was enormous, consuming the other thing he was. For the moment, leave that as it stands — the 'other thing' will serve. Was the same thing true of the wood? Was the wood any condition other than its physicality? He searched for a formula that would acknowledge that the wood existed in time and place and was not to do with time or place.

Had he not been holding his breath? He breathed out. The activity distracted him. Intensity ebbed, left him tired. Things of him which had been released, drew back into the frame of himself. Denser, he felt at once diminished and because smaller, stronger. He could make no value judgement of the change but felt it profoundly.

It might be expected of him that he would lie down on the moss and sleep and rising, refreshed, turn the experience to account. But he was not even sure if there had been an experience, and did not want to lie on the hard ground. If he were discovered standing, his mouth half open, he would be seen as daft. If sleeping, as poetic/artistic, something like that. But he remained standing with his mouth half open, though wondering whether he would have done so had he not been so certain that he was alone. That is, that there were none of his kind around to interpret his actions, for he had been thinking that in some way he was not alone. That there was an alternative presence for the apprehension of which he was inept. But now he could do nothing but think; whatever change had taken place in those few seconds — or it might have been ten minutes (and suddenly he was quite curious to know which) — was over, and the retracted form of himself had no contact with the other thing the wood was, only with itself.

He moved a little deeper into the wood, because in fact he had not gone very far yet, and made an effort to be aware of amongst what trees and over what surfaces he moved. For example, now that the path was steeply uphill, he had never before noticed that just under the mosses and grassy tufts, showing here and there amongst the green, the ground was a jumble of flat, slaty stones which could, by an accented footstep, be shifted, even dislodged. He visualized some climatic or orogenic catastrophe splitting the hillside into flakes in an obscure time, full of noise and silent, magnetic savageries, and regretted that his time might be too short to learn about geology.

Picture: this middle-aged man with the palsy, crouched over a solemn geology tome in the wee hours, frantically reading about the Ordovician in case he died next week in ignorance . . . Daft, really. He might as well let his mouth hang open. He was grinning a bit and saw a fox slink across a small, sparse area to his right and it was gone under the thorn bushes.

He stopped in astonishment. Quite conventionally, stopped in his tracks. He had seen a fox. Hadn't he? There was no evidence of it, but he knew he had. He had never seen a fox before — not wild, doing its own, self-initiated thing. Lots, of course, on films and in zoos and parks and in the old days hanging down his aunt's bosoms with their tails in their flattened mouths; foxes' heads on wooden plaques in pubs . . . but not in a wood. Not in the same wood as him.

It had been absolutely noiseless and it had gone. Where? What was it doing now? It must be very close to him still. No birds were singing. They knew where the fox was. Where he was. That it was a killer. Of course, it was only a tiny animal, not much bigger than a cat, really, and scared out of its wits by his big, human frame. Wasn't it? How did he know so exactly which bush it had gone under? How had he marked the precise spot so definitively? It was darker than it had been; colder.

The sun had left. Time to go home, isn't it?

. . . *and if there were no home to go to?* Cathal turned around slowly, with a sudden knowledge of desolation. With something in his blood which recognized the wood as all there was, or could ever be, for him to belong in: the essential locus; the womb of the present, whichever present; the where from which all going out and to which all coming in pertained. His veins knew it already; knew also that night and, after the night, winter would come. Prescient, they shrank a little deeper into his flesh, shielding the vulnerable blood deep down, burying it far from the coming night, tonight, all nights. The veins remembered. The skin, left pale, took on a bluish tint. He stared at it, at its knowledge, which was different from his knowledge.

As he watched the skin of his hand, something which it remembered caused every minute hair to stand up slightly. What did it fear? What was coming, that it remembered and which he was going to suffer? Afraid . . . Afraid, he looked hard at the blackthorn and the dark gorse, at the faded campions and livid brambles; at the sky blowing up clouds now, grey and sodden and wickedly out of the north-west with the smell of cold on the wind. Which wind, with winter deep in its *id*, came from Dyfnwal's land and MacErca's; from where the Picts were and, closer to Cathal, off the flanks of Eryri.

As he turned about, the slate scraped under his feet, so close to the surface was it.

How large a predator could cross here unheard?

A shadow?

A polecat? A fox? A wolf?

A man?

The Tracker could cross here, unheard —

Slates scraped. So cold, so unhouseled a sound . . . Certainly no kindly thing visited.

He should have gone home before this.

Ocha, ocha — wind caught in the groin of an ash branch, keening across the lip of a void in the heart-wood? Is it the wind? That flare of russet, a swirl of turned leaf? That soft pad, the slap of wind-thrown fern against bark? Something wicked — his left hand ran with cold barbs, blue when he looked at it, white-nailed. There is something. Something for which this is home. Is it he? For an instant it was. For that instant when the first spicules of rain and the north west wind went for him, when his left arm was dying at his side and he was utterly homeless, this was his locus. Then he ran. Ran desperately, noisily, back across the slates and into the path along which he had come questing for something, ignorant that he was.

Once back on the road he forced himself to walk, but belligerently, as if he were not afraid but had only been roughed up by the weather. The cottage door was wooden — made of a tree killed, cut into planks, and nailed implacably on to a frame. Serve the fucking trees fucking well right, said Cathal, lighting a fierce wood fire and holding his left arm out to the incipient heat lest it die there and then, suspended from his living shoulder.

The dinas lies across the summit of the low hill like a mist. The wooden sides of the ramparts have greyed with age, the stone infilling between them is grey. Birch roots and ash roots twist the stones out of alignment, feed on the ghost of past vitrification. Lichen blurs their outline, as they blur the shape of the ramparts and the canopy covers the form of the dinas. There but not there. Now out of then, but not the same as. The dinas is unrealizing itself, like an aged animal before death; loosing its sure grip on the hill, its lines wavering, becoming a spirit dinas, visible only to certain men at certain times. Then and again it is as if it has already gone, and under the moss and mould is only an arcane tracing buried by later nights, forgotten. After will come after . . . What comes to the dinas, comes.

Down below, in the valley, Cathal cannot see the dinas. It has left, o, a long time since — a when out of the reach of even the Tracker's shifting pelt-dreams which he dreamed when he came in from the forest.

The Tracker always left the forest slowly, as if returning

to the dinas were something dangerous which must be achieved with great care. In the llys he would communicate with the king, by one means or another, bringing the king and his territory into each other, and watching the king's mind when it withdrew into quiet places. Then there would be a signal: a whisper, a flight of birds, a shadow of a smell at the back of the wind; and he would return, silently, to the deer tracks and the beaver dams and the rock clefts where the bats swung and chattered — the tight interlace of animal life. And this he thought of as a pelt which was also his own skin and within which he had his only life, his only bloodstream, his nerve endings: the soles of his feet and the ground had no interface, but were one thing; the lingering warmth of a lair and his fingertips feeling it were one thing with the animal who had lain there; and he and the creature or the snapped bough or the death that scented at the back of his throat were one long thing, like the wind or the rim of a waterfall. This becoming of all things wore him, drew him from inside himself out to the pelt, so that when he returned to the dinas it was as a sick man who had sweated blood out; whose vital fluids had been sucked. So he would lie around, eating like a man, sleeping like a man, listening to words and the ideas that words made: through the ear into the brain pan, and so into pictures which were not real, but could be seen as no animal, he thought, could see them. And the binding pelt would relax, and free his finger tips to touch an infant's cheek and make it smile as no animal, he thought, smiled. And he would become a naked man, staring at the spirits as the first men and the first gods had stared at each other in the morning.

He had been out for several days now, watching where the carrion birds made for and whence they returned to roost. They came in from the south-east, straight towards the sunset, faster than the night which ran along the sky behind them. Somewhere, out there to the south-east, there was a darkness which was extra to and outside the night. There was killing in the south-east. He came into the dinas with the news, not knowing if it were good, bad, or merely of an event which had nothing to do with them. The birds had come in heavy-winged, though, and slow, the ravens last. Glutted.

3

It took Cathal only a couple of days to realize that the purely secular needs of his body, sick or well, were going to interrupt his discipline for dying if he did not attend to them coherently. For example, in the bread bin there was no bread, only a short list of injunctions above the large black circle which he had hidden in there to keep it out of sight. Since he was now resolved to put bread in the bin he retrieved the piece of paper, intending to find another dark place for its safe keeping.

It was an unbalanced work, he saw: the lines of manuscript too small and scattered, the circle ill-formed — words and device disparate on the formal rectangle of the page. Using the back of the kitchen knife as a ruler he pencilled in a neat frame which enclosed the two and related them to each other. In this way, he perceived that he had re-created the Structure which the great circle had obliterated, and composed a representation of himself with his design, by limiting them within a continuous margin. Protecting them, too, he thought, from intrusion, as in the earliest of the great illuminated manuscripts sacred words were sometimes protected by green, red and yellow margins of elaborate interlace and knotwork. He had scripted and drawn his existence; and now he bent over the page anxiously searching for any break, however minute, in the surrounding lines, through which malice or disruption might come. In the great gospel books any interstices in the interlace were

THE BOOK OF PANIC

blocked off by Sacred Signs, and the lacunae in the knot-work themselves took the form of Sacred Signs, thus rendering all spaces impenetrable. Standing where he and the circle now were, within a margin of intricately drawn and blocked interlace, he could watch the integrity of each coloured strand as it turned and returned about him. Nothing could be thrown to pierce it, nor anything break into it and destroy its involved continuity, but he would know it.

He held the piece of paper up to the light from the window, searching it fearfully. Not until he was satisfied that not even a loose particle of its surface interrupted the completeness of the four pencil lines, did he thrust it behind the unused plates and pans skilfully arranged on the kitchen shelves.

It was Mrs Post Office (her name was, in fact, nothing more difficult than Bowen, but Cathal found it hard to label her with anything as intimate as a name) who put Cathal in touch with the dinas. Gemma, with what seemed to Cathal to be wicked efficiency, had already sent a cheque for six hundred pounds to 'tide him over'. (Tide him over what? Life? Death?) She had also enclosed a leaflet about Opportunities for Retraining, and had ringed a paragraph on forestry in blue biro. Ha! Go out in the jolly sunshine with a green hat and a chain-saw, is it, wife — because you are not, or are, aware of the palsy in the left arm? (O, God damn her. This is my affair.) At least in the Records Office he had been a conservator in a sense; now she was inciting him to arboricide. What sort of an apprenticeship was that for death by palsy? Or even for living, until same came along?

Picture: an overheated, overlit vestibule with kicked tables and a green form on which Cathal is scratching Death in a box labelled Career Objective. At the bottom of the form is the stricture that telling lies will result in prosecution. At this Cathal squints in awe.

Last time Cathal had confronted Mrs Post Office he had been unarmed, in a manner of speaking. Now, armed with a cheque book and cheque card, he felt emboldened to utter a dim war cry. He asked for a stamp — first class, mind you — and stuck it on to an envelope already addressed to his London bank, into which he slowly put the cheque (Gemma's writing was very large and round; 0s showed up well). Then he sealed the envelope, left it on the counter facing Mrs Post Office, and inquired mildly if she had any idea why his cottage was called 'Castlegate' when there was no castle marked, even in Gothic lettering, on the Ordnance Survey map.

Mrs P.O. weighed Cathal's three parsnips on a page of the *Shooting Times* which the terrier-man had, she said, failed to collect last week and could therefore be spared. In return for this vicarious generosity Cathal kept his left arm down by his side, lest the tremor make her anxious for the safety of the sweet-packets. He had made an enormous effort to write out a list of the things he imagined he might need, and was not to be starved into submission by unilateral sanctions applied by Mrs P.O.'s derision of his single situation. She knew for a fact that he was short of cash; he was obviously extremely foreign (native, most likely, of Nowhere At All); probably rejected by his wife, and no wonder, and therefore on all counts the epitome of the immigrant Poor White. This she conveyed to him by the manner in which she talked at him, allowing her round spectacle frame to shield her eyes, as if it made no difference whether he were on the other side of her counter or not. Dropping the envelope into the mail bag under the counter without the merest glance at the address, she slapped the parsnips down in its place and said blandly,

'You've not been up to the castle.' She entertained no question mark.

'I didn't know there was a castle.'

'You stop at the bottom of the road up to it.'

He did? It was in the forest? 'What sort of a castle?'

'It's very old. Nothing up there to see.'

'How old?'

'Very.' She added, gnomically, 'It's gone, anyway.'

But he persisted. 'Is there a guide book about it?'

'A book about that? Huh! Now, d'you want tea as well as coffee, or which?'

'Coffee.'

'Coffee's expensive.'

'I know. I want coffee.' The parsnips looked dreadful. Cathal the Strategist saw his opportunity: 'How do you like your parsnips cooked?'

'Never eat them.'

Defeated. 'How do I find out, then?'

'You could ask Gethin. He owns it.'

He does? The castle — not the parsnips — but being a man, Gethin might be sympathetic about the parsnips, if not knowledgeable. He perceived that he had lost no more face by the question. 'Where do I find him?'

'Black Lion on wet nights'

'O? What does he do on fine nights, then?'

Fall, spectacle frame; and Cathal vanishes from the Post Office world. He paid humbly by cheque and card and slunk out with the same bright polybag as before and an uncomfortably sharp cardboard box which would not quite fit under his arm.

Please, God, let the Black Lion be in a cheque-cashing mood when I find it. O, and if it would suit Your plans, might tonight be rather wet?

By evening the wind had swung round to the south-west and rose, beating up the road like a heavy bird taking flight off water — a heron, grey, with sheets of water streaming from its undersides. There were salt and mud smells on it, and the high-pitched, cold smell of exposed shale and dolerites and the thin smell of fast, cold water. It lashed the road with these faint smells, slammed them against Cathal so hard that he could not detect them, only feel the wind's power, as he bent into it, as something hard and blood-swelling, going for him. An enemy. Personal.

The Black Lion was nearly four miles along the valley, and every mile was a bout against the rain and the dark and the wind. He felt driven. It did not occur to him that he need not go — that there was no basic necessity for him to find Gethin; Gethin would not light his fire, give him food, give him a coat. What Gethin had which he, Cathal, needed, was of a different order, yet he sought it out with the same urgency as if he were starving or under attack. Was he under attack? What was the smell on the wind? That cold, thin, grave smell that might have been of iron battle weapons; of burial in the rain. Hostile. Did it make him think of these things, or was it, in fact, of these things? A stink of something elsewhere or elsewhen, or just a smell left on the wind? Was not blood salty? But the rain, running down his face and on to his lips, had no taste of salt. Some things were, here — now; some things were not. Which? Who?

Who?

'Where are you?' His shout, sounding small and childish, was as if it had never been, in the wind.

How, for God's sake, should he know what a battle smells like? Even film out of famine zones has no sealed perfume sachets to release in the lounge while you watch the news. So how is Cathal Kerr supposed to know what battle smells like? Recognize Badon or Llongborth or Cat Coit Celidon by smell when he needs to? A hound or a fox or a cat could, but he, Cathal, has forgotten how. Pack-dogs and wolves know how. Ravens know (Carne, carne!), and common crows (Where shall we our breakfast take?).

* * *

The public bar was nearly empty. A noisy radiator with a wicked red eye clicked in the corner. Cathal's legs and back were filled with cold aches and his thighs chafed where his trousers had chapped them in the rain. The formica counter was chipped at the edges and wet with wiping. Two men buckled under the subject of BSE, their arms spread round ashtrays and half-empty pint glasses. They wore caps, and one was rolling a cigarette, moistening the paper on his lower lip. The fucking cost of fucking vets . . . They sat on stools pushed so far back that Cathal could not pass between them and the faded pool table behind them. There was no one behind the bar. The kennels were feeding the hounds on porridge and meal, not carcasses, fucking hell, this fucking year . . . The single ornament, a bright Rugby shirt in a dark Victorian exhibition-case, bumped slightly against the wall as the draught from the door took it and shivered the pool cues in their bracket. Not taking into account the fucking French and the lamb war; shit, man, if I'd been there that fucking night — shit!

Cathal was not there for the men at the bar. He thought perhaps he was not there anyway, that he had dissolved and petered out in the wind and rain on the road. A stain left by wet ink, a word, a name, washed out and run away. Roads had such ghosts that walked them, perhaps forever. Perhaps forever bringing news of burial in the rain, forever washed out and run away. He was one of them, still out there on the road.

There were ways, though, by God, of shifting cattle — o, fucking hell, man, ways . . .

Could one of these be Gethin? Could Cathal make himself real enough to ask? An elemental transition.

'Cathal,' he said, 'Cathal Kerr.' Naming names. Naming Names. Then knew that he had not said it; had only imagined saying it. Yet he would have sworn he had spoken. Fear came in in a rush like a gale's gust from the ridden cattle mart behind the pub yard. The Rugby shirt bumped on the wall,

There was no reason for fear. He had set out for the Black Lion. He had arrived. Nothing had happened to him on the way. The two men at the bar had shown him no hostility. They did not know about the palsy, had no reason to fear him or shun him. He was just not significant to them. Not in any way significant. In fact, here, now, only actual at all as a symbol, or mark of some epitome of the ephemeral. He thought, is this Death? Is this dying? And, what, then, is the difference between life and death? Is this what the farmers know, fucking and shitting at the bar? And I, because I am on the instant neither fucking nor shitting: is there anything for me to know, precisely now?

Cathal realized that he would not now inquire after Gethin. He had no right to Gethin's knowledge. He would leave before, as it were, he need arrive. His muscles flexed to turn up his coat collar against the things outside the narrow door.

'Is it you that is asking after Gethin?'

She was so instant, so physical, that Cathal actually jumped, like a clumsy actor. The bar-girl — bar-person — had materialized through a little slit between the rum, vodka and sweet port shelf, and a pock-marked screen that shielded the bottles from ill-thrown darts. She was overt and smelled of talc and hair mousse, and the black, armless T-shirt advertising Southern Comfort revealed little sprigs of dark hair under her arms. He reached furtively to feel for his penis before seizing the wet coins in his pocket.

'I've been told he comes in here on wet evenings,' he said abruptly, as if he had just arrived. He had just arrived. 'It's wet enough, tonight.'

'My aunt's sister said at tea last night that you wanted him.'

And that I'm a Poor White, haven't any money, can't cook parsnips, my wife has left me . . . Anything about my life expectancy that she wanted you to know?

'Gethin, is it?' The First Farmer wore a cap the check of

which was almost exactly the same as that on the cap Cathal's father had always worn when he took his family to visit the grandparents. 'In-The-Country' was the name of where the grandparents had lived, and one dressed appropriately, as one did for going to the dentist, or School Sports. The familiarity of the check pattern gave Cathal a chilly shock. But this cap had greasy patches over the ears and on one side of the peak.

He said, 'I'm told he owns the hill behind the cottage I'm living in.' He was afraid to say, My cottage, as he would have done in Cash-and-Nooky Land.

'Castlegate, you're staying in.' It was a statement; not necessarily hostile.

The man's eyes were old, pale blue, with a dark fleck in one iris and veins netting the corners. There were so many lines leading out from the eyes that it was impossible to guess if the expression were kindly or shrewd, bitter or amused. The forehead was pale below the cap; Cathal had seen gardeners' foreheads pale like that when the cap was pushed back. Thin mouth, tough nose, tough chin; cumbersome cheekbones with hard flesh folded over them; a man of about his own age, but with these old, old eyes as if another man were within, present, but not concerned. Not bothering with Cathal Kerr.

'Holding the rain out, is she?'

'O, yes. It's dry enough. Not that we've had much rain, lately, until tonight . . .'

He did not follow the Second Farmer into the labyrinth of woes occasioned by mud, cracked heels, foot-rot, fucking and shitting, scouring. He knew nothing additional about any of them — just the words.

'Won't be out with the ferrets in this,' First Farmer said, possibly optimistic, but it was hard to tell.

'So that's what he does?'

'Does a lot, Gethin. Ferrets, too. You go out with the dogs?'

Cathal did not want to answer that. He did not know what it meant. 'Have another?' he offered, resorting to pastiche.

'Don't mind.'

'And your friend?'

'Married the sister.'

The brothers-in-law drank two pints and a double whisky, all at Cathal's expense, and then said that they did not, in fact, know where Gethin was. Cathal asked if he could cash a cheque. The bar-person, surprised, asked why not? Cathal thought of a lot of reasons but since none of them applied to him, asked for twenty pounds and gave her his cheque card. She did not know what to do with it, turning it over in her hands and then reading his name aloud. Cathal had never met anyone who did not know what to do with a cheque card, so he had never bothered to find out for himself. Nor had he met many people who automatically pronounced his name right. So it was suggested that he should sign the back of a cheque — which he did; take a couple of tenners — which he did; and a have a drink on the house. The transaction was so artless that he suddenly observed how dirty his nails were, and curled them round the glass so that the bar-person should not see how grubby an emanation he was, coming from where he could be said, in one sense, to come from.

Second Farmer had disagreed with Cathal's observation, made well into the first fiver of the second tenner, that there was a lot of bloody night around, these days. From where he stood, it was more a question of a shortage of fucking days. This was a ponderous truth to Cathal, for when would the palsy get him, was the question. This he said out loud, then wondered if he had not said it just as he had not, earlier on, said his name. But Bar-Person had known his name, so maybe he had actually said it, but in some way his saying it had run away. That could only be true if he had run away, as when his name was written in ink on the wet road and the rain had washed it out. Very clearly, then, and listening carefully for the sound of it, he said:

'Would you be considerate enough to tell me if I were drunk?'

Very considerately First Farmer, Second Farmer and Bar-Person assured him that they would be considerate. Cathal was pleased, for there was a potential here for clearing something up. 'It's this question of day-shortage — I have it, you see.'

'Time . . .'

'Precisely, time. I don't know how much I've got. Any? Too much?'

The voice that went on saying 'Time' was very seign-eurial. Might, another night, even have been God or someone like that. It was a very big, bass voice with an archaic accent — which is much what you'd expect from God. Cathal said that it was delightful how easily the indoctri-nated mind could pick God up in the Lion, and the fact should be recorded. It was interesting, wasn't it? Socio-logically speaking. These days — these damn days of which there seemed to be such a shortage. Like now — bloody dark!

The lights of the Landrover picked him up among the pens of the cattle mart, and Second Farmer humped him over the tailgate, where he threshed about on something alive and cross. As they swung out into the light of the village street-lamp Cathal saw that it was a cattle-dog with bared, sharp teeth, one white paw and a star on its fore-head. Nervously he withdrew his ankles, and the bitch cowered against the cab-back, snarling. Once out of the village there was no light to watch her by, and he could only see the red reflectors swooping about in the puddles on the sluiced tarmac. He held on very tight as the vehicle swung around the road and bumped, he was sure, against the banks from time to time. Each time this happened, the canvas, which was wet and heavy, hit him painfully across the arms and neck and shot spits of rain into the small of his back. When the Landrover slewed heavily into a field wall and stopped, he fell out.

Absolute terror sobered him as the Farmer reversed out of the dented wall. He screamed; the bitch in the back barked in frenzy; the Landrover's revs shrieked. Cathal writhed and twisted in a mud-grappled jerk as the exhaust pipe roared scorching fumes into his eyes, and then went icy cold as the great back wheels ground away on to the road and, with a final flirt of the red lamps, vanished round a corner, the dog barking triumphantly.

DEATH . . . Himself drunkenly maundering about its Coming, and within a fraction of an inch of receiving it with his sternum playing chords on his backbone. He thought unsteadily of that coroner waiting to pronounce between Death by Misadventure and Death by Incompetence, so that he could have an accurate label tied on to his big toe.

They were not on the straight and ancient road. They were not behind the stone walls, stalking parallel with him through the sour, sodden grass which he could not see in the blackness and the rain. They did not come howling down the track where the old road ran up to the wood and the modern way swung left below the trees to Castlegate. He had expected them to be in all of these places. He had wandered in the road, unsure of its surface, its potholes, its deep drains tipping over with fast water. Once a great head had swung up at his passing, and hooves scappled hurriedly away from him on the other side of the wall. He had stopped. Listened to whatever it was moving quickly away. A cow? A horse? He had no idea what would be out in these bitter little fields at this time. Would a farmer know what it was by its movement? He did not know. Once a dog had barked elsewhere in the valley, and not at him. The wind shoved his wet clothes against his back so that he shivered continually and uncontrollably. The wind said nothing. Brought no words to him, no ideas. The alcohol was dead in his stomach, chill and heavy. He was alone on the road; no person, now or once, even came into his mind.

Here, where he had been afraid the other evening, running out of the forest as if someone had been after him, he felt nothing at all. The gateway, as he passed it, was empty. The track up through the forest was empty. The trees swung, nerveless, on the wind. It was seven minutes past twelve when he stumbled into the cottage, slapping at the wall with his numb hand, to turn the light on.

And this was where they were.

Cathal closed the door very gently behind him. As if it was someone else's door, and he an uncertain caller. There was no space for him, the room was full. He stayed there, crushed against the planks of the door. There was absolutely no sound. Everything was still. Held still. Captive. There was no smell in the room. He stood as still as the air, back against the door. Looking — looking. Nothing. Listening. Nothing.

His heart beat him soundlessly from within; his breath came and went as swift and minute as a moth's. The strip light cast no shadows. On the shelf over the fireplace the used envelope said, 'Fill the room'. He looked warily at it, at the pattern of shapes that realized an idea. Transient little artefact with transient little marks on it. Rain from his hair trickled down across his eye. Water would wash away the signs on the weak paper. As he blinked, his seeing of the signs wavered and blurred. They were washing out. He strained a couple of steps forward, and the space he left closed in behind him, pressing against his cold, cold back. His heart pounded. In the centre of the room he almost stopped, but there would be so much danger if he did — he pushed on another step, disturbing so little, so very little. At such peril.

Once he was through the kitchen door he crashed it shut behind him to keep the chill little lean-to safe — like a cellar to hide in, be buried in, go to ground, burrowing down, deep into safety and o, it was lonely in here. After the density he had passed through, he could not keep his shape in this void, this desperate, icy emptiness — NO. He spun round, stumbling, reaching for the door into the living room, which he had just slammed — anything to break this terrible, cold emptiness.

There was nothing there. They had left. The fire was out. The wind bumped erratically against the outside door, jittering the latch. In the kitchen he blundered about, turning on the Calor gas; putting on the kettle; lumping sticks out of a cardboard box to light the fire and make flames jump about and move, smoke swirl. He made noises, any noises, deliberately bumping into chairs so that their legs scraped on the floor; banging the coffee jar and the mug on the draining board; slamming the milk bottle back on the table.

Then he stopped to listen. To look. There was nothing to see. Nothing to hear. He was alone.

He had never been alone before. Not in this way, as he was in this empty room; as he had been in the cold, unhoused wood. The gates of the Civitas had dropped below the horizon of the present and the wilderness was a lonely place.

So who had emptied the room?

He sat on the edge of the armchair, the Calor gas fire scorching his left leg and raising a stink off the sole of his shoe; the new, bright young flames in the hearth not yet hot on his right, but their colour and light flicking and dancing. Between them he curled his hands around the mug, the fingers shivering and blue at the tips. He heard his own breath snuffling in his nose, his coat rustling as his ribs moved. So alone that he could listen to his existence. The sounds told him little — just that there was a body there. An alive body, doing nothing. Signifying nothing . . . And then is heard no more. Already it was unheard except by itself. Then in the future and then in the past growing towards each other, and for him, the centre of it, there was no sign that time was passing. For him, just breath going in and out of his body, blood flowing through his arteries, a muscle in his chest moving monotonously. Perhaps time was only the cartilage around his joints shrinking, or the sun cooling down there over Papua New Guinea . . . Whatever had been in the room had left nothing behind to make signs. Had left nothing behind to which he could make signs to see time passing through his veins. So he was alone. Isolated spirit. And if the physicality was alone, so also was the spirit. Could the spirit (whatever that was — Cathal had never solved this problem, being an atheist) exist in isolation?

What was the worth of all the fine spirits that had been and left no record? The same as that of the unrecorded, unsuspected bodies where there are no longer stones — no mark to show *quis jacit?* Hectares of rocky ground where the graves have not been deep enough, and whence the ravens fly to the north-west, glutted . . .

In another habit the raven is the spirit; or the raven is glutted on spirit, stuffs its crop with the transcendental, grinding eyeballs and finger joints against the bitter vision of a Patrick or a Gildas. If there were no spirit, would that raven starve? Fall dessicated from the winds, the fine geometry of bone and pinion spinning down the margin of its habitat in a strict pattern of interlocked, running knots? The ultimate design.

The pattern — he must see the pattern of his own margins . . . The instant he saw that image of the safe interlace framing him, the fear and the rawness dissipated. He was fully and totally aware of himself, as if he had never been otherwise; of the burning shoe on his left foot, of a full bladder and a wet shirt and a graze on his leg from rolling on the roadside behind the rear wheels of the Land-rover. He lurched sideways in his chair, swearing aloud. His shoe stank. The room was a room. He sat in a chair. It was night. No more, no less. He was a fool — a burlesque figure pricked out in raven's flight feathers with flames on his feet and shapeless trousers. But the coffee was good for him. It went down his gullet hot and thirst quenching, and took away the chill leadenness of the dead whiskey.

He threw some thicker bits of wood on the fire, and the tangy odour of spruce drifted out on the down-draught from the wet chimneystack. He threw off the raven's feathers and kicked the acrid shoe from his foot — right over to the door where it lay upside down, reeking by itself and with a blackened slackness on the sole. It would let the water in, now. He felt better. He made yet more coffee and sat on the floor with it, sniffing at its steam and the spruce smoke from the forest and the wet wool of his jersey. He had, after all, merely been drunk. Being drunk, even quite drunk, was commonplace in Cash-and-Nooky Land and had frequently produced depression and funny feelings. One aquaintance of his who played golf and holidayed vigorously with jet skis and snorkels, regularly cried when he had had too much, and no one thought any the less of him — they were used to it and indulged it with good humour. As far as Cathal was aware, no one he knew was dragged by carrion birds spinning down an illuminated margin or press-ganged by voids in their lounge; but then the jet-skier had never revealed what it was that made him cry.

After a while Cathal turned his back to the fire and sat in front of it, facing the room. Looking right into it. Looking right at the uneven plaster covering the big stones of the wall. White emulsion covered the plaster, but the shape of the stones beneath still showed. In the kitchen — which he had not painted yet; now never would — the stones were worn bare, red as if they had been burned in a slow roasting fire, their surfaces gritty and rough. He wondered, where had they come from? What had burned them? Amongst them? And before that, who had brought them together and taken them out of the ground? They were ground. Not like brick, an artefact, still less like the concrete blocks, with or without foam-filled cavities, with which he had often seen new houses being built. These great bulky things had once been the ground on which people, animals had walked; within whose interstices the roots of trees and tillered grasses had crept; on whose bared upper sides water and sunlight had gleamed.

When? Where? What living and dancing, dreaming and baptizing had passed among the stones when the stones had been the ground? And now the stones were the wall, and walls were synonyms for homes. He, seeking home-lessness, passed his hand over them in their vertical arrangement; leaned against them, watched the sunlight or the firelight pass across them. If he found a similar stone outside, would he bring it inside and sit on it? Would he leave it in the garden and sit on it? If the wall fell down, would he pick up the stones, one by one and place them up, one upon another, or leave them strewn for those pinkish red weeds with the jagged petals to sprawl over and amongst, and himself picnic there on a mild day? Sitting on the again ground . . .

Mosses would come, lichens and butterflies and ash-flights and snail mucus; and there would be sunshine and drizzle and children, and sheep when the children had gone home . . . In his dream he felt the warm sun and the damp soil under his back, and watched his cottage become land like all the rest of the hillside, until it was not his cottage but a stony enclosure with ash saplings left growing on the ridge of the bank. An enclosure which he knew intimately and without surprise, as he did his father and mother.

He slept there that night with the stones his father, and the trees his mother.

The ravens flew in, glutted, from the south-east; from the direction in which Carac had thrown his spear. It was from there that what was to come to the dinas would come; so when the Tracker left the dinas it was in that direction, searching for any shadow which that coming might cast before it.

The old Roman road was closing. Saplings leaned in on it, and the swathe on either side, that had once been cropped low so that it could provide no hiding place, was now a tangle of bramble and haws, blackthorn, gorse and rowan. Overhead the great image-road of starlit and moon-lit sky was narrowed to a curved blade of numinous shinings which gleamed in the puddles and glinted on the tiny pools in the forks of branches. The strident yell of a she-owl crossed between the cracked paving and the shivering sky, and travelled on eastwards — beyond the last known milestone, *Imp.Caes*; beyond the known.

The Tracker smelled the presence of another of his kind somewhere in the dark behind the road. Not a soldier: no smell of metal or leather on the damp forest air. No horse, no honey, meat, cheese, chains, blood, resin, cattle dung — a man on the edge, travelling with nothing to sell and nothing to eat. A man who, moreover, had not eaten for some time, for there were no faeces near.

The Tracker came close, like a viper, on his belly. There. The heap of black that was not shadow. Breathing that was nasal and regular and fluttered sleepishly on the soft palate. A lunatic? Lunatic was unsafe. Lunatic and Sacred were too closely knotted.

The Tracker watched, belly pressed down on the shrivelled leaves of a harebell. The she-owl moved south, towards the moon, and then west. Later, rain came, noisy in the trees. Later still it ceased, and a spider's web grew out of the dark and lay naked in the dangerous light.

The lunatic stayed asleep until the pigs were almost on him. The sow came first, shoving her way breathily between the brambles, gruffling, wheezing and flapping her ears. Her bonhams came after her in a line, skipping through the prickles, their stripes bright with infancy, but their little eyes already wicked like those of the boar who would rip a man from throat to bowel with his tusks, and grind his testicles between massive, many-cusped teeth.

The squeal of one piglet hustled by another woke the lunatic, who sat up with a jerk, eye to eye with the sow, who was about to investigate his black garment and the little iron bell beside him. He gave a yodelling bellow and wiped his face with his hand, which trembled. From where he lay, the Tracker could see a vein beating violently in his throat.

'Swine!' the lunatic shouted suddenly. 'Swine, swine, swine!' He raised both his arms, clenching his fists. The dark sleeves fell back, and the Tracker saw the white inside of thin arms, with deep grooves between the fierce tendons.

The pigs crashed back into the brambles. So much wrath over pigs? But the strange man was turning now, circling round the tree so that the focus of his anger shifted from the animals to the forest. Then he lowered his hands, clasping them and wrapping them round himself as if he were cold.

This was the moment to approach him — while he was uncertain.

But the lunatic was not uncertain. He turned, stared at the lightest part of the sky, and raised his hands, palms out to the morning. His voice, when he spoke, was clear and curious, dipping and curving over the words as if speech were a shore upon which some vision lapped:

Deus noster, Deus omnium hominum,
Deus coeli ac terrae, maris et fluminum . . .

As line followed line, his eyes became unfocused. The rhythm of the invocation took him in the spine, and he swayed with the flow of it, supple under the beat, curving in the arms of a Beloved:

> *Inspirat omnia,*
> *vivicat omnia,*
> *superat omnia,*
> *suffulcit omnia . . .*

The Tracker felt the elements of the poem rising around him as if great, smooth boulders of blood-red sandstone and blond limestone, of blue slate and milk-white quartz, flint, translucent as honey and basalt with the night on fire in its heart, were logically and inexorably mounting around him . . .

> *THIS DEUS WILL ROOF ME OVER —*
> *dowse the gleam in the hare's eye;*
> *shut out the perfume of the gorse;*
> *inhibit the incoming of the hind —*
>
> *et stella in ministerium*
> *maiorum luminum posuit . . .*
>
> *AND CLOSE THE STARS ON ME.*

For the first time since his mother had been eaten by the dogs, the Tracker felt loss.

Very softly he said, 'Go away —', raising himself from the ground, to his knees, then to his feet. Leaves clung to his body, some gold, some green. His hands, where he had clenched the muds and mosses, were green. There was a thin streel of bramble caught in his hair and small droplets of blood stood on his forehead where its thorns had torn his skin. He rose, green, sudden, powerful; the vehicle of a great rage and a deep pain — (*I, Deus, will roof you over . . .*)

The stranger lifted his hands in fear, and a single black-bird lifted song.

Birds of ill omen, heron and crow, flew in the malign quarter of the sky as the Tracker and the presbyter moved through the trees, southwards towards the dinas. Out of sight, up above them and near where the wolves laired, ravens croaked and thin, pallid clouds covered the sun bringing a chill, grey drizzle that dripped monotonously among the dark branches, rap-rap-rap on the ancient trunks of the oak and ash and occasional elm. Every few steps the presbyter stopped and took up a posture of prayer; standing very upright, arms straight out sideways from the shoulders, forearms raised and palms open. 'Kyrie eleison, Christe eleison,' he called out at the holly boughs and the lichens and ground-ivy and the rattling, shifting leaves on the forest floor. 'Allelujah!' So he called at every turn in the path, every looming, fern-hung, grasping bough. Viperous ivy stems leaned in and insidiously stroked the backs of his hands as he groped about his robe for the missing bell.

A shiver of fear bristled on the Tracker's back at the invocations from behind him. All around him the all-present, all-formed, all-joined lives of life heard the words, the insult of the Allelujah. The rutting stag and the mistletoe alike; the maned and bristled boar and the spotted, poisonous fungi; the red-pointed bull and the scarlet yew-berry; the raven and the drowning black water below the cascade all breathed to him on the shivering air, 'This Deus would steal our spirits and put our bodies in chains — *ocha, ocha*.'

Through the doomed trees the enclosure of the nemeton lay uphill to the east of them, the air here clearer and lighter without the heavy, arboreal presences of the closed forest. The Tracker was about to turn south again to the foot of the dinas when the presbyter pushed past him with a wild eleison towards the emanation of open space as if towards a shining vision. The raucousness of his cry put up every mourning bird and fowl into the echoing air and, in the terrible silence which followed, their frantic wing-beats threshed the wet mist into flying spheres of rainbow-brilliant prisms. Before the first of the black, wooden idols on the perimeter of the enclosure the presbyter crumpled like an empty hide and fell to his knees, howling.

The bulging, white eyes of the image stared over him; the inset, richly painted priapus jutted out above him. Implacable, the image stood in his path, oak heart-wood exposed.

'Christ Saviour,' — the high, rattling voice like a she-wolf in the scree. 'That I, Fiác Macciarus, crubthir of Patrick, am sent to baptise these idolatrous and evil unbelievers — Allelujah! Eye of God, look before me!' His voice rose higher, spittle and soil clogging his lips, sobs twisting his throat, until he choked and grew quiet, shivering.

The Tracker retreated into the leaf litter and lichens which still clung to him, shrank inwards behind the stains and smears of the forest, crouching as close to the ground as his ankles could bring him, flexed for action. The man lying shaking on the ground in front of the great image was either in the grip of an influence from outside himself or was about to become a road for intervention from outside. His whole body writhed and arched, and his outflung hands tore up great divots of earth and sharp slate chips. Suddenly, flinging back his head, he screamed out: 'Be left to wither and rot like a solitary tree struck by fire from God!' And fell forwards in the soft susurration of forest.

The stillness that held the forest was absolute. No live thing stirred, plant or creature. Only when a wren briefly music'd deep in the eastern glades, so far off that she might have been in another world, did the Tracker move out towards the motionless body and drag him gently out from under the stare of the Heartwood image.

It was some time before Fiác came properly to his senses and was able to shuffle, weak and still shuddering, along the dim paths away from the nemeton.

At the gate the Tracker reached behind him and gripped Fiac's robe, attaching the stranger to himself. The porter looked, assessed and moved slightly, allowing the Tracker and the bruise-eyed ecstatic to move through the gaping inner posts.

Torchlight and firelight reddened the enclosure. The Tracker chained Fiác in among the deer-hounds and left him shouting 'Allelujah!'

4

The hierarchy of the dinas stirred. It was the wind, perhaps, chilling towards winter now that Samhain was past, which rattled the hierarchy. It rattled the sweeping, dry twigs at the ends of the ash branches and rattled the coarse feathers on the backs of the geese. Dead wood-ash blew from the hearths where black, bony sticks showed like exposed bits of burned skeleton. The king of the dinas, who had been more or less dreaming for many years, there having been no battles to harry him into his warrior shape, woke from his dreams of still water and stood on one leg in a patch of cold sunshine, looking critically at the thigh and calf muscles of young men. His poet stood near him, gazing into the depths of a beaker of mead, whether in anticipation or meditation was not clear, and close by his charioteer was putting his wrists in hobbles and snapping them to test their strength. There was not much sound of voices, but some clinking and clattering and fast footsteps. Because the waning sun was low in the sky it showed up all the failures in the ramparts, shining its way along splits in the wooden beams that held the stones laced together; poking its light between stones where courses had fallen away and never been repaired; casting heavy shadows behind the grass tussocks in the overgrown ditches. Giant Herb Robert, crimson-leaved with autumn, sprawled amongst the overgrown slates of the abandoned glacis, and the last of the year's butterflies, some tabby, one harebell blue, dithered over the ragged flowers and the bright-cut leaves, sun on their wings.

When the Tracker was not working, he did absolutely nothing. He lay about in the sun, if it should shine, or like a vagabond, in front of a cooking fire. He was usually in the way, usually asleep. Sometimes he would be asked to help with something: to carry stones to the workers on the rampart, or to hold a mare in front of the stallion; but he would smile a little, shrug and not do it. Doing nothing created spaces in his body and his head. He thought of it in the way he thought of the pale spaces that balmy summer evenings make: a baring of essential structures; a ritual nakedness before the crisis of night. He ate little, after the first spasm of gluttony for cooked meat; drank sparingly despite the scorn that was occasionally thrown at him, and had no woman of his own. Children, who mostly liked him, had begun to watch him out of the corners of their eyes and remember what he said to them; herdsmen were always welcoming when they had a sick animal on their hands. The king's stare followed him.

Like all animals, the Tracker was part of the sun. He moved to the sun's ascent and ebb through the day as through the year, without calculation or counting, rounding to the great festivals as the stag came to the hind and the seal to the haul under the cliff.

His mother's uncles' father and his father's grandfather had known days of tax and levy; had had names for those days and systems for computing their return; had marked the year's paved street with precise milestones cut with sharp figures. Theirs had been a geometric life, he thought, laid out like the streets according to an instrument-drawn paradigm, disregarding and overriding the flourishes and balance of the land it was imposed upon. Since then, somehow, there had been more rain; the rivers had swollen, the marshes and bogs become more treacherous, the winters longer and the snow deeper. The streets had run with water, and the geometry of the Empire had blurred, its precise lines had faded out and washed away, and there was no one left who knew how to re-draw them. Eventually a nesting season had come round when the heron had found it safe to nest in the crook of the river where the kingcups are always early. That season there had been bright green, succulent nettles between the paving stones of the straight street below the dinas and a tough little bramble had rooted under the cornerstone of the guardroom in the fortlet at Erglodd. By the time Loegaire's pirates were using it as an overnight pen in the Irish slave-raids, the guardroom was a ferny bower in a secure thicket of blackberry and haws and scarlet thornberries. The Tracker used it himself now, having ousted a dynasty of black foxes who had claimed it after the slavers in Vortigern's time. He used their dried faeces to smear on his palms, soles and thighs, their scent being stronger than his when he had been out for some time. Only when there were wolves about did he make full use of his man-stink.

He lay on his back in the chilly sunshine, sprawled against the outside slope of the ditch, where it turned inwards to shield the gateway to the dinas. From here he could see the king and the fidgety hierarchy through the remains of the old gate, because they had gathered there, pointing out to each other the inadequacies of the defences; the collapsed state of the entry; the total absence of the walkway over the passage; all the things they had been living with for nearly a generation; letting happen. Now they had happened, and fighting-men were called heroes if they had driven off a few cattle from some wretched collection of huts, or because they had a scar on their forearm from scrapping in a shallow brook with an adolescent from a local rath who had nothing better to do, either. A generation of nothing better to do, because the markets had closed down, the villas were crumbling, and the taxman never came now that there was no legion or administration to feed; and men like himself and Echw and Carac, who had been bred specially for battle — dams and sires put together to get sons like Carac and him and Echw — had looked aside and found their dreams elsewhere. He in the sun, Carac, more dangerously, in the Bear.

Only the horse-trade was left; the continual, feverish demands from the Bear for horses, more horses, more horses. Every time the Bear's men came clattering up the old street from the south, bringing bundles of rope and whips for the round-up and the drive, silver, glass, looted jewels and a cartload of wine for payment, it was Carac who showed off the horses of the dinas: the spray-white and wild-strawberry roans; the golden mares with amber manes and tails like the hair of a king's daughter's; the silver greys and lake-blue roans; the heartwood browns and jet-blacks. It was Carac who would thrust everyone aside so that he alone would display them savagely on the flat field beside the river: wheeling, galloping, throwing the javelin, vaulting. And every time they took the horses away and left Carac behind with dead, bewildered eyes to turn to the mushroom and grow a little older, a little more soiled, until they came again. *Ocha, ocha.*

The stink of man eddied above the Tracker's head, the wind chilly enough to raise it breast high to a running hound, but not strong enough to shred it. He lay below it, down among the roots of the tussocks, his nose scenting the cropped, late grass, nostalgic of summer, milky where the goat herds had grazed now that their browse was brittle and falling. It was a frightening stink, complex as it was with the hot rancour of piss and sweat impregnated with beer; warm with greased leather and tannin, roasted flesh and honey, but cold with the sour, acid tang of bronze and iron and tarnished inlay. As always, when he first came in from the forest, he felt nervous, cornered by the smell. Trapped. After two meals and a night in the huts he smelled the same himself and would dream repetitively of being blind or legless; set, hopelessly maimed, before a great peril. He never stayed long, now, in the dinas. He had come to think that he was afraid of the dinas.

Cathal Kerr — in a way, 'also' — lay on his back in the chilly sunshine, sprawled against the outside slope of a ditch where it petered out near the top of the side-path up from the track through the wood. He had found his castle, but it was turret-less and unromantic. It was indeed, as Mrs Post Office had said, 'gone'. It was nothing but shallow, overgrown ditches running around most of the top of the hill. He thought it was a highly defensible position, with its steep, rock-face on the far side and that it must have had a commanding view over Castlegate and the valley, and over the other valleys behind, when the trees were felled. He had followed the ditches in a rough circle around the hill's crown, stumbling through the ash saplings and hollies in the windswept area on the very top. There was no trace of any motte, just this scant ditch overgrown with wind-scoured trees, the shifting, noisy slates under the mosses and ivies on the slopes, and some stones set upright like shark's teeth where the ditch levelled out: an entrance, perhaps — but to what? And why the evil, jagged stones, more appropriate to defence against spirits than longbows? He wondered vaguely if perhaps it was a hill-fort or a sacred enclosure from pre-Christian times. He felled the ashes; filled the valley with horses and cattle and long-haired men wearing torcs and gold brooches, erected neat

77

round huts with golden thatch and stood a druid beside a pyramidal bonfire . . .

There was no knowing. He rolled on to his stomach, his flippant scepticism cold and dirty like a cloud across the running, winterward sun. Even that was wrong. The sun was as it always was in late autumn; it was the earth which moved, not running but spinning towards its own black hole in time and space — supposing that were true. It was not true for him. Not true for the Tracker. For both of them the earth was flat and the running sun whipped across it on a windy day and beat from it in high summer. How could he tell which was true?

Later, standing on the lip of the lower ditch, looking across it and upwards at the dinas, could he tell? Could he, as it were, at least learn how to tell?

Later again, kicking at loose stones on his way down the hill towards the path out of the wood: because, *Who the hell is the Tracker, anyway?*

Road — Road — Road. His eyes knowing every stone in the walls, every drab ewe trailing around the thin fields, every blocked drain where rotten leaves fouled the slate-built culverts, and brown floods seethed out over the tarmac. His feet knowing every mended patch as a trap, his thighs knowing every gradient between Castlegate and the Post Office in daylight, Castlegate and the Black Lion in the dark. His shoes leaking, his wet, wind-chilled hands blue and shaking. A tramp, going because he was going, with nowhere to go. Gethin did not exist, Gethin was the local word for 'We-don't-want-ones-like-you-up-there', or even, in Cathal's glummer moments, for 'shotgun'. Gethin was the local word for illegal trapping, for shooting protected species, robbing hawks' nests and poaching trout from the lower reaches of the river. Sheep-rustling was probably called Gethin too, maybe even horse-theft. There were notices in the Post Office about freeze-branding and cattle-rustling. Gethin was the reason for them. Fuck Gethin, for turning him into a tramp in the ceaseless rain.

Last night he had become so angry about Gethin that Bar-Person had suggested that he go and talk to the priest who was 'well into olden days'.

He peered at the gatepost in front of him. First Farmer had said that even Cathal couldn't miss Hengardd, where the old priest lived, it having such an old stone for the gate to lean on, and his being keen on old things, isn't it? In the last of the November daylight Cathal squatted on his heels among the dark, wet nettles, clawing them aside and peering at the shadowy inscription amongst the lichens and the drip-stains.

IMP.CAES.TRAIAN. . HADRIANUS . . .
A . .GONT . . . M.P.LXX . . .
A MORIDUN. . . .P.L . . .

Imp.Caes.
Trajan?
. . . more than seventy thousand paces from one city; more than fifty thousand to the next . . . A long way from the Civitas, this — from any Civitas. For nearly two millennia the implacable Flavian lettering had been scoured by wind, rain and sleet. In some places frost and sun had worn it quite away; in others it survived, impeccable. Imp.Caes. Now rain trickled down the upright of the I, hung in the serifs of the T, and had washed away the civitas at . .GONT . . ., so far away; had weathered MORIDUN. . out of measurable distance; would wash away all Names written in ink on the flowing surface of the straight road — all except Imp.Caes., which was cut in stone: a milestone on the street, mark of the Cities.

The building rose sheer, black against the darkening

night. No windows in this wall. No ingress, no welcome. Hengardd.

He stumbled through the narrow gate held up by Imp.Caes. and along a stony path to an unlit doorway in the side of the tall house.

'Are you a priest?' he said, when the door was opened.

The old man said fondly, 'Time is such an inconsistent old hussy,' as if he were talking about a faintly regretted mistress from his past.

Cathal nearly shouted back his denial, but the long years in Cash-and-Nooky Land made this impossible for him yet. Instead he mumbled, 'Time is perpetual. It can't be messed up. It's not a clock or a bowl of soup that runs out. It goes on and on. Before, after, all the time. Times end — that's it, really. There's a time, and then there's another time. Like that Imp.Caes. of yours at the gate. What's Imp.Caes. to me that I should weep for him?'

The priest smiled his old man's unbothered smile and indicated that Cathal should fill up his glass with more gin and bitter lemon. 'Stronger — stronger —' he said petulantly as Cathal's hand hesitated with the square gin bottle poised over the beer tumbler. Surely it could not be good for so old a man to drink like this? Worse than harm coming to him, might he not become drunk and fail to answer Cathal's urgent questions? Already there were bright little spots of scarlet on the stained, old skin over the sharp cheekbones, and a blurry, incoming tide washing the faded eyes.

'No head for drink, Time,' he said mischievously, grinning at Cathal. 'It's always been a good way of making her back off a little. Get drunk enough and she'll keel right over and go out like a light. Surely you don't need me to tell you that? But that's not what you want, is it, Cathal Kerr? More like rape and plunder — that your idea? Rape the old whore and plunder her of the truths on her fingers and ankles — and her gold teeth besides. I know. It's been tried before. But who knows? You might be the very man to succeed. I wonder, now. I wonder . . .'

Cathal shifted nervously under the old man's speculative stare. Surely the old bugger was drunk. He cursed Gethin for turning into a euphemism, and Bar-Person for sending him along here to question this derelict old cleric about the lumps and hollows in the wood at the top of the hill. Perhaps it had been a nasty trick played on a gullible outsider to keep him, Cathal, from turning up in the Black Lion on wet nights and nagging the farmers with questions about Gethin. Now this old crab was sitting, slightly sideways, tip-tilted with the gin, and with a pincer locked into Cathal's viscera.

'What makes you so anxious to get at her? Or is it that you are in love with the old —' Cathal expected an antique word like 'besom' but the old man said 'hooker?' in a rudely contemporary fashion.

'I'm dying,' Cathal said flatly, holding up his left arm, although since there was nothing unusual to show except a wavering which might have been due to the gin, he looked as if he were claiming a goal scored.

'Aren't we all?'

'Not at my age, we aren't all. Knowingly.'

'At mine, though. Gin?'

'No. No more gin. Have you nothing else to drink? I hate gin. It comes from horrible places — like the Marina Bar or a filing-cabinet.'

'Not at all. This one is distilled in London.'

'Exactly. Cash-and-Nooky Land.'

'From which you are running away, I hear in the Black Lion. Tell me, did you have a nice place there?'

'If you like prisons — institutions and prisons and rehabilitation homes. If you don't, you jump the wall. Doing time then looking for time.' Obviously it did not much matter how he expressed himself — the old man was past understanding anything except the gurgle of a bottle — so he might as well use metaphors and symbols and plain facts and allusions to facts just as they came along in his head. Saved a lot of trouble. If the old crab would just release his clawhold on Cathal's gut, he would slip away and leave him to sleep it off. Cathal wondered if he did sleep it off, or whether he started again before that had time to happen?

Vignette: old man's head on a tear-stained pillow, a gin bottle on a chair beside; and a giant candy-striped straw, one end in the bottle, the other between the old man's teeth. Overhead, an illuminated Bleeding Heart lit by a red bulb.

'And what do you call the place you live in now, Cathal Kerr?' the old man said sharply.

'Land's End?' Cathal said, embarrassed by the inaccuracy of the vignette.

'I don't think so.' He grinned like a skeleton in a sagging museum case. 'My *alma mater* had a place called the Examination Schools. A big, austere hall all got up with Corinthian pillars that never quite came into full leaf, if you know what I mean. Interested in architecture? No?'

'*Look on my works, ye mighty . . .*'

'Quite so. The ambiguity, at least, remains quotable.'

'Being snubbed has always made me angry,' Cathal said meanly.

'In that case, it would seem to be time to ask you why you are here. Anger is an excellent aperitif to conversation. Gethin never sends me visitors idly.'

'He didn't — and please don't mention Gethin to me. I've had a bellyful of Gethining. The pub sent me here — Gethin doesn't exist, I'm quite aware of that, thank you.'

'No? Ah, well. Nonetheless, because of Gethin, you have arrived here. You wouldn't dispute that?'

Cathal searched for some up-to-date mockery, wanting to get out from this meeting which was turning into an

interview between Father Time, Imp.Caes. and a panto-
mime sidekick (played by himself).

He said, 'I'm dying. I have some sort of muscular disinte-
gration — there are several sorts. It's getting worse, and I
haven't enough time for perplexing encounters. I want
simple, believable explanations to fusty, dull questions
which are outside the scope of fucking and shitting farmers.
They told me you were a priest and had some history, and
I assumed you might be willing to give me a little local
tradition. Probably my cheques have bounced in the Black
Lion, and you are a New Age *competens*, and they saw this
as a comic way of getting rid of me —'

'What? A brush-off, as they call it? No, no. Gethin has
much more unsubtle ways of doing that. Ferrets, for instance. Truths, terrier bitches, vulgarity — that sort of thing.
So what did you ask that interested him enough to have you
sent here? Answer slowly. Think about it. What have you
been asking?'

He was still implying that Gethin was a person . . . Well,
Cathal was prepared to humour him, not to force a dead-
end argument. Perhaps he could get hold of some coffee
and make his escape while he could still walk and before
he felt he ought to put the old man to bed.

'I asked about the castle on the top of the hill — over
there,' he waved his arm vaguely at the window. 'Where
there is no castle. I live in the cottage at the bottom of the
path — Castlegate, it's called. You know? I want to know
about the castle.'

'Why?'

'Well, I would, wouldn't I? Living in Castlegate, naturally
I'd want to know; what castle?'

'Naturally, yes.'

Had he imagined that dryness of tone? Was he imagining
the length of time it took for the old man to say more? The
old man said no more. The length of time stretched into a
silence between them.

'Go on,' the old man said. Cathal could not see his eyes; how far the gin-tide might be coming in, as it were. He was beginning to think: bloody gin — but the old man's voice had been sharp and clear, not slurred.

Defensively, Cathal said, 'I don't think anything else. Just, what is this castle? Whose?'

'Why "whose"?'

'Most castles are somebody's. Castles have people — Bayard or John o' Gaunt or some story or other. It may not be true — doesn't matter, if it's a good story. That sort of "Whose" castle.'

'Whose castle do you think it is, Cathal Kerr?'

O, mine, he said in his head, or probably in his head, for the old man did not move but just watched him. It's my castle in some way. That's what I want to know. Why am I the Who for this non-castle? But he could not say that, nakedly. Nonetheless, the old man was expecting him to say something of the sort, otherwise why was he looking at him like this, wryly or dryly or whatever word best described that mixture of suspicion and arrogantly with-held knowledge? The look was making Cathal feel small and defensive, and the smaller he felt the bigger grew the knot of anger that had already been generated. Lacking the authority to say, I'm asking the questions, he said sarcastically,

'Perhaps Gethin thought you might know. I'm sorry I have bothered you — I'd better go now, it's getting late —'

The old man pressed the tips of his fingers together — beeswax-coloured and smooth; hands that had never dug terrier bitches out of a trappy hole among the brambles; priest's hands, come to that. 'It's never late. Only, some-times, too late. We could pray that that is in the future.'

'Which,' said Cathal crossly, 'is in rather short supply. I said, I'm dying. Not like you; like me. Only me. Obscurant-ism won't get me out of it.'

'Are we talking fact, whatever that may be, or fear or

hope? What is this "castle" you have to reach before the future runs out on you? Who holds it? Against whom?'

Is that what is up there in the wood? A stronghold of some sort? A defensible position against the palsy — even, perhaps, a position from within which to defend the very palsy itself? Gin was no good to him as an aperitif to thought. This was not the castle he was talking about — this was the old man's castle, somewhere quite else. Wasn't it?

He said carefully, for his consonants were slackening as the old man's were not, 'The castle I'm asking about is a lot of lines and hollows in the trees at the top of a hill. S'not a psychological fortification. It's lumps of ground and lacks of ground. It's really there. I've found it. I walked around on it. Clump, clump, my feet went on it. Clump,' he finished positively.

'And who did you find up there?' the old man's voice was silky.

'Nothing much.'

'Not what. Who?'

'Ah,' said Cathal. Then, 'Some woodlice. Butterflies. There were crows, too. I thought even ravens — big gluttonous ones. And something in the ferns. Perhaps a fox. Almost certainly a fox. Gin?'

The old man held out his beer tumbler. Cathal poured for them both with his steadier, right hand.

'Go on,' the old man said.

'I thought someone was there,' Cathal said, suddenly giving in; suddenly wanting help from this powerful, knowing magister. 'Someone — I didn't see anyone, but there is someone. There's someone I want —' And then he was shouting, violent, like a drunk or a Panic, 'but they won't come — he won't come in, close . . . close to me —' and felt saliva at the corner of his mouth.

The old man leaned forward, staring at Cathal, rheum making his eyes shine like stars, like holes made by a throwing spear cast at the sky.

'Can you say his name, Cathal Kerr?'

'He is not Cathal Kerr,' he shouted. 'No, not. He's some-one else. You tell me his name — you know it — I can see that you know.'

The priest said, dreamily:

> *'I am the silence that is incomprehensible . . .*
> *I am the utterance of my name —'*

He sat quiet, staring at the floor and seeing, hearing, some-thing inner, something supremely sad. After a while Cathal, all the anger and the panic dissipated and leaving him cold and directionless, said, 'Is that all, old man, Father?'

'Leave me alone and go home, Cathal Kerr. Go home.'

5

It is dark back here, or in here, or down — wherever. The tunnel is not lightless, but murky, indistinct. Old men sit against the damp walls amongst the drip-stains and the genesis of slime, their legs bent up like storks' under their small bodies. Corpses, perhaps, wrapped in cloths and unstill as if responding to wappe and wan. Ambrosius is here, for some reason eyeless, the purple dye faded almost to pale pink in the damp and running from his sheet in blenched stripes. Soon it will be gone entirely, and there will be nothing left to show whatever it was he declared with such violence. O, such violence! The blood stains have gone dull brown; they are permanent, of course. Gildas will know that when the time comes. Vortigern and Hengist and Patrick, propped up against the wet stonework and left dreaming of immortality, or Germanus in Auxerre, or barrows harbouring perhaps drag-ons out there among the hushed islands. Icel of Angel and — far on along there, where it might be that there is a bend if it could be clearly seen — is it Cunedda? The shreds of an old plaid, fallen from the shanks, maybe, or the fleshless collar-bone. Where is the brooch that held the plaid in place — still wearing it, as he was, when they brought him down from the lithic north, sons and all? Jutes and Brits, Saxons, Picts painted unintelligibly, Irish, dolphins and one Goth. Why only one Goth? Why any Goth? Theodoric knows. Are they his feet, booted, ringing on the stonework, sloshing in the black pools on the floor? Who is that, coming back here — who shall we have, eh? MacErca or Cadwallon? Cato of Dumnonia or baby Maccudeccetus? Little fingers in the murk — o, phalanges, but informed phalanges — pointing: Eeeny, meeny miney MO! *Manus Dei* slowly drawing a name: graffiti in half-uncials in the half dark where the unstill old men are watching.

This the Central Tree knows, having its roots so deep. And the Tracker knows, being in his shape so much a tree that with his toenails he nudges Patrick, St., so that the old man sways and perhaps would rattle were it not for the effects of the damp . . . But the tree was old, desperately and dyingly old. Hairs on the root system had shrivelled, grown brittle this last year or two, loosened and fallen into mouse burrows and beetle holes. The Tracker, leaning against it, could feel that the tree had died; that the cells which had carried the spring sap-rise every year since Paul the Chain had flayed the tree-loving pagan British soul, back in Constantius' time, had crumbled inwards to decay, hollow as leeched veins, as marrowless bones, as Ambrosius' sagging femur. Leaning against it, the Tracker knew the lifelessness of the tree through his vertebrae. Knew that this mid-winter the ultimate sunrise would not reach this ash tree. Felt it dead at his back. He touched it gently with the palm of his hand — not for the tree, the salute of its passing, but for himself. Just a marking of its existence in his own pattern; less than a rite — perhaps a tally-mark in his being where one line in his pattern had completed its knot.

There were wiry little stems of growth in the leaf litter at his feet. He hoped that one of these was from this tree and was careful with his foot in case he killed it prematurely. He hoped that it would survive. He smiled at the ground, in case. Someone else's pattern, he thought, without following the idea, merely brushing against a sense of time that would come after the tree and after him and therefore not to do with either of them. Though in fact it could have been greatly to do with both of them, if there was a sapling from that ash tree, and if it were to survive.

Cathal Kerr, standing under the ash tree which was in his pattern, knew none of this. But he was attending to something, because he felt that something was attending to him. There was nothing there in this part of the wood where he was; nothing but trees. Benign? Hostile? He was a Fool, lurking under a bough, anxiety-ridden about whether a tree was going to be kind to him. Something in the hollow of his back crept with self-ridicule, and something behind his eyes stung with self-pity. The old man, last night, had not been kind, could not have cared less about Cathal's acknowledged dying — which, as a priest, he ought to have. Perhaps the old man was so familiar with the knowledge of dying, old as he was, that he found nothing interesting in it? Perhaps that was what degraded livers did — sillied the mind with fantasies about spirits and Utterance so that the essential difference between the living and the not-living drifted away on a tide of gin slings. Or perhaps, again, the old man's knowledge was that there was no difference, so that he could sit there, gated in by Imp.Caes., impervious to the footfall in the tunnel — which might have been Cathal's or his own or even that of the Bear. No wonder then, that he was so hard. Hard and unkindly, as if he, Cathal, were no more closely related to him than a piece of old wood —

Cold, the chill of sudden fright — he was coming to know it so well, that clutch of fear in the vitals.

What am I afraid of now?

Look up, up at the tree where you are, at all the old wood (How old?). Unrelated, is it, Cathal Kerr — so many of its branches gone, so many that are left, barren and shrunk. And here and there, dangling from stalk joints so thin that the next wind gust must snap them, rags of yellow, sodden leaves quiver uselessly. Like your arm?

Like my arm — SHIT. He reached behind him and beat his left fist savagely against the ash bark. He could still use his arm — of course he could still use it: carry things with it, hit things, hit men, cut throats with it . . .

Still cutting throats, Cathal Kerr?

He had never cut anyone's throat! Had he? Perhaps a sluglet in lettuce. He thought of the holes in the potatoes he had cooked, and made pictures of who had lived and eaten in the holes. What had become of those lives when he had sliced the potatoes and himself eaten them? Perhaps, he thought in a rush, they had survived the boiling and the scum and were even now making holes in his . . . Was it nausea or hysteria rising in his oesophagus? Or a grub? Cut his throat and let it out? His physical body was black with blight; the palsied arm would not hold still enough, after all, to cut CATHAL'S throat.

Where was he? Where was Cathal now? A fever started up in him, or a panic. He could not tell which, but knew they meant widely different things; things that might be intensely important. Mad or sick — sick or mad? Deep in his brain, deep in the bone marrow, somewhere the knowledge was in him, but he could not reach it.

He stared around him at the figures under the other trees. There, a sick Cathal, dark red flush on the cheekbones, waxy pale at the temples, with starting hair and his own, shivering limbs. He was holding the sapling behind him, gripping it with his right hand, so that the young thing stirred restlessly, bowed and twisted by the man's clutch, as if it would get away, ducking and dodging through the undergrowth. But it was a rooted thing and could not move where it would. A captive thing, and Cathal hanging on to it, for help, for rescue, disabled by fever and fear of fever with death at its end; hanging on and distressing the child to the very depth of its tap-root so that it would be weakened, probably, for life, never able to fulfill what it might otherwise be: great or beautiful or useful.

A thrush, sensing it strained and distorted, flew to more stable branches deep over the second rampart of the dinas. In the depths below, a mole, disturbed, moved in a reactive jerk.

Cathal shouted, 'Don't — ' at the violence done in the feverish man's name. 'Cathal, don't, no, no, no —' His wild cry put up the woodpigeons with a clatter, and he lurched forward into the clearing as if to pull that Cathal away from the child before he injured it beyond help. Behind him his own voice struck the stone blocks in the walls of the dinas and hit back at him — 'No, no' — whipping him round to respond, face to face with Cathal under the thorn tree, its low branch tangling his brow so that the blood ran down over his eyes. That was where the panic was, answering the echo from the vault of the tunnel — 'No, no, no' — to the old, old men propped in cloths against the dripping walls, and the booted feet still coming closer, ringing out in the dark down there or back there, wherever. (Whose feet?)

Jesus Saviour — that is a name to conjure with, to stir old men's bones with. Say it again, shout it aloud this time, as if there were no one listening who might think you were crazy; or — and this came very quietly — as if it were a prayer.

He was thinking now, he realized. Not feeling, or hallucinating or whatever he had been doing — or that some part of him for which he had no name had been doing. He thought of the names in the vocabulary of fiction — image, psychic extension, vision, trip, fantasy, delusion. Of them all, only Vision was not diminishing, and he had had no vision. Vision had become unacceptable at about the same time as horse-dung had, in Oxford Street.

There, it was over. Linear time had re-asserted itself. The sapling had straightened, the thorn receded. He wondered, Will it blossom on Christmas Day? He felt the grimace twist his lips and shook his head, tired, almost tearful like a child after too riotous an occasion. That the blackthorn flower at mid-winter —

That Grace come

And that the world pass away —

I have been having visions. I am dying, you see. Yes, probably really, whatever really is — but that may be part of the vision — I don't know yet. Anyway, I have this shakiness and weakness in my left arm, and it's — well, strange, you know? I'll die of it. No, I don't know when, but —

He was standing with his back to the fire, talking to Gemma. The fire was going well, freshly sawn logs crackling at the rims and pulsing in the heartwood. He was blissfully warm, and it was probably that which made him so easy about the palsy. Gemma was sitting in the chair which he had moved away on the night he had stayed and she had gone back alone to Cash-and-Nooky Land. Now the chair was back by the fire, and the room receptive to two. He went on trying to explain, at the same time attempting to work out what it was that made her look so slightly unfamiliar.

. . . usually, when someone is dying and knows it — o, I don't mean the very old, I mean, well, us — usually the people around them try to make things as good as possible for them. You know, if the weather is good, and they like picnics, someone takes them out into the country; or to the opera, if that is their thing, or buys them something special — a salmon pink cyclamen or Russian Sobranies or a gorgeous bathrobe. Nice, special things, to like.

It was going very well. Fluently, really. He was cradling a glass of his favourite Irish whiskey, but not actually drinking it —

Well, I want something nice, too. Several things, in fact. I want to know about these bright things I see. And then there are some people I have to get to know. And to fit it all in in the time before the — you know — gets me, I have to live here. Here, alone. Alone, you see. Alone . . .

He said it again — *Al-one* — making the long, round syllables draw out like the dim sound of an old prayer. He saw it transmuted into graphics, and containing his death in an arcane pattern. With knowledge, with a priest or a *magus* to guide him, he might be able to draw it.

He held his hand out towards biro or brush or stylus —

'Good God,' said Gemma, 'Your hands have got shaky. What have you been doing? Drinking?'

Ahh — *Gemma*. He had forgotten about her coming. The pattern had gone — the interlace, the knots, the controlled border. The roads through the forest were closed and tangled, impenetrable and dark.

'I am not lonely,' he cried out, turning — desolate, abandoned — towards her. He saw himself, heard himself Panic-ing, flapping round like a song-bird on a thorn, bleeding high, thin jets of blood that sang as they darted from a body he had never had before.

He said (thinking, How did she recognize me in this new form?), 'I didn't hear you arrive — how's the car?' and 'I'll just fetch the other chair — use this one — sorry about the stones in it . . .' and 'Would you like some coffee — you mightn't like it . . .' And so on and so on, looking for sticks, an old cardboard box, anything, to light the fire with — and shit, the wood was damp, he'd forgotten to dry it last night, out as he had been, in the Black Lion; asking, always asking the same questions, Where is Gethin? Who is the old priest?

He tried frenziedly to remember what he had said last, what she had said; to make logical sense, secular sense.

'There's as much pub crawling here as anywhere in Docklands. Only here, when things get hairy, there aren't any taxis to take you home. I nearly got killed the other night, thrown out of the back of a Landrover into a stone wall. Local fellow — pissed out of his mind (no, no, the stones can sit on the floor — or me, I often do). He didn't realize what had happened, and nearly backed over me, getting out of the ditch . . .' And so on and so on.

How was she? He could not tell. Who was she? What was she saying? Her smell bothered him. He knew that he knew it well — that freshness, but artificial freshness, not like the damp trees or the rain or the woodsmoke in his jersey. The kettle called to him from the kitchen, shrilled at him like a wife, and he hurried in to it, fussily, distracted. He realized that he was wondering how to entertain her. He used to wonder, anxiously, in exactly the same way, how to entertain her mother and his mother, and her god-daughter and so on and so on. What could they talk about? Would she eat a biscuit? This woman whose thighs around his hips were at one time as familiar as the clasp of his office chair — would she like a biscuit? How could he tell? How could he ask her, whose nipples' tint within a white bra was as ordinary as the shape of his own knee? He opened his hand and put his palm, meditatively, sensuously, on the smooth handle of the kettle. He did not know what Gemma was saying.

He brought the mugs in one at a time, pretending that he had forgotten his own, so that he did not have to carry one in his left hand. All his efforts to teach himself how to relax or control it had still come to nothing. He thought she noticed, but was not sure. It was as she took it from him that he realized that there was a dislocation of realities between them. He did not so much feel it, as find the words in his mind and wonder what they meant. But there was never any time to wonder when Gemma was around.

With the mug in her hand, she withdrew it and herself into the back of the chair, managing to look invincible by this act of condensation. They made small talk — about the London flat, about her work, her sister's family, her projected collection of antique maps. About bills paid and social responses deferred. They were both waiting for him to say: I am dying, you see, as he had done before she arrived. The circularity of it confused him.

He asked after the sycamores in their road — whether they had turned crimson yet. Outside the window he could see the ash tree by the gate swaying, its yellowed leaves dead on the grass where the dogs couched at night in the grand pattern in which his knots formed and reformed and slipped and repeated. He hoped he would not become dizzy thinking of it. He moved his wellingtons from the log box so that he could sit there. He felt her watching him — and watched him, himself.

She said, 'Why did you put the other chair out in the kitchen? Do you sit there? On your own?'

He snatched at the excuse. 'I had no idea potatoes took so long to cook,' he said, obliquely. Smiling a little.

'What do you do all the time, Cathal? I mean, do? Really?'

This was the time — now to begin: I have visions . . .

But he said, 'I walk a lot. Think. You might say I do nothing.'

'I see. Why?'

'I need a change, Gemma. I was getting tired.'

'The Gormans went on a cruise when he got tired that time. He was all right when they came back.'

He eyed her to see if she was attacking him yet. Had her

94

remark been a threat, a statement of disbelief, an objective or, veiled, an offer of help? It was possible that she could so misunderstand that she might genuinely think that a cruise might help him. Cocktail bars, swimming pools, cha-cha and chillies and bodies and bodies and bodies all talking in a very very small space with the salt sea boundless and binding in all dimensions. She was capable of thinking that.

He said, 'I don't need distraction — I need to be — ' He was afraid to say 'Alone' in case, at the sound of the word, the great margin came back — but damaged, askew, never to lace together again because it had been called up in the wrong place. So he changed 'Alone' to the in-word of his generation. 'I need space,' he said.

'What for?' She used words, but he saw crude blows. With a cleaver. He thought of her striking at him with that plain, elementary weapon — which would go straight through the leather, straight through the wooden frame of the shields, so heavy and plain was it. Behead a goat with a cleaver, you could. He was silent, watching the cleaver. Watching the assailant. If there were magic you would become invisible — not slog it out, blow for reeling blow, slithering in sweat, red-eyed at the ford, but evade; become a mist pearl on the thorn bough where the sweet white flowers uncurled in the evening . . .

He stayed silent, minute, an atom in a pearl of moisture, invisible to the naked eye.

She searched for him. 'Are you eating enough? You've got very thin — what do you eat?'

'Oh, I do very well. You must tell me how to manage parsnips.' He felt a little thrill, as if he had parried a thrust.

She told him briefly about parsnips. 'I brought down some avocado paté and consommé. Perhaps I should have brought beer and sandwiches — or beef tea?'

He tried to smile, imagining her in his kitchen, replacing things. How long would it take to undo her visit? It had not occurred to him before that her effect would outlive her material presence; that she would come for measurable hours and last for days. He could not live for days without the Tracker and the priest and — what were their names, the great ones still in the twilight? Would they pause, would they wait, or recede back beyond the dinas while he fought for his life on the stones in the ford?

To get back to the dinas, to get back — he felt the insidious numbness of loss.

'What?' he said.

'I said, Aren't you letting yourself get on your own mind a little?'

'What a ridiculous thing to say!' He heard the words — he'd spoken aloud. He knew the extraordinary expression so well, and the undertow of scorn that went with it. 'I am bound to be on my own mind — it's my mind, after all.' The emergency of her being there (how could his mind have dodged the responsibility of reminding him that she would come today?) made him fluent, rapid in reaction. 'Even if it's only a decision whether to pee now or be uncomfortable for a few more warm minutes, it's my mind thinking about me. Perhaps you mean something more precise.'

'Perhaps I do. Cathal, I think you ought to try and talk to somebody —'

She did not mean herself. That was sad, really. A huge relief, but sad. It ought to absolve him from any feeling of duty or even guilt towards her, but somehow it twisted itself so that he knew she had rejected him. He had not realized that before.

How long ago had it happened? He found that he had no idea. He thought of the dark shadow in the cup of the white bra; of the curve of her spine in a sundress; of avocado paté and a lost earring and the line of her shin in a winter bed. She would not stay the night, tonight. He would worry about her on the road, among the slippery fingers of the dead leaves. He felt a huge emotion, but could not identify it: reprieve, isolation, glee, hurt? It had been that easy for her to nullify him?

I have visions. I am dying, you see . . . But he did not say it this time, either. She was spending Sunday with 'new friends' in Knighton, she had told him. He had imagined how she would have noted some nice little hotels on her drive over, just in case the visit turned out unsatisfactorily. He had nodded, and she had left avocados for two. When the little car had hummed purposefully round the bend at the foot of the dinas, he had stood at the gate and cried.

There has never been a night so dark.
Never has the ground been so solid, or the air so
  dense.
In the thick soil, no creature. Grass tussocked, its
  blades coarse;
Some drops of rain fall, slow and heavy. Below, in
  the dark,
the river runs over stones; its banks sheer, cold earth.
We are waiting.
Up on the hill they, too, are waiting.
Rolled in plaids, heaped around, waiting in the dark,
there are many men.
Not men, closer than that,
kind.
The dark goes on. And the drum, now and then.
There will be a dawn. I know that. I am waiting for it,
here by the ford.

There has never been a night so dark. Dawn must come.

6

The Goth came in through the gate of the dinas with the cold lying across his shoulder like a brand. Theodoric: the same name as the great Goth who had turned the last of the Western Emperors out into the cold. He came in with the grey of the seaways in his beard. His chain-mail was dull after the journey and glinting only in the creases across the lower belly, in front of the shoulders and in a deep dent over the right breast. He carried an ugly Frankish throwing-axe in his belt, the grip bound in dark raw-hide, and a long sword in a plain, heavy-duty scabbard, the hilt hidden under the folds of his cloak. His horse was tall: a foreign, dark animal with dapples the colour of sandstone pebbles on its heavy haunches and shoulders, and a black mane and tail, tangled and coarse after days on the road. Its hooves were shod in the Roman manner with iron shoes, which clattered coldly on the slates of the track.

The raw new wood of the defences perfumed the gate-way; the horses of the Goth's five men sweated and stank, calling and screaming at the small, bright horses of the dinas who wheeled in the corrall. The people stood back suddenly as he came in. Words of praise or greeting fell aside, unused. He was not like other men. He came from too far away. It was almost as it should have been: the dinas shaking off a generation and becoming a war camp once again, singing like a struck anvil. It should have been like a poem that beats along the bloodstream and bursts from the throat. But there was no poetry in the Goth. They had hoped for hope, but this man brought none. For the first time since Badon, they were afraid. Leave. We are too poor for victory. We cannot pay what you will cost.

The sour smell of metal worn for nights on end disturbed the Tracker, who lived by animal stench. Watching the people's eyes, he tasted blood on his gums. It was not as it should have been; but the flaring autumn sun that flashed on the damage in the Goth's mail shone around Carac like a mandorla.

He moved along between the dwellings, parallel to the king, who walked beside the mounted Goth. He could not hear what was said but he watched. The king was making statements with his walk. He had left off his bright, trailing cloak — trailing the distance of three strides behind him, demonstrating like an Emperor that he felt he had no need of a protector at his back — and was this evening swinging a hide cloak edged with marten skin. So, tonight, the king was very much one of the *cymru*; gristle to the Bear's bone, supporter, nourisher, bodyguard; unmounted while the warlord's Goth rode through his dinas. No expensive, foreign wine would appear in the llys tonight, the Tracker thought dryly. Nothing exotic, nothing that suggested the remotest source of wealth-pride would be served as long as this dangerous man was in the dinas. He would be offered boiled pig and native beer with the king, as if that was all the king ever drank. He would take back to his warlord no suggestion of luxury, no hint that the king's loyalty had a price or his allegiance a particular significance.

The king would invite the Goth to persuade him of the strength of the warlord's power and purpose, his allies and his armies. The Goth would convince the smiling king of the necessity of the warlord's cause and of his inevitable victory. They would discuss a battle plan: so many fighting-men, so many smiths, so many swords, javelins and spear-men; this many battle horses, that many chariots and carts, at such a time, in such a place, for the coming battle season. Then he would leave some acknowledgements (loot for the smith to work — a silver brooch from the Pictish north or a glass one from the Franks; honey, perhaps — the king had an exceptionally sweet tooth); and he would turn his dark, driven face south and return to the great halls behind the Dyke and the riding passions of his warlord, the Bear. That was how it would be done.

The evening was luminous in the sky — green as glass sherds out of the wreck of old Segontium. There was a sharpness in the air that sent the coralled animals galloping and bucking to raise the heat in their blood before the night closed in. Their hooves thundered in the pounds — the same sound that they made in the Ride, the Tracker thought. As if the Goth had spoken to them of the horsemen of the night, touched them with his god as he came in . . . . He was dismounting now, heavily, treading with certainty on the beaten ground at the door of the hall where the torches, already lit inside, blazed. The king entered in front of him, his head on one side. The Goth, huge in his armour, filled the space between the doorposts so that for an instant, as the Tracker saw it, the heart of the dinas went dark. But it was not for him to interpret signs of that nature — his business lay in bent bracken stalks and the rumour of feathers.

The Tracker, who had not been back in the dinas long enough to be quite yet a man, ran his tongue around his gums and touched his thighs with the tips of his fingers.

The priest brought the Ford to a stop in a series of little pianissimo darts at the verge. After a jab at the grass, indistinguishable in result from any of its predecessors, he switched off the engine and peered through the spotty windscreen at the gate into the wood. He had driven the entire journey with his left foot hovering like a dragonfly over the clutch, which for no obvious reason he would suddenly depress and then release, so that even when potholes, ill-repaired drains, subsidence, acute corners, cats and natural caution had not caused irregularity in their movement, the vehicle would wail, hesitate and leap forth.

'I wonder,' he said, surprisingly, 'if you are taking this seriously?'

100

'Well . . .'

'Perhaps, if you carried the chocolates, lest I stumble — you must be more sure-footed than I.'

He sat sideways on the car seat, removed his shoes to reveal pink socks with one dirty toe-nail coming through, wrapped his trousers in a tight roll around his shins and drew on a pair of hairy brown oversocks and black wellingtons generously dotted with red bicycle puncture patches. Swinging a green canvas bag on his shoulder and grasping a hefty stick, the priest was heading for the gate while Cathal, seeing himself as slow and awkward, was still struggling into his anorak. He could not think that liqueur chocolates were appropriate to the occasion — nor the car: hand-painted bright yellow, with laughing daisies and a brilliant rainbow on one side, butterflies and lightning flashes on the other.

The track up to the dinas was as it always was — or a little lighter, perhaps, with more leaves shed; a little more dimly gold; more derelict and ragged with the dying off of the last weeds. Ahead of him the priest strode slowly but purposefully. He was wearing a college scarf and an aged green jumper, long and misshapen, with the elbows carefully darned in brown wool. The sun slanted down through a complex grille of filigree branches making steeply angled flights of light. A pigeon rose across them along the opposite diagonal. Faint paths, Cathal saw, ran across the grass and mosses, criss-crossing, into small gaps and tiny tunnels, and between the major trunks around the clearing. Walking behind the old man, clutching the chocolates, he felt angry. He had not come here with this man to have a silly picnic with bright bits of silver wrapping left behind. There should have been dignity, reverence even; this was farce. He stopped. He could not go on with this.

'Dying, is it?' the priest said, turning round in the middle of the clearing and putting his canvas bag on the ground. 'When?'

Cathal stared. 'I don't know. You expect me to actually know?'

'Tomorrow? Easter Monday? Five years?'

'I don't bloody know. Does it matter?'

'I would have thought so,' the old man said, smiling.

'Do you believe me?'

'Do you believe it yourself?'

Did he? Do I? Do we? *Jesus*, how tall those trees are, going up and up, branch and limb climbing and closing in, the sky tiny and unreal at the end of the long shaft . . .

Now the priest was lowering himself ponderously to the ground. He held out his hand. Cathal was not going to help him — o, no.

'Chocolates?'

Tempted to hurl them at the old man, Cathal put the elegant box down on the grass with extreme care and gentleness. Underground, he conceived of vast, tilted surfaces of rock strata streaming with water as pure as crystal, underlain and overlying other strata tilting at opposing angles, so that the waters ran across and over and below each other in a great, moving, multidimensional lattice. Magnetic fields, lines of resistivity and electric charges laced the earth's surface; and in the air above, the gold threads of the sun shafts and the silver flight of the bird intersected precisely above his head. Target? Core? Prism, bending all illumination, sending it out on new alignments to be received, or not? Where? Nucleus or vacuum?

He sat poised, in the active and the passive moods: the epicentre of action.

' — to follow it forwards and backwards, not stopping at a contemporary now, just because we happen to be sitting in it.'

Cathal did not know if the old man had begun the sentence in his head, or whether he had simply not heard the beginning of it.

'What?' he said.

'Time, Cathal Kerr, time. Is it curved or straight? Does it exist or is it a convention of physics made in our own image, like a god is? Or is it God? Is it a creation of the forebrain, stumbled upon amongst the bones of sabre-tooth tiger and cave bear, and crudely shaped to answer an immediate fear? Once upon a time, will it die?' The priest was taking the Cellophane off the box. Of what might he be a priest or magus?

'I don't suppose you expect an answer?'

'I might hope for one, mightn't I? Grand Marnier or Benedictine? The red ones are surely cherry brandy. In fact, I might almost suppose that you might be the answer.'

Cathal chose a chocolate — Curaçoa.

Was the world really shot through with lines? Were the lattices and the diagonals and the streaming water sheets really there? Were the great roads to gnosis to be found here among these present trees, lacing and interlacing, inturned — and somewhere a path which Cathal Kerr might follow and so step on to the Road?

He said, 'I thought I saw a fox here, once . . .' — here where he was sitting now; where all the paths and lines crossed and recrossed. He had not known for certain what it was. Now, he would accept that whatever had visited could have come either through space or down the ravelled roads.

He said, 'Am I going mad?' — making it a question like any other.

'O, no,' said the old priest. 'Good gracious me, not at all. Whatever made you say that?'

'London has gone so far away.'

'It is far away. Other things are closer. You have moved. The geography has changed. You take things so literally, Cathal Kerr. You can't take geography literally — it's too personal for that. I'd like the Benedictine — or do you want it?'

'No, no. Please.' He held out the box and the old man

scratched about in it, looking for the Benedictine chocolate as the fox might fuss over a buried splinter of tibia.

'Geography is an attitude of mind — yours in this case. It's a bore. Let's not talk geography.'

'And I asked if it was I who was going mad!' Cathal said. 'Look, Vicar-or-whatever-you-are-' He paused, waiting for a name but the old man raised his eyebrows, waiting for Cathal to go on. 'All right, then, don't tell me your name. They'll tell me in the pub. Geography is what we are sitting on. It is x miles from London, sort of west. I'm not quite sure how many miles or exactly what compass points, but I do know that if I gave someone a ten figure grid reference and an Ordnance Survey map, they could arrive right here and take all the Benedictine chocolates. That's geography — there's nothing personal about it.'

'Only now when you think of where we are as a point with numbers and a third person who can look at them and interpret them in exactly the same way that you do. And, moreover, who wants to. Gethin might call this the place where he set the trap with the yellow peg. The tree might call it the place where there is room for a seedling. It depends on the divisions of the times. It might be a main road —'

'To where? O, come on —'

'To whatever it is that is up there on the top of the hill. You know there is something there — you keep asking about it — so it must be there, mustn't it? And this is on the way up — so it's a road. It depends on when you are. Sometimes it's a bush, this spot. Here, in the side of the slope, it was once a river — that river. It had to get down there, and this bit would have been in the middle of it as it cut its way. A map showing it in green with contour lines is wrong. It's blue. Look — stickleback at your big toe! Ha, you moved. See? It's a river, your big toe knows it's a river.' He giggled happily.

'Death by piscine consumption. On the coroner's label —

when I die,' Cathal said unclearly, hating his toe now for having moved as much as he hated it for waiting for its label.

'Big toes know all sorts of things; they turn up at burial time. It may be prudent to bury some face down, or crouched, as the ancients did, because of the things big toes know that make them turn up. That's what I mean by its being personal. You may think your big toe is there for the coroner to tie a label on to, but it knows it's in danger of being devoured by a carnivorous fish. Given an aeon or two, an ice age or so, the water will come back, maybe, and the stickleback will pounce again. Or this may be a desert — and it will be a hairless rat, or a lemming in the tundra. Geography's a when thing, as much as ten figures and a square. Ten figures is for the ignorant; wisdom is in the twitch.'

For a moment this seemed to Cathal to make sense, and he believed in the rat and the river and the road he was sitting in the middle of. 'We could get run over,' he shouted in an alarm that was private and consecutive to the old man's logic — and therefore, logically, not private at all. Might a community of dry toe-bones, intoning wisdom, sweep along and crush him underfoot so that he could not stagger up and run with them?

'You have to be moving before they reach you,' the old man said.

Christ — how do I learn to do that? Christ, how did he learn anything as huge as that, coming from St.John's Wood and Gemma's oddly wrong, now perhaps right, old maps? He knew he had not spoken aloud, yet the old man had heard him. If he now looked at the priest, what would he see? A sage? A geologist with a little hammer to break his bones? Or a wizard writing the Names of God in the dust thrown up by the collision of times? Afraid to look, he closed his eyes and lay back, trying to conjure up rats, lemmings and piranha fish in order to annihilate them at will, his will, when he chose to open his eyes again and look at the high, autumn trees and the reality of ignorance. Slowly, he said, 'You have moved a mountain . . .'

'No. You have. It is not me lying in a blue river — it is you. I am sitting beside the chocolate box.'

A river . . . Glacier waters rolling thick and shingle-loded, building banks and shores in its curves, and reaching into an unstable world; dragging rocks, tearing boulders, devouring slopes and angles. Hills where there had been plains, valley and gorge where there had been upland sweeps; changing geographies . . . He opened his eyes, and there were valleys; he could hear the river thrashing below in the gorge, and the uplands had indeed gone. 'What have you taught me?'

'Time and death are not always contiguous.'

'Death,' Cathal said, thinking of the coroner and the extreme physicality of his own picture of his own corpse, 'is an immutable boundary. My life has contour lines in time. They have been drawn, and there is no river to change them —'

'Boundaries shift outside the City walls.'

'Because we are dying?'

'We are always dying. All along we have been dying. More or less, you see. But that is not the same as believing in death. Death is not for all of us.'

' "Half in love with easeful Death —" ' Cathal said, understanding what the old man said until, suddenly, no — he did not understand. 'What do you mean, death is not for all of us?'

But the old man said no more. Sucking at the Tia Maria chocolate, he was sitting on the grass like a figure in a childish drawing, his feet stuck straight out in front of him.

Who believes in Cathal's dying? Cathal said, 'I'm married, you know.'

'Many men are.'

'And I've left her. Only it seems that she'd already left me, and I hadn't noticed. Maybe she believes in my dying. But I think it is more likely that she disbelieves in it. She likes to make progress.'

'Geography again?'

Cathal looked at the priest — who had never once indicated any qualification for any priesthood, any special sort of knowledge. He had accepted all Cathal's anger and misery as if he had been crouching there in the dark of Hengardd, clutching his chocolates and waiting gleefully for Cathal's dying to break his fast. Was it he, Cathal, who was on the verge of knowledge and the old man who was seeking for a guide? *Were the positions, perhaps, reversed?* The old man had said, 'You might be the answer,' as if it were Cathal himself who might be the initiate.

In that case he, Cathal, was without a magus; was alone in the dark.

'Do you want to see more?' the priest said, softly (slyly?).

See? What sort of see? No, no, he could not take any more — not now. Never. He did not want to understand. If there was any more than just the grass and the over-gold sun shafts, it was something too terrible. But if there was nothing — if there were no crimson and verdigris border to his existence, no roads beyond the Civitas, then this was an unbearable deprivation . . .

No, he wanted no more. If there is some terrible thing, it can only destroy Cathal, split him open, fragment and twist him away with unimaginable agony; draw him out in wires of madness teased out from his brain.

'Take me home,' he shouted. 'Take me away — home —' But the great margin was there at the cottage, glowing in antique hues; and outside it carrion dogs licked their flanks . . . 'O, God, take me away from me.'

'Aah . . .' it was the old man, sighing.

Cathal took his hands from his face and looked at him. What bright eyes. So hard and so bright. Beyond pity.

7

In the evenings he cooked potatoes and parsnips for supper. He had forgotten what Gemma had told him to do and treated the parsnips as he had learned to treat potatoes. Then he would sit by the fire, drinking coffee and wondering if he was tired enough to go to bed. Wondering why he was wondering. He should not be wondering; he should know.

One evening he took from the mantelpiece the envelope which said 'Fill the room'. It was grimy from the fire, the paper yellowed and brittle. He turned it over in his hands but lacked the courage to burn it; so he folded the envelope and put it on the window sill. He would find something ornamental to put on top of it, and eventually he would become immune to its presence. Not to force things, that was the thing.

He thought: I have lost my way. I am alone; I am sick. I am unable to structure this 'dying' thing.

The following Tuesday he thought: I am not even afraid, not even sorry. I should be listening to the draught in the lintel of the poor, murdered wood of the door who cries to me for recognition and know that when this season comes round again that draught will be myself — '. . . imprisoned in the viewless winds /And blown with restless violence round about the pendant world'. But still I am not afraid. Not touched by grief.

On Thursday evening he thought: but the palsy is real enough. All I have to do is pick up this coffee mug, and it is evident. Look, there is the wool of the jersey, once the fleece of a sheep on just such hills as are out there in the dark beyond the door, crouched under the line of a cold wall, delicate black legs curled on the sodden ground, wool weighty with rain and mud and scragged with bramble, innocent of the stun gun. For the soulless today is only daytime; tomorrow, nothing. Beneath the wool of the sheep

— now dead? now eaten, her last substantiation spun off a used plate in a tumultuous dishwasher? — tomorrow is nothing. Here is cotton, exquisite fibres brought to harvest half a world away — heat and dust and sweat and loud cries in unknown tongues; flower blossoms huge and brilliant; birds hued like a Gospel Book. And within, bones: tibia and fibula curved like a viol's bow, shaped like Everyman's, yet mine alone. Break them — only I will ever feel it. Fleshless, marrowless, colourless — are they Anyman's then, or mine? Were one to come, now, in through the wailing door and offer to break Tibia or Fibula — o, I would be most afraid. Sweat, piss probably, squealing and begging to be let off. But dissolve Ego off Tibia, drop Tibia casually there where the dented Pepsi can and the twisted fork are rusting under the umber sorrel stalks and the virulent nettles, there to whiten and snap in the frost like the rabbit's mandible and the stillborn lamb's scapula — weep not for Tibia . . .

NOT EVEN FOR MY TIBIA? Where is my own grief? Bring me my own grief. Bring me something, anything, so long as it is mine —

Come, I am sick for your coming . . . Under the ash trees the watchdogs lie crouched beside the scapula of the stillborn lamb and me.

On Friday he heard: 'What is it you would have, Cathal Kerr? Fire from the Pleistocene gravels? Watch this — see — the spark from the flint. What more would you have, Cathal Kerr?'

Who says this? Does it matter? Perhaps. Let the voice die away, and listen —

But there were no more words, only the crying in the lintel of the door.

He ran out of food, and found that the Post Office was closed because it was Sunday; so he lay in his chair, his feet stretched out to the fire which now and again he would stir himself to rebuild. He thought: how quiet the cottage is in its cradle of wind, its wicker of abstract trees and trans-substantiate trees and relict trees in the soil. He thought how the cottage nestled into the boulder-strewn ground; how, when it had collapsed and its elements dispersed, there would be a sheltered hollow on the hillside where its weight had rested, like a hare's form; how the stout little building had nuzzled its back into the rising ground, the trees and the ideas of trees bent round it; how the hill curved to right and left, and how the hill itself lay in the embrace of higher hills, circling round and around the valley so that the Cathal Kerr in the chair was held, a nexus, safely kept by the guard dogs.

Then he saw that although the little Cathal Kerr in the chair stayed motionless, the whole entity of which the tiny figure was the nucleus was moving, very slowly, down-wards and to the left. He wanted to turn away and not see what was happening but found he had no power to move his head. 'Paralysis'. Just the word — no voice speaking it. Now Cathal was having to strain a little to see clearly. At a certain point both in its linear diminution and in time that whole entity was going to vanish.

There was ice in the sky now, sharp as flying glass, spicules spinning in the ether which pricked his back and his scalp, and from which there was no shelter. Darkness — with the little entity so far away now that its reflected light was dim and blue. When it went from sight, down there, it must cease to be — *and the world pass away.*

'*Ocha,*' Cathal cried aloud, '*ocha, ocha . . .*'

He sat on for a while longer, watching the fire go down and listening to the wind in the crying door. *Ocha.*

All the next morning he swung between acute anxiety and a peaceful lassitude. The recurring image of the thing that

slipped away, encircling him as its own essential, over-
whelmed him each time he saw it in his mind. The fear that
came with it was cold, complete. Each time the contact
faded, he was left feeling either weak or peaceful, he did
not know which. He would find his hands fiercely clenched,
deep crescents in the palms where the nails had dug in; and
his jaw would ache as it relaxed. Once he felt his teeth
grinding as the mandible returned to its ordinary place. If
his fists and face could contort without his knowledge,
what else might his physicality learn to do — without him?
But the separation was so beautiful. He did not know why
he thought that, nor what the beauty was, but could find no
other description for it — indeed, did not know what it was
that he was calling beautiful. It was something which was
there, or which happened, while he was away.

Cathal found the priest in the vegetable garden behind
Hengardd. He was digging for carrots, the college scarf
wound twice round his neck and the patched wellingtons
smeared with mud. A grey-striped cat watched him from its
place on an old board balanced on the bank which ran
round three sides of the patch, and a white goat at the end
of a heavy chain tore at the last of the little blackened
leaves left on the thorn hedge growing out of the stones in
the body of the bank. All three turned and stared at Cathal
as he scrambled through the mud in the narrow gap
between two stone outbuildings across which a broken
farm gate keeled, leaving just enough space to qualify as an
entrance. Cathal sidled round the rusty metal with its loop
of barbed wire for fastening and stood transfixed by the
three pairs of eyes — emerald, agate and slate — which
blazed out of the wintry vegetation. He froze, immobilized.
He had never been an enemy before.
    Immediately in front of him rows of Brussels sprouts ran
between lines of darkened pom-pom dahlias, the orange

111

and deep crimson heads still partially coloured. Roses, circled by parsley, held their last pink and yellow and white blossoms, floribunda and standards growing in a circle within which a cobbled round held the fading stalks of marjoram and mint and wormwood. Hydrangeas and cabbages and underground parsnips interwove in a long plait, and a feathery pampas sheltered a wheel of bare beds, each spoke a raised trench of celery heads, the hub a knot of hellebore. Basil and thyme, rosemary and lavender hedged dug squares, and the base leaves of tall perennials ran up and down between trenches laid with dark manure.

The priest stood in a V of raspberry canes, each arm of which ended at half an old water-butt spilling out gold and bronze chrysanthemums. A wide, straight path of camomile was arched over by a wild rose, its hips and haws hanging like festive toys from a rough trellis grounded in chips of blue and chestnut tesserae. A line of aged bushes alternated thorny gooseberry with dense currant, and Chinese lanterns and Michaelmas daisies flowered among their fallen leaves. Slabs of pale limestone, the colour of buttermilk, made stepping-stones amongst groves of sunflowers, now petalless, whose seeds protruded sharp, striped spines like swarms of living things. There was a dung-heap and three beehives; a potato clamp; a high run enclosing a juniper bush and clumps of honesty and fern in which a pair of Lady Amhurst's pheasants stalked warily, and a low one in which a group of long-legged gamefowl with blood-coloured eyes prowled up and down the wire. A collection of rabbit hutches was laid out like a star in a bamboo grove. The rabbits were huge and spotted brown in white, or else fawn with long spaniel ears; and in each cage was a collection of old chimney pots and sewer pipes into which they bolted at Cathal's entry. In the same disturbance three lavender guinea fowl went up with a brittle clatter and lit on the ridge tiles of the house, screaming. There were pale coronae of amber sunlight in the drizzle, suffusing the damp

112

with the colours of rainbows and drawing the odours of the plants and the soil into a web of perfumed iridescence.

Uncomprehending, Cathal stood at the gate, the garden circling, interlocking the circumference within circumference in front of him. He had come only in a passion of anxiety, but the garden made him its enemy. The animals and the priest and the fowl stared at him, waiting, watching. No breeze stirred any leaf. The pheasants, eyes like Fabergé narcissi, stalked, prowled. From the tendrils of a vine trained on the outhouse wall, the damp ticked regularly to the path: rap. Rap-rap. With minimal movement the cat's ears flattened. In the centre of the garden a pale rose petal sank down the silence to the cobbles. The priest's eyes flickered to its fall and came back to Cathal. Rap. Rap.

Serial music of fountains behind lyre and thrilled cymbals; gathering ground for Demeter, copse for Diana, groves for Juno, parterres for Venus; roses painted delicately in faded ochres and pinks against the pale grey blues of fresco; birds in silver wire cages: it had to be so, but was not. Where had the young girls gone, got up as naiads and dryads, and the red, garlanded bowls of olives ripened in Levantine noons? The perfumes of sweet oils and incense, of garlic roots and viscera suddenly exposed to the sun; of oysters from the sea margins and lemon trees at evening? With terrible pain he watched the melon leaves blacken and shrivel over the rude manure; the fragrant mimosa die down into the dug earth's crudity; and the mosaic laid for a caesar — prancing, martial horses cavorting at the *piaff* in white, blue and Samian red tesserae — turn to dull cobbles under a broken garden seat. The cat was there still, and the goat and maybe the priest, but not he. Not Cathal Kerr, standing at the entrance to Elysium, an exile. In the heart of the garden the wormwood leaves loosed bitter, silver drops.

He cried out, 'Why am I the enemy?'

He had already turned away, and the clatter of his feet knocking one stone against another in the mucky gateway

113

drowned any answer there might have been. Out in the yard the painted car squatted on the rank grass outside the disused stable. Cathal rested his hands on its roof and beat gently on the gaudy metal. After a while he heard the old man come up behind him,

'Gin?'

'Why not?' Cathal said.

He took his handleless cup of gin with poor courtesy. Last time he had been given a tumbler with *Regal Hotel Cooden Beach* enscrolled in thin gold letters. The old man took a mouthful of gin and bitter lemon from a beer mug and wiped his lips.

'Where have you been, Cathal Kerr? Where did you go when you came through my gate?'

'You tell me, priest.'

'I am not your guide.'

'You have to be. You live there.'

'Where?'

There was silence in the room. No clock; no puttering fire; no wind under the door or in the window frames. No sound in the old man's breathing. Around the room the house was silent. Beyond the house the light was fading. The drizzle had softened into a mist. The windows grew grey and then bluish. The old man's question stayed in the room, there in the dusk between Cathal and the priest.

After a while the old man lit the fire. Cathal roused himself enough to watch but was not now surprised by the economy and dexterity with which it was done, nor by the fact that the hearth was cleanly swept and the kindling prepared in advance. The young flames were very bright and lively, but in their light the room became suddenly darker, shadows moving in from the corners and from behind the great bookcase, which took up the whole of one wall.

Cathal said, 'I seem to have been living in nothing but nights. The days are getting shorter. I don't mean because it's autumn — I mean that the living I do is all tied into the dark. And it's a crowded darkness, full of voices and people — or like people — whom I can't quite hear, can't really see. If someone else told me this, I would say that they were mad. But because I'm inside it, I know it's not an illness I have — though there is the palsy and I do sometimes feel things I know are not healthy — like getting dizzy or nauseous or desperately cold. But they are not from within me — they happen because of the things that are going on in the dark. Are you listening? I am all right — I go for a walk in the woods, maybe even in the sun. And the wood grows dark (though perhaps not actually dark), and there are people — or like people — and creatures. The sun is shut out, and everything is about something else which is happening somewhere that has nothing at all to do with me. It is just happening. Not in me, or to me. When I get away, or run away, it goes on happening — I think.'

'Are you telling me something, or asking me?'

Cathal was again aware of the peculiar brightness of the old man's eyes. He had seen that stare as merciless. Now he wanted to see it as incisive.

He went on, 'I can't think with all these other things happening around me. And if I can't think, I can't sort out this "dying" thing.'

He stopped. He had said something important. He looked into the old man's sharp, bright eyes — and saw his words blocked by a shield of frontal bone. The eyes gleamed — light caught by top-tines upon which, if he dared to say any more, his thought would be impaled. Here was danger . . .

He burst out, 'You're destroying me — for your own ends. Whoever you are. I can't tell if you are real. I don't know what "real" is any more. I don't know if I saw a garden out there or just a row of decaying cabbages. What do you want with my empty skin?'

The old man showed no surprise. He sat by his fire, unembarrassed, as if Fictions and Realities were familiars like a dozing cat. As if the desperate dark now outside the window were a natural concomitant of day. His fingers, pressed together so that a bloodless crescent showed pale around the tips, were as still as carved stone. As Imp.Caes. Cathal's left arm, hanging by his side, trembled and twitched.

The old man said, 'But I don't want your empty skin.'

Clenching his hands together so that the knuckle-bones grated, and thrusting them between his knees so that the priest could not take one of them in his old, cold grasp, Cathal leaned forwards. Darkness had come into the room. Was that the stem of the lamp, or a tree? Was that a heap of books, or of boulders and dead fern stumps? Was the soughing in the chimney the breath of a wild thing that would kill?

Is that you, priest? Who is there?

He looked up. The old man was bearing in on him, trez tine and bez tine lined up on the fourth and fifth ribs on the his left side . . .

'Go home, Cathal Kerr, go home.'

8

'**Go home, Cathal** Kerr, go home.'

But if there were no home to go to?

It had been dusk when he had first come up this track. In the wind and the cold rain he had known that there was another life in the undergrowth, and it had terrified him. Now he was coming back, driven and drawn. He had arrived in the clear space where last week he had stopped with the old man; where he had sat on the grass and eaten liqueur chocolates and been afraid to go on in the priest's company. Not far from here stood the Central Tree where he had placed his hands and known that the tree was; and the tree had not cared that he was or was not. That had not been a beginning. This was the beginning.

It was dark now, fully night. He looked back, and behind him the track up which he had come was pale and open to the drifting sky, as if it were a way that led on, rather than returned. He waited in the clearing for a while; not for anything and not listening for anything, but just being there, wanting to bring together a place and a time and a self which he could call 'Cathal', and with whom he could then move on up the hill. Now and again there were movements in the wood, shiverings amongst the dead leaves on the ground, and he knew that they were occasioned by entire forms, assemblages of habit and flesh and temporality which were free to go about wherever they must because they were entire. It was of things which were not entire, which for some reason had become fragmented, that he was afraid tonight. Turning back to the narrowing path that led deep into the trees, he moved uphill heavily, as if with grief.

He was wearing wellingtons. The big soles gave him grip and security, and he felt safe on his feet. He put his right hand out on to the trunk of a young tree which angled across the path. Gripping it, he felt safety in it, too. It did not bend under his weight. It would be there when he returned. Somewhere below him he could hear the sound of running water. It tugged at his memory but this stream, wherever it was, ran too lightly and fast, and he could not bring the earlier, fuller river sound to recognition in his head.

There had been something, something also at night and very dark, beside a river once, where it ran over stones. He knew it had been running over stones. Then, that it had run red.

But nothing more came to him. So he went on with no

sense of why he was moving up the wood towards the ghosts of great ramparts and empty winds but keeping pure the knowledge that it was so.

His feet touched the first of the hidden, shale-like slates of the glacis. He stopped. The trees were thinner here. Between the banks, the old ditches dipped into remote shades without definition. For a long time Cathal stood and looked at them. He thought of the grey echo of light hanging over Britain; over the thousands of other wooded hilltops ringed round with dim earthworks, and no sound, no movement in any one of them; and of how, every pale night for however long his life might now be, he would know that they were there.

A mouse-scream from a quarter of a mile away whipped along the owl-roads between the low cloud and the thin branches, as distinct as the creak of one bough breathing against another; as the sourish smell of the leached thin soils up here amongst the slates; as the man-shaped — or almost man-shaped — movement among the trees.

Hanks of silhouetted ivy or desiccated fern leaves swinging from an outstretched branch? There was nothing there now. Cathal, in his shabby anorak and firm wellingtons, stared around him, searching. No movement in the quarter-light. No visible movement, but a sensation that the cause of his own presence was moving about — from over there, to closer, to somewhere below him where the cover of the trees was denser.

He ground his feet securely in amongst the stones. They rattled and scratched upon each other and a small moth, dislocated, fluttered by his knee; a wisp of life put up by his being there, mother-of-pearl in the silver starlight.

He cried out: 'Come, I am sick for your coming,' and 'I am so lonely' — which he had never told before.

It was exactly then that the man came from among the trees immediately in front of him: merely the gleam of giveaway eyeballs and teeth and something else where the hand might be. It was too dark to see a face. He had been very close. He was holding out his arms as if to embrace. Cathal was swept by a great sigh which fetched up from nowhere. He put out his hands blankly like a newly blinded person, as if to touch, but felt the chill winter breeze on his still empty palms. *Ocha*, come — but he did not say it aloud. Aloud, only a she-owl called out in a great scream like a triumph, and the twigs crackled as if fire shot across them.

The man was tall and his reach greater than Cathal's. Now he had Cathal by the forearms and the thing he had been holding had fallen, sounding on the slates and rolling a little downhill, still ringing like a heavy-tongued bell. The sound thrilled in Cathal like honey or adrenalin; his arms swelled, strength came back; and he burst the other man's hold suddenly sideways and stepped back, heavy boots grinding into the broken slates. The man was crouched, disadvantaged by the angle, but coming up again, his gaunt face rigid, his glittering eyes staring at Cathal's hands: which way to move; which way to grip; where to get in to the soft parts, the pressure points; where the angle that snaps bone. They were both panting, each hearing the other sucking for air, hauling in oxygen for the high blood, for the extreme action coming. Their breath stank over the nightwood smells.

The man struck upwards, so that his head took Cathal just below the collar-bone, and his right arm locked around Cathal's neck. Cathal thrust his arm up between them and got his thumb under the man's jaw. His fingers groped for nose and eyes; and he pushed his body down and his fingers up. The man began bending away from him, straightening upwards and backwards until they were level, eyeball to eyeball, tongue to tongue. They strained, swaying, left shoulder to left shoulder, the great round pommels of the joints grinding together — and suddenly he felt the pain of teeth biting deep into the ball of his thumb and closing over the side of his hand like a jagged trap round a fetlock. He was held. Breath for breath. Hot blood was running, its mawkish, costive smell the stimulus to terror. His only need now: flight from the smell of his own blood, which filled his nostrils, flooded into his mouth, flowed into the back of his throat. His slithering, slipping hand caught the man's hair. Winding his right wrist in it, he let all his weight haul on the back of the man's head.

It broke them free of each other.

The man said, 'Look after that which is committed to your trust, and' — looking into Cathal's eyes — 'taceas.'

He turned and was gone, down into the trees.

TACEAS — KEEP THIS SECRET — TACEAS: the great word rings around the thin trees of the outer bank, clangs on the slates of the glacis, stoops in full strike down the slope of the hard hill, tears apart the silver vapours of the air and beats upwards again among the echoes of the owl and the magnetics of the stars — TACEAS TACEAS — calling and hunting among the motes and the atoms and the results of annihilated causes. Soaring upwind now, on the currents that rose from the Dubglas and Tribruit, into the sky; circling higher and further until only the sound of the jesses reaches earth; fading, although the command itself is still going on out there, beyond. A thing spoken is a thing which is; word-giving, the God-act.

The Tracker did not so much hear as acknowledge Cathal's fading retreat from the outworks of the dinas. He collected Fiác's bell from where it had fallen among the brambles and, holding it by the clanger so that it would be silent, made his way back along the track. Now that Cathal was no longer there it was again clear of trees, but was almost equally impenetrable with stashes of firewood, baggage heaps, hobbled pack animals and the bendies and skin tents of smiths and armourers and horse-traders drawn by rumours of the Goth's presence and the certainty of coming war.

In the llys he darted alongside the wicker screen and into the chamber from the body of the aisled hall.

The king of the dinas sat back against a chestnut sheep-skin, his head in shadow. It was very quiet in the chamber. The painted cloths which hung against the wattle panels swayed slightly. There was a small fire for light, one pitch torch guttering, and a chipped Roman oil lamp which smoked blackly from inferior oil. The centre of illumination was low so that all that could be seen of the king, seated on the high bench, was the glitter of his eyes and his jewellery, and occasionally the dim line of his lip. The hierarchy of the dinas sat below him: Carac, the king's disfavoured grandson; Echw, the king's foster-son; the king's poet and the king's charioteer; the king's uncle, the Oldest of Men, who with his thin, aged hands was carving a bird's head on the end of a long, delicate splinter of bone; the king's smith, the king's foster-brothers and the king's cousin. Theodoric the Goth sat amongst them, gripping a wine cup, the sinews of his forearms like ships' rope under the short black sleeves of his tunic. Bulked there, in black and unlaced leather, he stared down into the cup, seeing in the lees the geographies of exile. Marcellus the Horse Master, come in to collect the horse tribute to the Bear, lay curled on a black ox-skin, dressed in full, old-fashioned Roman red. His short, dark hair was oiled, and he smelled of the gum of exotic trees.

The Tracker, standing by the entrance, looked hard into the king's mind.

'Barrectus,' the Goth said, 'will be the shield when the Bear leads his armies north against Illan and his Leinster men. And you, like the javelins beside him.'

'Magnificent,' murmured the king, his eyes hidden now.

Carac: 'His horses are thin —'

Echw: 'His men are unsettled and his youths are restless
— '

Carac: 'He is still looking for a sufficiency of winter
pasture and he has not cattle enough for all his people — '

The smith: 'Travelling is expensive — it has to pay in the
end — '

Marcellus: 'He came for fame and battle. He wants booty,
not honey . . .'

'We know Barrectus,' said the Oldest of Men. He was the
king's mother's brother, very old now, with silver hair like
frost by the lake shore. He had been there all through the
old wars, even at Badon. He sat on a low stool to the Goth's
right, and the Goth had been at Badon, too. It made
something between them, something deeply sad and un-
breakable. When he and the Goth looked at each other it
was like a tenderness, a communion, such as is found
between some women. 'Why would Barrectus, of all men,
fight for peace?'

Echw: 'If he has come for fighting but all he gets is peace
he will turn, as a matter of course, on his nearest neighbour.
That will be us.'

'And,' the king's charioteer said softly, 'you will have
taken all our next train of horses down to the Bear. And he
will have ridden them into a pile of carrion on his great
Dyke. You have an eye for horses, Marcellus, Horse Master.
You have chosen to take as tribute to your Dux every
animal I have been keeping for my king and my king's
fighting-men: chariot horses, carting horses, riding horses
— all bred for my king and all marked down by you to
drive south. Mounted on what are we to face Barrectus
when he turns against us?'

Marcellus: 'When the Dux has the enforcement of the
Law in all Britannia again, there will be no need for me to
take your horses in tribute, or for Barrectus to take your
winter-grazing. That is why we need the horses. To estab-
lish the Law.'

'The Law came. It was called Rome,' the king's poet said slowly. 'It ran on its own spears and died.'

The king of the dinas leaned forward, bent into the light, rustled among the reeds on the floor of the chamber under the skins and brought up in his hand scrapings of the soil below. He held his hand out into the light, the dirt in his palm among his rings. 'This,' he said, 'is the Law.' He let it sift away between his feet. 'Your great Dux,' he said, looking at Marcellus and his military style, red tunic, 'does he remember this Law?'

'He knows the Law,' said the Oldest of Men softly, looking up from the bird's beak to hunt in Marcellus' eyes.

For all the cold outside, it had become very hot in the inner chamber. Gusts of wind whinged under the thatch and bumped dully against the rounded, outside corners. Inside, they were so many men laid, the Tracker felt, like wicker, criss-crossing each other in their minds or their blood; and a single light would send them all up in a rage of shooting fire. There was sweat on Marcellus' arms and the Goth's forehead, little beads of it on the bleached temples of the Oldest of Men and the hairlines of the hierarchy. He smelled it, vaporous and rank with drink, thinking that it would flare like oil or bitumen. Who would torch it?

Marcellus: 'That is what the Law requires: allegiances and alliances, so many horse, so many spears, so many battles to a war, so many wars to a conquest and after the conquest, rule.'

The king's face was still hidden in the shadows above the light. 'Of whose war is this Dux Bellorum of yours "Dux", I wonder? And after the conquest, whose rule?'

The Goth: 'To Marcellus he is "Dux Bellorum" — but to you? You have your own name for him — you have named him, too . . .'

Still, from the shadows, the Tracker stared into the king's mind.

O, yes. We have called him in. We brought him in by the God-act of naming. It is the Bear who will torch the dinas.
And the kind. *Ocha*.

TACEAS TACEAS . . .

The great word rang around the thin trees of the outer bank, clanged on the slates of the glacis, routed out the entire beings and drove them before it through the silver vapours and the gut-black organs of the wood. Beyond the wood on all sides the forest went on and on: secret oak limbs and ash limbs and spaces where moths danced in the falling dew. The roots of the old ash tree slither and twist down into the viscera of the forest form, clasping, taking, giving and raising up *fraxinus* form, new every eighteen decades in the shape-changing forest lands: one time virgin, blonde and golden haired with six-row barley, swinging promises, promises; one time gravid, plaided in purple vetch and white fat-hen, waiting brown warps and fertile green wefts; one time crone, shrunken, unkindly bared; this time a ragged wood. In the beetle holes and the root holes the forest form gestates darkly. Stringy and desperately strong, yearling growths cluster at the height of a man's ankle, with eighteen decades to endure at random risk before crashing back into the cyclical matrix of the changing form.

Cathal Kerr, turned loose among the great trees and the grappling boughs, the boulders under the humus and the man-trap roots set across his path, was screaming; running and screaming although, in fact, he made no vocal sound. The screaming was in his muscles, tearing as he lurched from lump to hole to ridge; in the gristle stretching to breaking point, cartilage and sinew twisting and spraining; in his heart muscle, grabbing for the next breath before this one was caught; in his veins, seething as the adrenalin and blood burst through the narrow valves in massive surf-

124

rollers from the driven arteries. Slowly he curves over, the white line of breaking streaks across the crest of his mind and he crashes, massed and formless, creaming across the forest floor. Released from shape and rhythm, he too is loose in the forest.

The Bright Road shimmers amongst the trees. Street-straight, up from Moridunum and the rank amusements of Leg.II Avg., as it was maintained by the First Cohort Sunici to run north from Erglodd to Pennal before swerving round the great mountain and returning to true; thence to the fork, and dexter to Deva and the XXth Valeria Victrix, sinister to Kanovium and Segontium. All ways to Annwn. Quercus, Fraxinus and Ulmus tower behind its verges, lupus and vulpes padding softly between the great trunks. Starbursts of eyebright are cast like moonbeams where the turf meets the dimmed paving stones. The wind is from the north, travelling the road singing of whales beyond Ultima Thule and perfumed with yew charcoal glowing in Dinas Emrys. From time to time light chariots pass, and although neither the wheel-rims nor the horses' hooves make any sound on the stone street, the creaking of the chariot body and the whistle of the wind in the reins and traces swing in and out of the sounds of the forest, and the odour of horses drifts on the night air.

There is much traffic on the Bright Road tonight as dawn comes coldly nearer. Cathal himself moves lightly, his body as lithe and many dimensioned as a playing lark's. He flies to the side in awe as a band of Leinster fighting-men runs softly past him, spears levelled at the dim horizon, and in the middle of them a man carrying a smiling, decapitated head whose golden curls brush the ground — *ocha, ocha* — like kelp on a lifting tide. Perched there, he watches Carac and Echw, armed for battle, come up from his right; but before they reach him Echw turns aside and is lost among the ash trees and the oaks behind. When Cathal looks for Carac again he is far along to the north, almost out of sight.

Quite often he sees the Tracker, stepping in the centre of the road, occasionally quite close, coming out from the trees on either side to make phrases of some long dance, swaying the trees and their branches and the spinning leaves thrown up by his soundless feet. When young Maccudeccetus runs by, a few very gold oak leaves stirred up by the Tracker cling to his green tunic and in his hair. The boy is laughing with pleasure as he passes Cathal on his bough and weaves his way in and out of the small procession of the Baptized, who carry tall wine amphorae high on their shoulders all the sweet and blesséd way from school to Ynys Môn. Allelujah! they call, Allelujah! on a single note, rhythmically: Alle*lu*jah 1 & *2* 3, Alle*lu*jah! 1 & *2* 3 . . . Cadwallon Longhand passes and Serach in a painted chariot, courteously turning his right shoulder to the bones of Patrick, St., where they are propped against a dawn-damp boulder set at the wayside to mark the road in the snow. Caw, pulling the child Gildas by the hand, salutes the bones; and the bleached skull nods, singing:

> *Inspirat omnia,*
> *vivicat omnia,*
> *superat omnia . . .*

It is all so happy on the Bright Road from Segontium to Annwn — so happy! The nuclei, protons, neutrons, cells and spirals which are Cathal Kerr spill off the branch, where he was a bird, and flow out along the road in iridescent droplets, twinkling in the brightening light from the east, to form a glittering diadem holding together the loosening occipitals of Ambrosius for just a little longer, little longer, little longer — and swirl in a shivering pool around the feet of the Bear.

The Bear is not dancing or running or singing. He stands as still as a milestone on the side of the street. As silent as stone with no lettering carved upon it. As Cathal reaches him the sun breaks over the eastern tops of the canopy and blares down on the hard paving and the blanked-out milestone, brilliant red with the first frost of the year, so that for an instant every smooth surface flares up, blazing blood, and all the dew and the shining, lying water vanish in a wisp of vapour.

Coming round was difficult. Where he had been on the hard street was now suddenly the past, and the memory of the Bright Road and the happy travellers withdrew into a grey blank with just a silver thread drawn through it and a milestone harsh in the distance. He was aware from time to time of the old priest's face coming quite close to his own; of a gross discomfort shot with real pain and of rainfall and movement; later, of light and warm feathers, and now of the square of light where the sun was coming through the window. 'Light is hugely significant,' he said to the window; and his mouth was swollen and stiff. The old man held hot tea to his lips, which was painful, but the warmth and sweetness of it comforted him and he fell asleep for a long time.

When he woke again the priest was still there or maybe had returned. Cathal moved under the warm eiderdown so that he could see the window and the evening sun lighting the ash trees sideways as it set. He had thought there should be a north wind, but the tree was very still. He felt a spasm of grief for a cold, ancient wind which he could not quite remember, and a great relief that he was sheltered from it.

He said, thickly, 'Warm. I'm very warm.'

The priest said, 'It was cold out there,' and for a moment, for Cathal, he was speaking of the north wind and the forgotten place — and then obviously not so, for this was Cathal's cottage, and the back bedroom with the gas fire.

'Would you like some tea?' the old man said politely.

'Would you mind? Or maybe I haven't any. There is coffee — o, hell, I —'

'I brought some over with me. And milk — goats' of course — and sugar. All the standard rations for the sick. I'll go and make it. Don't move, you've hit your head quite hard.'

He was gone for some minutes. When he came back with one of the hand-thrown craft mugs which Gemma had bought especially for Castlegate, brimming with musty, sweet tea and goat's milk, Cathal said, 'What is your name? I don't think anyone ever told me your name.'

'No, I don't think they did,' said the old man.

'Tell me. Tell me your name. Or what they call you.' He did not know why he had put it that way.

'McKier. My name is McKier.'

'McKier,' Cathal said slowly. What had he expected? He could not remember what he had expected or why. The name was new to him. It meant nothing. Except that it was the priest's name, and the saying of names was important.

When it was truly dusk McKier fastened a deep brown cushion cover round the light with an old safety pin so that it would not be too bright, and left Cathal with a dented vacuum flask of tea and a gin bottle filled with milk. As he was going, he turned round at the bedroom door and said, 'Where are the dogs?'

'What dogs? We haven't got any dogs.'

'No . . .'

He left the door slightly open. Cathal heard him go out of the front door and then, dimly, the car starting. He was certain that he would come back during the night and lay comfortably waiting for him. Then he thought about McKier's cold, merciless eyes and was afraid that he would come back. But no-one came that night.

It was a hard pillow he had elected to rest his head on, he thought. McKier had left a worn black rubber bucket beside him for obvious reasons, but Cathal preferred to wrestle with his sense of balance and manoeuvre himself down-stairs to the lavatory. He was very bruised and suspected a broken rib or two. His teeth felt loose, but he did not look in the bathroom mirror to find out about his mouth. With whom had he fought up by the ramparts? Because he had fought — he knew that. The bruises of the other man's grip were clear on his skin, tender to touch (*but McKier had not asked about them, had he?*).

It was dawn when he came downstairs. Chilly and half-lit, the living room was partly emerging, partly still hidden. He glanced at the stones in the chair, at the painted planks of the outside door and the cold fireplace. He was, in a sense, amongst his own. It was a phrase usually reserved to describe a human family, he thought; but just the same, it was the one that had come into his mind. He weaved weakly into the kitchen, with the idea that a cup of the coffee he had grown used to might strengthen him more than the old priest's ageing teabags, and watched the spring water gushing out of the tap into the kettle with the same sense of relationship. The tie was not that of familiarity — that was the relationship he had with the London flat — and with Gemma (*Gemma* — how long since he had considered Gemma as one of his own?). No: the planks — the murdered tree in the door — the water and himself shared a mutual tenancy of somewhere — some when? They were together in a now which was temporary and therefore would come to an end. Not an end, no, an alteration . . .

He made the coffee and brought it slowly into the living room, staring at the stones in the uneven wall, round the hearth, in the chair. The stone in his memory was as real a stone: a milestone, or something of the sort, beside a bright road. It had been unspoken for, and that had appalled him — it appalled him now. The stone was somewhere. He could find it. Reach it. Where it was, was where he was.

He thought that he must have lost all grip on reality to be

thinking this; that he must truly be sick and mad. Yes, he acknowledged that he was sick; not just because of whatever nasty fall he had had in the wood last night, but because of the insidious corrosion of his muscles, which he knew was speeding up. But he had not so acknowledged the madness, thinking of it more as part of the palsy, or unrealized fear of the palsy and the death it portended. Now he had to think, I am actually mad.

He could not think that of himself. He stood there in his room in Castlegate holding the coffee, sipping it. There was nothing of madness in him. The dawn, emanescent, cradled the valley outside the lightening window. He stared through the uncleaned panes at the pale ring of the hills; at the cold lake of mist lying below, the lines of bent thorns and holly that clung to the walls' sides running above its surface like dark causeways; and at the solitary stand of ash and gorse on the little hillock in the marsh. He saw it as a silhouetted island that drifted away as the white mist shifted and deepened; and the valley as drowned, a lake flooding tenderly up the hillsides and bringing, or returning to, a strange landscape with different landmarks: the islet, coves and landfalls where the mist crept into hollows and lapped at foreign shores; the tough autumn tussocks standing bunched like reeds.

A bird called, trilled, fell hushed. He thought it looked desperately sad, this landscape which was not a landscape; this lost lake which would fade, as a dream fades, in the morning; from which no woken deer nor returning hare would ever drink.

THE BOOK OF BATTLE

At Llongborth I saw Arthur,
Where brave men were struck down with steel,
An emperor, Director of Toil . . .

— *'Gereint son of Erbin', from* The Black Book of Carmarthen,
trans. Gwyn Williams, The Burning Tree

So Cúchulainn's training with Scáthach in the craft of arms was
done: . . . the feats of the sword-edge and the sloped shield; the feats
of the javelin and rope; the body-feat; the feat of Cat and the heroic
salmon-leap; the feat of the chariot wheel thrown on high and the feat
of the shield-rim; the breath feat . . .

—The Táin, *trans. Thomas Kinsella*

. . . in the presence of the Spoils of Annwfn dolefully he sang . . .
Three shiploads of Prydwenn we went thither;
except seven, none returned from Caer Siddi . . .
A flashing deadly sword [or, The sword of Lluch Lleawg] was
    sought[?] from it,
and in a fierce hand [or in the hand of Leminawg] it was left;
and before the gateway of Hell lamps were burning.
And when we went with Arthur, a famous task, except seven none
    returned from Caer Feddwid.

—*'The Spoils of Annwfn', Poem XXX,* Book of Taliesin,
trans. Kenneth Hurlston Jackson

9

In the crooked little cwm the river rears high over the boulders. The bank has been swept away and the roe deer no longer drink between the two willows but further downstream, below the bend. There have been no horses sheltered in Camlann these last four winters, no cattle. The north wind is bitter, and old wounds ache. Snow edges down from Eryri, already incandescent on the peak at dusk, white above Cadwallon Longhand in his shrewd hall.

Three times a day Fiác, the holy man from the woods, climbs part way up one of the heavy ladders that lead up to the walkway over the gate of the dinas and weeps, howls, prays and exhorts: 'Come out of your drunken dwellings and your adulterous stupor, follow the commands of the Lord, and the might of God and his saints will strengthen your right arm against Illan . . .' His eyes are hot, but the cold has turned his thin face yellow and lumpy like frozen oil. Ringing his bell furiously each time he speaks the word 'God', he leans from the ladder into the wind, his long black wrap whipping about his bare legs and snapping like a cloth pennant. Fiác is trouble. The king houses him, stands his mind on one leg elsewhere when Fiác talks Christ at him and suggests that he should not be encouraged to wander in the forests or among the homesteads talking Christ at anyone he meets — for Fiác is burning up from inside to have the dinas, king and all, baptized and set on some wild warpath against the heathen Saxons, as much because they are heathen as because they are Saxon. He has even been heard, one night, to call out to his god for the mission to baptize the Bear! Comic as that may be, it caused a little run of shivers to raise the hair on the spine of the hierarchy.

In the llys, where Fiác howls psalms in the men's company, denouncing the beer and the boasting, the beef and the honey, the horse-talk and the sex-talk, Marcellus the

Bear's Horse Master sits bunched in a great cloak, staring out at the weather and swearing that every year it is more terrible, that the rivers are roaring for the drowned. Marcellus, for all his rhetoric and drinking, has a Roman way with the fighting-men as well as with the horses, a sort of detach-ment. He sees things from high up, as a hawk might: great plans and wide patterns and the significance of incidents within a huge scheme. And the scheme he attributes not to the gods — any of them — but to the man he calls the Dux.

He has no place for Carac in his 'cohort' — in any case, he is not taking on men in the winter, no matter what imagining he may have of the next battle season. However, he feeds Carac wicked little tales about the great battles and the Dux's passion for horses: how he will choose such and such a horse that Carac has ridden o, so well. What a pity that Carac cannot see what the Dux will do with that horse . . . And Carac's eyes go black and his lips twist with the pain of his burning. He is, Marcellus says, like him — he will become a brilliant battleleader at the front of the war-band of the Kind. But Carac is not like Marcellus. He is burning away while Marcellus, drunk, talks horses, horses night through: harness and armour, Gallic bits and Allan stirrups; himself always on the fittest or the tallest or the fastest, and the crowd roaring 'Marcellus, Marcellus!' or the helpless running enemy vomiting blood over his shoulders and shitting down his painted legs.

To all this Fiác, too, listens; and his lips grow tight and twisted as Marcellus dreams horses, horses aloud while the tall, expensive wine amphorae empty in their cradles in the chamber. When Marcellus grows maudlin about the size of a particular stallion's prick, Fiác rushes about shouting, 'Put not thy pride in stiff-necked horses . . .' or crying that Christ his god rode an ass.

Marcellus and the Goth and their men have eaten the dinas wretched. But now Marcellus is leaving, moving the bright little horses out down what is left of the road, going south to the old fat lands running east from Leucarum to Venta, and to the great Dyke where the turf is springy and the grass comes early, Marcellus says — on white rock! There the villa roofs are still tiled; there glossy, round-bummed mares with their tails up, squirting at the screaming passion of a stallion, stand wide-legged on a mosaic floor laid once perhaps, for a Caesar; now swept bright for a horse.

The snow has come early again this year. Very deep and soft. It is still falling now. The land has gone down under it; the trees stoop; the ash trees bow down. Blood sinks from the skin of man and horse. Yesterday, when the wild sow was slaughtered, her blood was dark and ran out thick and slow.

'Come to me, come, come — I am sick for your coming,' he said — over and over again, tramping up and down the room in Castlegate; up and down the stretch of road between the gate up into the wood and the cottage; up and down the track through the wood itself, but never, never going as deep in as the Central Tree. He had tramped October through and now November, calling and searching for the almost-man in amongst the tree trunks, the child Maccudeccetus skipping along the Bright Road, and the blank milestone. But there was no stone, no boy, no man to touch with his cold hand.

He stopped going to the Black Lion on wet nights, since every night now was wet or bitterly cold and neither had raised Gethin in any tangible form. Instead he went occasionally to Hengardd, sometimes cadging a lift in the Landrover from one of the farmers, exchanging little foulnesses with him and the white-pawed bitch in the noisome cab, and picking up random information about EU subsidies, the sexual proclivities of the Second Whipper-In and lucrative and foolproof methods of relieving the Foresty Commission of a surplus of Christmas trees.

134

At Hengardd he avoided the sinister little wynd into the Garden of Livia, and if McKier was working in there, would wait out in the yard with the silly car, sometimes surreptitiously kicking its worn tyres. He grew used to the guinea-fowl eyeing him, the goat lipping elegantly at his coat buttons. A long-haired bluish rabbit, who peered out from under the car from time to time, would shake its drooping ears and retreat — disappointed, Cathal always felt, by some failure in himself. He resisted the urge to pull rank on the rabbit by aiming one of his kicks at it. And always the high fortress walls of the house rose sheer and impregnable from the ill-kept yard, and Imp.Caes. bestrode the entry like a Colossus.

Still he came to Hengardd, questing. Offered some of McKier's dreadful tea or, worse, gin in a clumsy tumbler from Yarmouth or an antique sea-blue glass (from Gaul?), he would continue his tramping up and down beside the monstrous bookcase, up and down outside the locked doors of McKier's learning. McKier would light his precise, vestal fire in the ornate black grate and close his eyes, feigning uninterest in Cathal's distressed tramping up and down the frayed rug, round the one-armed sofa and among the maidenhair ferns, aspidistra and spider-plants in their cracked chimney-pots and tarnished fish cauldrons standing upon and among the piles of journals and second-hand books which did for furniture. Cathal would talk endlessly — for example, about the sound of wind in chariot traces, and the child dancing in the bright leaves; watching McKier — who made no response, gave no answers.

One evening he said suddenly, 'You know.' He turned from the dark, south corner of the room towards McKier, who was not looking at him but into the bright, clean flames of the young fire. 'You know exactly what I am talking about. You know I am not mad. You actually know.'

'Who has ever said that you are, except yourself?'

Cathal was remembering something, something physical. He stood very still, smelling the sweet wood smoke from the fire and feeling no heat from it out here in the middle of the room; feeling deeply cold and damaged. He spoke very softly, afraid of what he was saying: 'You came out on to the Bright Road and carried me in. I remember being carried — the feel of it. How painful it was where I had been hurt by . . . No, don't tell me to go home — tell me what you were doing out there.'

'Why should I have anything to tell you, Cathal Kerr? Why do you assume that I know anything about your doings at night?'

'But you do, McKier. You do. You actually know — you were there, too.'

'Where? Where "was" I? Where "am" I now, Cathal Kerr?'

There was a long silence in the uneasy, clockless room. Cathal felt a blank fluidity within and around himself — as if he were being washed away by flowing water . . . He could hear it now, rushing through and over his head. He struggled against the current, dragging himself, gasping, back to where McKier seemed to be —

He shouted, 'You are doing this to me. I'm not mad — you're making me think I am. You're trying to kill me, to keep me out of something. You're trying to kill me because I've come too close to something. I'll get you. I'm real and I'll get you . . .'

But McKier was not there to kill, only the hot dark and the bitter north wind.

McKier was there but over by the door, bringing mugs of tea that smelled of goat.

'Fucking tea,' Cathal cried, burying his head in McKier's empty chair and weeping desperately.

Later, sitting crouched up by the fire on an ad hoc stool made of the *Journal of Roman Studies* and a split cushion, he said miserably, 'What do I do, McKier? I don't know what to do.'

'What do you want to do?'

Cathal looked at him wearily, but the priest was asking

honestly, not rebutting him. In the weakness of relief he answered, 'I want to go there — for it all to join up,' knowing now that he did not have to explain.

'Are you sure?'

'O, yes. I'm quite sure. I can't go on like this. Not knowing what is now and what is different.'

'Real?'

For a moment Cathal thought the cynical, goading tone was back, but he rushed on, 'No, no. It's all real. It's just differently set out — in a different arrangement. I just want to see the pattern.'

'Perhaps everyone who thinks they are dying wants a pattern,' the old man said. Yes, the slyness was back.

'Don't mock me any more tonight — please, McKier. Help me, just help me this time.'

'Look at me, Cathal Kerr.'

But he could not. He was afraid. In McKier's eyes he would see scorn and a reflection of himself. He would see a hunched-up, grotesque little Cathal, made small and stand-ard issue by the pandemic act of dying, one amongst all — except that McKier had said, 'Death is not for all of us . . .'

Slowly he said, 'Join up life and death — life and life — is that what I want? The position in the interlace where the knot ends and starts and isn't an end or a beginning but a position — is that what I want, McKier?'

'Is it?'

'Not to unravel the knots, separate out the lines — process them into a theory. But to understand, to lie in them as in a hammock, or climb them as a ladder or net, up and down and sideways — to travel the strands —'

'A long journey, Cathal Kerr.'

'It's always a journey — across the Styx or through the aether on the backs of angels . . .'

'We bury our dead in hobnailed boots. There is so far to go.'

'Put my feet on the road, McKier. That's what you are for,

isn't it? To put my feet on the road?' Suddenly he saw why McKier was in his life. McKier was not in his life but was already inside him, was a position of his own mind, a level of understanding: a preliminary.

'You are my Preliminary,' he said, looking up into McKier's eyes with a dazzling smile —

Not into McKier's eyes. Into the mouth of a tunnel in slate: perfectly round, perfectly lightless.

His own fire did not catch with the bright clarity of McKier's, but fluttered red and smoky amongst the pine cones, snapped sticks and woodland litter with which he tried to light it. His back was cold from walking home in the rain. He had forgotten to buy any bread, and the milk had solid little blobs floating near the top of the container. The room was cold, the bed upstairs would be cold. The door rattled sadly against its latch, a little trickle of rain creeping under it and into the room. He knelt by the fire and blew anxiously at it, craving heat if he could not have enough food. He would settle for one or the other. He could not shake off the feeling that the conversation with McKier had never happened, yet he could taste the aftermath of the goaty tea in his gullet. He could not remember at what stage he had drunk it — which words had gone with sipping or swallowing. It seemed extremely important that he should try to remember as he filled his lungs with smoky back-draught and blew hard at the side of a flickering stick.

And again... His belly vanished.

It was only lack of oxygen, he said — then, aloud: 'Lack of oxygen . . . Dangerous . . . Use it?'

He tried it again, and the centre of his head went.

He said, 'I'm coming —' and stared at the empty room. At the envelope saying 'Fill the room'.

He imagined the huge interlace, like a ship's net rigging without any spaces between the ropes: infinite, a million men swarming sideways and up and down and diagonally over and along it; and himself — indistinguishable from the others, among them — climbing, clinging. He imagined it, then he saw it. Then it was gone, and he was imagining again. The difference: his belly had not gone. It was there, sick and chill, a sack of bile and misery in the middle of him.

Use it — use it . . .

The idea and the words that reflected them ran on and on, riverine, flowing, borne on their own impetus. The fire caught and crackled into life, sparking and flaming, drawn by the rising wind now booming dimly above the roof, soughing in the ash trees. The light from the flames jumped and ran on every plane and surface in the room; the room was in action, roused, quick. Use it.

'I'm coming,' he shouted, kneeling by the hearth, gripping the arm of the chair in front of him and masturbating violently. 'I'm coming — in — in — in —'

That was the word. There was the God-act.

This was not the way. The distress of stopping made streams of sweat course down his thighs and back, pour over his forehead. His hair was wet, his hands shining with it, his eyesight blurred by it. He panted, gasped, until the pain died down enough for him to straighten up, kneel upright, and stand up giddily.

No, this was not the way for him. The perfectly round, perfectly lightless tunnel: that was the way in.

He sat quietly by the fire. In the morning he would find the piece of paper where he had drawn the black circle on his first morning alone at Castlegate. If it was not a good enough circle he would put a cup on the black wrapping-paper that the cookies had come in — there would be a big enough space that had no printing on it — and cut carefully round it, thus making a perfect, black circle into which to go.

To be so deliberate was frightening, but inevitable now. In the meantime, how companionable and pleasant the fire had become.

McKier stood in the open doorway. Had the lintel always been so low, the frame so narrow? The room was suddenly all in shadow, the white plaster over the bulky stones full of hollows and uneven planes. McKier cast darkness in front of him into the room like a black thing in a shrine.

Cathal, lying on his back on the floor under the black circle, raised his head with a jerk, stared into the darkness that McKier made, and saw the old man's eyes glinting down at him. McKier was standing on some brink, high above him. In this pit he was inhumed, its sides so close that he could not move his arms, only make this ineffectual raising of the head. If McKier took one heavy step Cathal would be crushed, his ankles smashed, his kneecaps, bowels . . . He saw the bright toecaps of the priest's boots closing on his lips and nostrils —

'Stand back,' he screamed.

' . . . wife for Christmas?' asked the priest, moving forward and letting the light from the door rush in and colour the cottage. Naked on the floor, Cathal sat up hurriedly and reached for his trousers and the pants inside them.

'Christmas?' he said stupidly.

'It happens every year. It's going to happen this year in a couple of weeks.'

'Should I care? I know it's Christmas-time, anyway. There are cards with robins on them all over the Post Office. I'm not having Christmas this year. Pass a shoe, would you mind?'

'I'm so glad,' the old man said, poking Cathal's shoe across the floor to him with his steel toecap. 'It saves me having to say that I don't do it. I'd rather thought you might. Or rather that the wife might come and do it at you.'

'No,' Cathal said. 'No wife for Christmas. No Christmas. Why did you ask, anyway? You were not thinking that I might expect you to slaughter your goat for the Nativity, were you?'

'And you are not suggesting that I would do any such thing, are you?' It was a statement.

'Shall I make you a cup of tea? There doesn't seem to be much point in talking about Christmas since neither of us is going to have it. Unless you would like me to buy you a robin in Santa Claus costume to thank you for looking after me?'

McKier ignored this. 'I left some teabags in your kitchen.'

'How thoughtful,' Cathal said, standing up. There was a wash of freezing giddiness, then he went to the kitchen. Out of the privacy he gained by being in a different room he called out, 'What do you want, anyway?'

There was no answer, but he felt that the old man was near the door, was moving in on him. 'Why are you here?' he shouted. If McKier answered he would know where he was. Eventually he carried in a mug of tea and found him standing in the middle of the floor, just where he himself had been lying.

'Why are you standing there ?' he said snappishly.

McKier pointed at the ceiling. 'What's that for?' He was pointing at, nearly had his finger on, the black circle stuck to the white ceiling-boards.

'Your tea is on the table.'

'I know. Why did you do this?'

'It will get cold.'

'And why do you have to take your clothes off?'

'That's my business.'

Cathal turned his back on the priest and stared into the empty fireplace, pretending to concentrate on drinking his coffee and then on finding the matches, as if he were about to light the fire. But he would not light it, in case McKier chose to see the action as an invitation to stay.

McKier said, 'You spend a lot of time in the dark.'

Cathal: 'What makes you think that?' He turned round fast to try and glare at the old man — to make him shut up without having to actually say it. To make him go away.

'When I go by in the night, your windows are nearly always dark.'

'When do you go by? You don't — I'd hear the car. It makes such a dreadful noise.'

McKier smiled slightly. 'Why do you spend so much time in the dark? By the fire, in the dark?'

Cathal said, 'I like to.'

'Where do you go in the dark, Cathal Kerr? Or do you go? Are you fetched? That is what I came to ask you. Do you go, or are you fetched?'

'Do we have to talk in riddles?'

'I think so, yes. We are living in a riddle, aren't we? It seems the appropriate form of speech.' The old man's voice was soft — it might have been beautiful were he not making such wicked use of it.

Cathal said, 'Until you tell me who you are, you are getting nothing from me. Nothing, McKier, nothing at all. Now go back to your garden and think about it.'

The priest put his mug carefully on the cork mat. 'I'll come back,' he said, and walked to the door. It had been open, but he closed it behind him.

Castlegate was empty of him.

Cathal stood by the fireplace, staring at the door and then at the small window, as if he expected the old man to tiptoe round and peer in at him through the dirty glass. He listened for the sound of the ratchety old engine but heard nothing. After a terrible pause which hurt his ribs, so lightly was he breathing — hurt his hands where he was digging his fingernails in again — he suddenly jumped at the door and flung it open to see the priest standing huge against the light. But McKier had gone. Cathal put his hands on the door jambs and beat gently, rapidly on them.

'McKier,' he shouted, 'Come back . . .'

The breaking-up of his concentration by the priest frightened Cathal and left him dizzy and quivering, wandering around the room holding on to the back of the chair, the edge of the table, the mantelpiece, as if he had been woken from sleepwalking over a precipice. He ranged around the cottage, between the lean-to kitchen and the living room; even outside where it was deeply cold and the sky was turning dark — almost brownish, it was such a lifeless colour. It would snow. The cold stung him; he felt it on his face and hands as if he were lying face down on ice, so tangible was it. Under his clothes it was insidious, fingering him. It made outside hostile, inimicable to the animal life in him that depended on warmth and food and shelter for its very existence. The animal was still there in him . . . He was so seldom aware of it that the understanding came brutally, and he had a sudden rage against the animal, a fury with it for intruding into his short time, his narrow space in time. In some way it diminished him, as if the thing in his veins, in the flesh covering his bones, were a vile thing which was extra to him, like a carrion-beetle or a rat.

He held his left arm out in front of him and stared at it. It shook. The wool of his jersey quivered. It would not keep still. It was like a rat running, scuttling in there, in him . . .

He was running — he knew he was running by the way he leaped over the pile of stones on the floor. The knife was on the draining-board where he had sliced bread some time (easy, the way things were to hand, now). He picked it up and poised the blade above the left sleeve of his jersey. The rat was running now, he could see it. He stabbed at it, right in the middle of his forearm. There was a dreadful jerk and the rat's blood sprang out, streaming through the cut in the wool and splashing on to the floor.

'Got it!' Cathal yelled, 'Look, I got it!'

He clutched his arm and shook it. The hand flapped — crazily — the jersey gaped. Through the slash he saw the opened flesh, the skin split back, white rimmed where the blood was not pouring through it. Something in there was very dark — purple: the rat's heart, intestine. He beat the arm, beat it, beat it, and blood flew in sprays over the table, wall, sink. Panting, he stopped. Gasping, leaning on the table, he let go of the arm. It looked very thin and helpless; bleeding, quivering slightly. Shock, perhaps. He stared at it. The rat was gone.

He threw up. Sweat dribbled coldly down the side of his neck. He was shivering. He had to sit down.

It turned his stomach over to look at the wound; he held a towel over it so that he could not see it. The sight of the inside of his own flesh made a black weakness in his head — it was a forbidden sight, one of the Forbidden Things. He had broken a taboo and the guilt sickened him.

After a while he realized that the arm should be stitched, but he could not think about that — the how of it; the smell of a casualty department; the implications of questions unanswered. He could not be questioned . . .

He needed a cigarette and some coffee — and that meant moving around. With concentration, wrapping the reddened towel tight, he managed both. Big red drops, frilled like decorative Xmas stars, turned dark on the floor.

When he felt better he stuck the skin together with strips of insulating tape running at right angles to the knife-cut. It was not too difficult — not as nauseating as he expected. Then he bound it up fairly securely in a conventional way, with lint and a bandage out of the First Aid box Gemma had installed under the stairs, and put the insulating tape into this with the plaster, as being more useful there than in the tool-box. Feeling quite efficient but very tired, he fell asleep in the chair without the strength to light the fire.

It was very cold when he woke. The door was still open, as he had left it after McKier had gone in the morning. He

144

felt sick and he was shivering uncontrollably — great juddering spasms. There were small, rapid flakes of snow falling slantwise beyond the door. Some of it had drifted in and made wet patterns on the mat. It was grey-dark, not night-dark. The air smelled of day. The light was blurred and mobile, but it was light.

There had been no rat. His arm hurt, now — a dull, heavy sort of pain that he felt as dark brown, not the shrill, psychedelic pain which would frighten him.

Had there been no rat? Had he made a mistake?

He gave himself a bad time cleaning up the vomit and blood in the kitchen, and then lit the fire and burned the soiled newspapers and the floorcloth he had used. It took a while before they stopped hissing and stinking. He threw some wet spruce fronds round the edge of the grate to sweeten the air as they smouldered. His arm was very painful, but he found that he liked that. It turned it into a wounded arm instead of his palsy-arm, and thus gave it a new sort of life; a validity. He kept looking at it, bulky in its bandages. A very real arm. His arm.

There had been no rat. He wondered what the dark, purplish thing had been — vein-blood, probably, or a big vein itself. He did not know, but thought that inside everyone there must be the same dark colours, the same involuntary runnings and beatings. Even inside rats.

He had never thought about his flesh like this: meat, like a pig's, or one of the sheep in the field across the road. He had read once that human flesh tasted something like pork and wondered how the author had come by the knowledge. He put his right hand to his neck and then to the side of his face, but he had grown thin and nothing he felt had the dimensions of meat.

The fire was burning well, now, the window dark. Was it still snowing? If it was, the sheep would be carrying it on their backs, on their horns, and feeling it in wedges between the segments of their cloven hooves. Under the snow

145

their meat would chill, wouldn't it? Their blood run dark and slow? They would be going about, or lying against the walls, enclosed in the weather and enclosing it, part of the weather. If he were to put a hand on one, the snow on its back would be no less cold than the snow on the ground. Or on the tree. It would freeze him just the same. He thought about them out there — the ash trees and the sheep and the carrion-dogs that sometimes came to the trees; winter all around them, and they partaking of it deep down in the flesh where it turned purple, or in the dark ring around the heartwood. He thought of axe cuts in the heartwood, axe cuts into the carcass, and the wound in his arm — the arm which was dying on his shoulder. And he thought that they were all, perhaps, in the same case.

It was warm where he sat by the fire. He could feel the heat on his right leg. Curious to look at the hot leg he stood up, slowly unzipped his trousers and sat again, staring at his right thigh. Would a sheep look like this with its wool pulled off? An unbarked tree? The skin was reddening, the flames strong. He could smell himself: the smell of man; the distinct smell of heated human flesh. He gripped his thigh — there was the meat! From hip to knee, then a bony, gristly bit, and then more meat down the calf. He was proud of it. He sat in his chair, gazing with pride at the proof of his carnality. He thought, I am a ram, a boar, a bull, a provider of meat. Today I can spring from rock to rock. Tomorrow another animal, fed on me, will spring from rock to rock, higher — further — energized by me. It is in my gift — I am a source, a giver.

For a few minutes it was a wonderful thought; an identi-fying, relating thought which gave him, half-naked by his wood fire, a unique position in a great, twisted rope of fibres and minerals and trace elements that ran with the water that flowed out of the secret spring in the wood; with the pigeon that drank from it and with Gethin, who shot and ate the pigeon. (Who would eat Gethin?)

A log crumpled, flared and spat. There could be wild dogs or wolves outside under the ash tree now, crouched there, hungry in the cold, snow sticking to their muzzles and over their eyes. If One came out of the dark corners of the room, he had nowhere to go but out there. When the dogs had done with him, there would be ravens — dark beaks probing in the eyeballs, the tongue, the genitals . . . He twisted in his chair, pulling his legs up and cowering back between the arms, staring around from corner to corner.

He saw McKier's face at the window. Stone, he could still see, with stone eyes, McKier's eyes beyond the pane. Stone, his eyeballs would not move, his lids blink. Stone, he did not breathe.

McKier was gone from the window. There had been no McKier. He had made a mistake —

McKier was opening the door, coming into the room, standing over him.

'I said I would come back,' McKier said softly.

Cathal screamed. His heart crashed at his lungs and ribs, and blood seethed in his brain. He flung his arm up, in terror, between his head and the vast dark that was McKier.

'Go away, go away, go away,' he shouted.

'Where are you, Cathal Kerr?' The old man's voice was low, almost a whisper. He did not want his question to be heard.

'Nowhere,' Cathal yelled. His sound was high pitched, ragged and stupid.

'Where are you, Cathal? Where?' He was leaning over him, asking the same question over and over again until Cathal could not bear his immobile bulk and broke, sobbing,

'I don't know. O, Christ, I don't know . . .'

There has never been a night so dark. Never has

147

the ground been so solid, or the air so dense.
. . . Below, in
the dark, the river runs over stones . . .
The river is rising. It is in flood.
No faces, but dark, humped forms, living all round.
There has never been a night so dark. That there be
not dawn . . .

'Where, Cathal, where?'

'Let me get up —'

'Not until you tell me where you are, Cathal Kerr — tell me —'

There will be dawn . . .

'I don't know — I don't know. I don't know. Can't you see that? You know where I am — why won't you tell me? O, Christ why won't you?'

'Because you know. All you have to do is say it.'

Cathal was crying. He was huddled as deep into the chair as he could go, as far from the brute magnitude of the priest as was possible, the broken springs grinding into his spine, his arms clutched across his naked belly, his feet drawn up against his thighs, jerking. In the depths of the chair, blocked out by McKier, it was pitch dark.

'You have to go — move. O God, move — I'm going to piss myself —'

'All you have to do is tell me where you are.'

'I would, I would — I don't know — believe me — I will —'

'Yes, you will.'

McKier had gone. The snowlight was in the room again, dim and rippling slightly where the ash trees disturbed it. Cathal lay in the chair, his hands over his face. He was crooning to himself, keening gently at all the pain. It was a soft sound, and had a sort of beauty in it. A queer sort of music.

148

There would be dawn, he knew that. But not yet . . .

For the moment it was over. He struggled to hitch the chair closer to the dying fire and threw a light log on the embers. The front of the seat cushion began to steam slightly as the flames grew brighter. It was over, for now.

10

In the mornings the soles of Fiác's bare feet go green-white where the frozen ladder burns into them. Above him leaden clouds roll across the sky, and the gate tower is picked out in white, its corners glittering with icicles. He shouts, 'Forge your spears in the hot rage of God against his enemies, King Illan and his vile house-cub, and no shield shall turn them aside' — and the men are tempted.

The holy man has a tale from Vortigern's time in which a sacerdotus from Auxerre, named Germanus, caused a whole army of the Kind to shout one of Christ-Saviour's holy words, and the combined force of Picts and Saxons who had come against them were so terrified by the Word that they ran into the rivers and drowned like rats. This he keeps repeating to the king and Echw and everyone else, frothing and begging them to believe that baptism in a lead tub and Fiác's leadership will produce the same results if employed against the raiding Irish. However, even Fiác looks shifty when asked if saying 'Allelujah' will really do instead of feeding the war horses, or re-covering shields.

The king has said that this may not be the time to anger Fiác's god — he understands that he has a widespread reputation for vengefulness. It may be best, the king has said, for Echw to continue to allow Fiác to whirl among the fighting-men, screaming, since he is, after all, on the same side as the dinas. His hatred for King Illan is quite extraordinary. Disgusted, Echw has threatened to nail the Allelujah-boy to his ladder if he appears among the fighting-men again.

The Goth is Wodan's man. It is to him only that the Goth promises and prays. He makes sacrifices of a sort — gestures, anyway, in a habit-formed manner, as if he is unable not to, but has no great interest in what he does. Echw has likened the Goth to a gannet held far inland in a flimsy cage. It might be fed bartered fish and shellfish, flesh and dried kelp; but that huge form, lurking in the cramped cage with the ocean in its heart — yes, that was like the Goth. And there is something about Fiác's god, Christ-Saviour, which particularly threatens the Goth. He walks away when Fiác starts raving about his Christ.

The Goth seldom takes part in the exercises down in the pastures but he frequently watches them. He stands, a black cloak wrapped tightly round him, and afterwards talks at length to Echw about numbers of men and numbers of spears and javelins. It is the Goth who has had the immature boys down in the icy river, bringing up round sling-stones and collecting them in caches at regular intervals around the dinas.

Now the Goth has ridden through the mountain pass to Barrectus' hill-camp, taking only his own man with him and staying there five days before coming back. The first thing that he says on his return is that he has seen the sea — that seems to have been important to him — and then that Barrectus will stand firm for the Bear against Illan. But when Echw asks him what Barrectus' price may be, the Goth makes no answer.

His business among the kings and chieftains of the mountains now done, it is not long before the Goth, too, leaves for the south, with the Bear's strategies and confederations for the next battle season in place. He sets off, with three men in single file behind him, down the track from the dinas. The snow has made solid lumps and ridges between the paving slabs which are already beginning to heave apart or subside after decades of neglect. There is thick goose-grease packed into the horses' hooves, and they carry extra ropes and bags. The Goth and his men go down the hill on foot, leading the animals carefully. There has been no departure activity, no farewells. The king stands on the walkway, watching, but no gestures are exchanged.

The Tracker saw the Goth on to the old road, where he and his men mounted their horses and turned south. He watched them until the snow and the distance closed the straight cut of the road, and they went from sight. The Tracker did not follow them but lingered for a while until the warmth went out of the dung and the hoof-prints, and there was no sound and no sensation left of anything of which he was not part. The snow closed in around him, wrapped him. He opened his hands and it lit on his palms, turned his face up and it gathered on his brow and above his eyes.

The dinas was alone now. It stood behind him on the hill as the fathers had set it, solitary in the winter, to exist in its own way, in its own powers. It seemed, he thought, stronger — as if it had in some way regained a purity which the red tunic of Marcellus and the sea-eyes of the Goth had stained. Under its covering of snow, smoke as straight and high as the trunk of a pine, walls and ditches sheer and ice-clean it seemed, the Tracker thought, like an everlasting thing — a thing out of the other world which might come and go as it would, sometimes in one substantiation, sometimes in another. As long as the Goth and Marcellus had been in its compound, the dinas had stayed steady on the hill, harnessed by contingencies and politics and the stink of eaten meat. Now they had gone and the snow covered over their absence and hid their prints. From where he stood, down on the dying street between the white brambles and the white hollies, only particular sounds reached him: the clang of axe and anvil and the iron note of the holy bell. The warm sounds of human voices and wood cooking-fires, of leather working and children — these blood temperature sounds were taken up into the cold air away from the empty road.

The silence of the snow sang to him. For a while he stood, listening to the snow's song, and after a little he sang with it, not with his voice but with the nerve endings in his skin; a rising and falling, an answering and a calling that went between them without meaning but which, at one level, coupled them to each other. He had been in the dinas for a long time, and his body felt thickened and congested, although he had trained with Echw and the fighting-men and hunted swans and duck, roe-deer and pig. The noises of the dinas, so many words and so much shouting; the blows of hammers, the clangour of metals and the thud of felled wood had coarsened his ears, and the thick stench of bread and oil clotted his nostrils. Now he pressed all his mind into the nerve endings in his skin to feel the snow's song and sing with it on the rim of his being. He stood as still as a partridge. He thrust out his mind — out of his head, out of his name — stretched and strung it out there on the surface of his skin, as far away from him as he could reach. For a long time he breathed, while the stillness took hold of him; waiting for the real stillness; waiting.

When it came, and he was stiller than any partridge of this world, he withdrew his mind and sent it softly into his breast where his life was, closed it there against his heart. He rode beside the muscle — beating, beating. The white light of the late day darkened. At one with the muscle and very slowly, he eased himself upon it and rode astride it — still beating, beating. For a long time he kept there, pulsing in the darkness until the heart gentled, reined in to his touch. It was ready. He drew it in and it slowed. After a while, again. And again. Then the snow sang to him, and he answered it from the stillness and the darkness, and there was meaning in their song.

Later he told the king of the dinas, 'I heard a song of great grief.'

'Whose song?'

'The song of the snow, king. And it was in me to sing, too. I am full of grief and my life is sore. *Taceas*.'

The king said, 'That is the wage due to a singer. I pay fighting-men with the blood of my fighting-men. It costs me less. *Taceas*.'

Now the dinas and its affairs had become strident and coarse. The air was crammed with noise and smells and there was no space in it for the silences in which news came to him. The king needed the Tracker's eyes, ears and muzzle out on the snow. After the winter, who will be the enemy, who the prey?

From the highest point in the dinas, the Tracker stared out over the new rings of defences; the great plank-laced rampart with its rebuilt gate; the oppressive walkways, men here and there, ready-laid signal fires covered with skins to protect them from the weather as the Goth had directed; the horses and some of the cattle, the goats and pigs penned in slushy corrals on the hill slope, haunches to the wind, black-wet with melted snow, heads hanging; geese in groups, legs black with mud, sheltering against house walls. The water-towers dripped, eroding little dips and holes where puddles formed under them. Snow lay deep on the thatched roofs, stained by smoke and embers, the tall crest pieces distorted by strange convolutions of ice, carved and twisted by the almost daily melt and freeze into threatening totems and shimmering insignia raised against the grey sky. Beyond the fields close in to the dinas the forest reared in cliffed islands, snowcapped and indistinct,

153

its margins creeping every season closer to each other as if it would close in altogether and drown the dinas and its starving territory. A vision-sea, he saw, rising from the stories of the fathers: the dinas become Caer Siddi, white in a white sea, islanded and alone. Secret.

Somewhere he could hear a child crying softly; and in his own place the king was staring into the deep inroads of his hearth, seeing the severed arms and split eyeballs of his fighting men, counting the cost of an embroidered cloak in spilled bowels at a red ford. The Tracker had a sudden need to see Carac before he left. He had seen how the king ran a crimson thread through his hands, weaving it into a many-coloured cloak as long as the distance a strong man might throw a javelin ('I pay in fighting-men's blood. It costs less . . .')

'Carac,' he shouted, starting at a run for wherever Carac might be sleeping off the wildness of the night: in his dwelling, in the hall itself, on the bench of the woman he favoured, on the windswept walkway of the ramparts, 'Carac — *ocha, ocha* . . .'

Carac was not in the dinas, and the Tracker was out in the woods before he heard him. He ran between the trees where there was no trail, for the anguish in Carac's voice acted like his own pain in his own bloodstream, and he had no mind in him but the running and the leaping to reach Carac. He found him, neck stiff and head thrust forward, crazy-barefoot on the bed of the fire in the roasting-pit. His voice rang from side to side of the pit, echoed and clattered among the rocks of the valley so that the ravens and the crows swung up into the heavy sky:

> Howl in the forest, wolf!
> Roar in the deepest woods, white bull!
> In the cwm, red bull!
> The voice of the live earth is raised
> the voice of the sky, the voice of the hero,

the cry of the Kind on the rim of the battle —

'No,' the Tracker shouted, 'Carac — no —' But his voice would not reach over the stone bank of the pit. He flung himself up it, the burnt boulders shifting and rolling away behind him and under him, grating and rattling on each other, wild things laughing in the deep winter.

On the raised spine of the pit enclosure the Tracker flattened himself and stared down at Carac in the fire. The pit had been used the day before for the roasting of a great pig which had been driven to turn into the spears in the rocky cleft downstream from the ford. The pig was known, was an enemy of the dinas, savage and violent; and not only was his meat an ecstasy after the lean days Marcellus' and the Goth's men had engendered, but his death had been a celebration and a release, for they had feared that a child might come across him in the forest and be impaled on those foetid, yellow tusks. Now Carac had brought the embers back into life; had rekindled them, coaxed them into resurrection and raked them through the stones which were still hot so that he had made a glowing platform on which he was raising a spirit.

The Tracker, knowing that the spirit was not his but was close to Carac, shrank down among the old fire-stones above and watched for a point when it would be safe to break in.

At this moment Carac was crouched at one end of the fire, dancing, running and ducking without advancing, his chest bent low over his rapid knees. He was naked and cursorily painted — not fully, but with his essential, own patterns in old blue; his hair was stiffened but not dyed, combed up into a horse-mane that tossed above his head, heightening him, making a crouching giant out of him. This was not battle against Illan; this was nothing that a turned and hungry Barrectus would ever see: this was battle between Carac and his spirit, and the spirit had to win. This was Carac's secret way through his own turgid flesh to the ancient battle-frenzy of which the old men still sang in wonder and awe. What Carac had learned from their antique songs he was now living in his own young limbs.

As he danced on the embers the pain in his feet lifted him from the glowing stones in a great arched bound, back hollowed and arms rigid as a salmon at the cataract. At the other end of the fire-pit he turned, eyes white rimmed, lips stretched, teeth bare and sharp, to run the embers with the spear low, then brought whipping up and forward to throat level with the great cry, 'Och! Och!' The sound hit the rocks by the river like sling stones. He spun round to face it, steadied his burning feet, poised the spear behind his shoulder and loosed it screaming through the air over the crashing river to bury itself in the far bank. There it quivered, swayed and grew still, the polished, upright ferrule glinting dimly in the tossing light upcast from the water.

Carac stared at it, stumbled and lurched forward, his hand held out, pointing. The Tracker was beside him before he fell, dragging him off the fire, Carac's knees and ankle bones banging between the scorching boulders. He was dribbling, and his eyes were bulging balls of sightless white.

The Tracker dragged Carac to the river, pushed his naked legs into the green, wild water, and flung handfuls of it over Carac's head and chest. The river thundered and frothed beside them, and the heavy spear rose on the far bank taller than a crested warrior in the old histories told in the llys.

'He would have me,' Carac whispered, 'as I was then?' With a great effort he raised his hands and pressed them over his unseeing eyes. 'The salmon-leap — the great throw — he'd have me for them?'

'He'd have you.'

'Did you see the spear fly? How it struck?'

'It is still upright. It stands.'

'Can you see it?'

'Take your hands from your eyes and see it yourself.'

'What will I see?'

'Carac's spear upright on the other side.'

'The other side. You know what is on the Other Side.'

'I know. And the spear knows. It has a home, now. You have given it a home. Come, take your hands from your eyes and look.'

When Carac let his hands drop from his face his eyes were a live man's eyes again, and he raised his head and stared across the river at the spear on the far bank. He smiled and said quietly to the Tracker, 'He'll take me — me and this spear.'

11

He had no lists, now.

He had not cleaned the windows, after all. He sat in his chair, as usual at this stage of the morning, drinking coffee and watching for the postman to go past the gate in his bright red van. On Sundays there was no van, and it could throw him into a panic, because he had come to rely on the post-van as being a marker that told him which world he was in. Sometimes he found this profoundly silly and at others he would sit gripping the seat of the chair, his knuckles white and his neck rigid, until he heard the buzz of the engine coming round the bend in the road.

Today the postman waved as he went by, and Cathal raised his arm in greeting (not that the postman could see him inside the dark room of the cottage), as a recognition of the world the postman inhabited. He had not found out why the postman sometimes waved and at others whipped past with the windows sealed, but it did not seem to be anything to do with Cathal's state of mind.

It was a bright day, blue and sparkling with frost on the trees and grass — perhaps dangerously icy on the road. The sun was melting the frost away from patches of the sheep fields on the other side of the road, and the colour emerged as if it were coming up from deep under water, muted and then pale olive with dark, sour patches which the sheep avoided, wandering in groups in the illusion of warmth that the sunlight loosed across the valley. He thought suddenly, It's beautiful. Then, what a long time it was since he had found the land beautiful. A long time ago, shortly after they bought the cottage, he had roused Gemma (*Gemma . . .*) on a spring dawn to come out and feel the hazel-sweet morning and hear the birds. Now Gemma was dying out and perhaps — perhaps there would be beautiful mornings again. This could be the first, couldn't it?

There was a thrush on the path not far from the door, pecking anxiously at something between the vast, worn paving stones. He moved his head slightly to watch it, and it must have seen him for it paused and set its head on one side, and he could see the brightness of its eye and the thread-like delicacy of its legs. He wished a rabbit would come and nibble the grass — he would have enjoyed that.

The frost made his arm ache, although it was nearly healed now, and he held it to his mouth and blew hot air gently through his sleeve and the bandage that still covered the wound. He did not think about the rat which had caused him to stab his arm; he had made a decision that he would never, consciously, think about the rat and had had some success, although rats came into his dreams sometimes. He had looked after the wound carefully, and to his surprise the insulating tape had been highly effective in holding the edges of the skin together. He had thought that, being rat-infested, it would almost certainly turn septic; but it was healing without difficulty. He stretched his legs out now in front of him and found that he was comfortable. A young fire was crackling beside him, and the sun was coming round and would soon shine on him through the open door. He was tempted to fetch a rug to wrap round himself and to allow himself to doze but he was sufficiently recovered to recognize that his body was deteriorating and that if he did not go off and buy food for it, service it as he would have done the car, then it would cease to serve him as a vehicle for his mind.

He had a cogent moment in which he saw himself quite clearly as a man in retreat, organizing his retreat so that it became purposeful: a man going down into a great (and ancient, even) discipline to wrestle with the problem of Time, the question of When, the theory of the Interlocution of Minds. He would write this down, he thought, in case it escaped him and he needed to tell anyone why he was growing thin in Castlegate in the winter — for he could now see the hollow between the two joints in his wrist, and that was thin; he could tell, too, that the groove was dirty. He must wash, therefore, and eat.

He was still lying in the chair, his legs spread out towards the patch where the sun would come. He would be in the bathroom, washing, combing his hair before setting out along the road. He saw himself pushing himself upwards . . . A quirk in his stomach reacted to the picture but he had not actually moved, only nearly moved. In a minute he would really do it.

It seemed an unusually long way to the post office. He thought that it was a great act of courage, this — exposing his condition and his rat bite to the populace. Was it comforting or insulting that the sheep on the other side of the wall did not bother to raise their heads as he passed? If they did not notice him as human, did not look up and shift casually away as was their habit, might it be because he was in some way incomplete?

The road was incomplete; the road was entirely tarmac and stone walls, no aspect of the Bright Road lightening its leaden colours. Only he, walking along it, had its bright aspect in him. If the road could lose its luminescence, could he lose his humanness? The pitch of a chain-saw rose, and he saw in his head how the wood of Door had been murdered and at the same time how the sawyer saw him; Cathal, ignored by the ewes and treading nervously between the patches of ice where he might slip: a reduced, negligible rendition of manhood which could not even lift a chain-saw, let alone use it. He thought of himself trying to explain how he could never walk up to Door again if he so much as touched the thing; and knew how the sawyer would look at him.

'Hello!' he shouted at the sheep closest to the wall. 'Look up, damn you — look at me.' He put his thumbs in his ears and waggled his fingers as he used to do as a child, behind grown-ups' backs. 'I'm not mad, sheep,' he yelled, 'I'm not even a real vegetarian — not in Gemma's flat, I'm not. Think about it.'

The sheep raised their heads and stared at him. They had oblong eyes with wicked, sloped pupils and thin, narrow faces curiously like a goat's. One of them was unnaturally white. No mud, bramble stalks or little balls of dung clung to it. Its lips were parted in a snarl. First it and then another took a careful step, not away from him but towards him. In the distance the chain-saw wailed.

He said, 'Fuck off — go on, fuck off,' very low and quickly. The sheep took another step.

No one was mobbed by sheep. Cattle stampede, horses charge, post office ladies look. Sheep run away. Why not these sheep? Why not from him? He must shout Boo, Baa, Yah at them. They were trying to turn the world upside down, stepping out of story, committing an atrocious error

160

which would set in motion a train of events leading to malformations, mutations . . .

He began to hurry, not so careful now of treacherous little slides of ice on deep-shaded camber. The sheep followed. He went faster — a stumbling, hasty pace, not quite a jog, clumsier than a walk. That sheep — *agnus clarissimus* — where was it? His arm hurt, jolting at his side. They would have to stop at the river — they would not swim after him? Sheep cannot swim, all that wool pulls them down and drowns them. Get to the bridge, and the post office is within sight from there.

'Fuck off!' he shouted one more time over his shoulder, not looking. Reaching the bridge and eyeing the water — wall-eyed, scared — he stopped, holding the stone parapet, gripping it so that his protruberant knuckles turned waxy, sick yellow. What had he done to himself?

'Can I help you?'

God, yes. Anyone could help him now. Even her. He looked hard into her round glasses, daring them to turn amber and horizontally slit.

He said, 'Ah . . .' with total helplessness, watching her bundle a group of papers to one side and carefully cover them with a paper bag saying Merry Xmas in red. That was all right, he told himself. He knew what Xmas was. Surely he still looked as if he knew about Xmas?

She snapped at him, 'More coffee and eggs, is it? And there's a nice Xmas slice come in a packet that I've sold a lot of. And the stamps for your cards have angels — well, I think they're angels.'

'No angels, no,' he shouted, aware of the terrible danger of shining angels in his path; and aware, too, that he must keep such knowledge from her, along with the fact that he had no cards to post — the one being as wayward as the other. 'Thank you,' he said, more quietly.

'You have to buy five pounds' worth before I can take a cheque. Rules. Coffee's up.'

'That will make it easier to spend five pounds, won't it?' he said, equally snappishly.

She stared bleakly at his coffee jar, box of eggs and tin of peas. 'Potatoes? You've not had potatoes for a while. Bread? Toilet tissue? How many angel stamps?'

'Whose are those sheep the other side of the river?' he said, loudly, refusing her hard sell and connecting only with the angels and the nativity and the sheep leaning into the crib with carnivorous teeth bared and no one but the Babe able to see it. 'They ought to be stopped.'

'Stupid, I call it, taking a sheep into the school all shampooed for the kiddies' Play, and hiding expensive chocolate biscuits in the feed trough to make it stare at the manger.'

So it did lean in, about to eat . . . The hairs on the back of his neck bore in on him how insubstantial and threatened he was. Mutations and malformations, mysteries gone quite beyond Mystery. God, let there not be Christmas . . .

'That damned sheep was creeping along the wall beside me. Maybe I should bring it a biscuit — yes, I'll take a packet of whatever it likes. And no stamps . . .'

'It'll be out over the wall, next thing, and the whole flock after it. In the night. Cause an accident. Death, even, these bad nights. Mark my words, it'll bring trouble.'

'But you'll give me its biscuits?'

'Trouble . . .' she said, incompletely, reaching for the choc-chip cookies. He knew, from the harshness with which she slapped them on to the counter, that they would be crumbled and broken. Buying something as daft as cookies did not make up for not wanting angel stamps. He wrote his cheque while she added up the total in her head. With cigarettes, it came to a pacifyingly large amount. He stowed his packages in the bright polybag, the cookies on top. She watched him, so that he wondered if she expected him to try and sneak in unpaid-for angels. The dirty bandage on his arm showed as he fumbled under her look.

'Rat bite,' he said, trying to be pleasant. 'Perhaps you have some disinfectant?'

'Ugh — filthy things — ugh. Down there between the stick-on nappies and the Ladies Things. Ugh.'

He felt grotesque, grovelling among such things on the low shelf, his back to the door, which suddenly opened. As he rose, clutching a bottle of Dettol, Mrs P.O. was saying, 'Ugh, he's rat-bitten,' to Bar Person, who laughed at him.

'Swab it with whiskey, why don't you? We'll have a go at it if you come in to the Lion tonight. Have you poison down?'

Was it a rat bite? He could no longer remember exactly. There was some doubt. He would take a knife-cut to the pub, and Gethin would come with dogs on a leash and set them loose after the rats in him . . .

'O, a mound of poison,' he cried, imagining the dogs.

Outside he was afraid of her disgust at his accident (that had to be the best name for it); afraid of coming across the entire man who wielded the chain-saw; afraid of the sheep; afraid of how far he had to go before he was safe from these. Afraid of what might be waiting in Castlegate. What had he done to himself?

He stood in the patch of sunlight which was now streaming in through the open door (who would not speak to him in his present mood) and showed the hearth to be cold and hostile. He had betrayed someone. Was it himself? Was it the Tracker (who the hell is the Tracker, now)? It had happened as soon as he heard the sawyer and became conscious of People. 'Other' people? He was no longer altogether one of them, therefore 'People' was correct; but he was still sufficiently one of them to alter as he came into contact with them. Therein the betrayal. Because of People he had understood that Agnus Clarissimus was not an emanation but a tame sheep looking for choc-chip cookies, and that the angels would stay on the stamps. If he had been alone, would he have understood this?

'I AM SICK FOR YOUR COMING —' exploded in Cathal's own voice, in a violence of gold fragments, hinges, pins, the curved forelimb of a dragon, the upper segment of a Chi-Rho, part of a bird's head, eye and beak; in an ecstasy of shattered garnets and splinters of spear blades; a toccata of sharply broken sherds of red pottery and the teeth of bone combs, of blue glass rods and flakes of chip-carved bronze, fragments of smashed stone with deep lines and parts of names the colours of blizzards and Welsh horses . . .

His undressing was a tearing off of something more than clothes, his laying himself on the bitter floor more than hope.

The black circle stuck to the ceiling was quite small, and for a long time it stayed that way, with the grooves of the ceiling boards visible beside it. From time to time it slipped slightly to one side and he had to force it back into the centre of his vision.

Later, it began to grow larger, and the cold of the smooth slate floor slithered away from beneath him. His heart missed a beat. The black circle grew and swam closer to him, or he to it. The air around him was warm, honey-warm and liquid. It was very silent — deeply, fundamentally silent; and the black circle became a sound which he was deaf to.

It grew to the size of his eyes and suddenly cut them off from sight so that the blackness and seeing, and the blackness and hearing, were all one sense — which tilted and suddenly dropped him. For a flash he had the ability to put out a hand to steady himself, but instead he reached out at the blackness, which was hollow. As his fingers came closer to it he felt it cold, and draughts blowing into the tunnel surrounded him, drawing his hand, his head and his spine with them; drawing him spine first into the black vacuum. Fear sprang from him as a rain which he poured into the tunnel, and which lashed the stone walls with a roaring and rushing in the middle of which he whirled, tumbling and falling, and then running down the passage which he now knew, stone for stone. He ran past the bundled corpses propped against the wet walls and heard the procession of the Blesséd rise behind him and follow him, singing 'Alle — *lu* — jah, Alle — *lu* — jah' in a high, humming tone which stayed just behind him and urged him forward. In front of him the passage turned a sharp corner, and there was brilliant light beyond, streaming up from the lip of the pit.

He stopped on the edge, stopped in the instant of falling, seeing the great strands of the pattern in gold and red and blazing green swinging down into the pit, which was where he was going, too. For the first time he reached out and caught hold of the nearest colour — the red. A heron rose from water somewhere below him in a burst of light. When the brilliance was gone he looked up and saw the raven spiralling down towards him, spinning into its own pattern, which was also his pattern. His hands and wrists turned to water, and he clung to the red, his grasp slithering and loosening in his terror, his legs thick and unwieldy as he tried to grip the strand with his knees, and could not.

The raven's shadow closed the pit, the high monotone of the Blesséd was shut out, and it was cold. The wing beats of the raven hammered the air as it dived. He saw the heavy, open beak, the yellow and black eye fixed on him, the bulk of the bird spiralling around the point of vision, the curve of the talon. He flung his arm up above his head, but the bird was immediately over him; its weight thundered in the strands of the pattern, and its wings crashed against the shaft's walls, so that the roaring of rhythmic winds deafened him. He could not look up and see the claws so close. He knew he was alone with the raven, that he had to close with it, that he was going to close with it; but he failed.

His screaming spun in an airy gyre up from his open mouth into the sky, and as he let go of the red strand in his pattern he caught a glimpse, swirling away below him, of the pale blue entity which was him, shooting like a sapphire comet into the void sky below.

He lay, shuddering with fear and shame. The black spot on the ceiling stood over him as a symbol of failure. He stared at it, wide-eyed, until tears stung his lids, and he blinked wavering, prism'd reflections over its perfect shape.

After a while he rolled over on to his face and then slowly struggled on to his hands and knees. He stayed there, panting like the dogs, his head hanging. A few tears dropped from his face and made dark spots on the floor. He lunged at the edge of the table and pulled himself to his feet. His clothes were cold from the floor, and he shivered at their touch, his skin shrinking from them; he felt abraded and raw at their contact.

The sun had passed the door and the room was chill. His misery curdled in his gut. He went upstairs and lay in his bed in the shadowy room, shivering under a heap of crumpled blankets.

Gemma found him still there when she walked in through the open door at twenty-five past five. He heard her arrive, heard the car being parked and locked (against whom — a blue comet? McKier?) and the slap of carrier bags on the cottage floor. He cowered under the bedclothes, invaded by an innocent idea that she might not find him if he hid under the bed. But he was too late, she was coming upstairs.

He sat up and shouted, 'I've got 'flu — I'm ill.' Because

there was nothing she disliked more than the role of nurse.

Her tread hesitated, and he heard her go into the big bedroom which he had left in the autumn. 'Where are you?' Then, 'Not in here, for heaven's sake? Why? This is ghastly, God, the bedclothes! Cathal, what the hell is the matter with you?'

Himself beating off supernatural carrion birds in a sulphurous canyon, clinging to a ledge, Tarzan-style with not even a loincloth was the Matter-With-Him . . .

He said, 'It's only 'flu. The whole village has it.'

'What village? There isn't a house for miles. Or did you pick it up from someone in a crowd in the telephone kiosk?'

He said, 'There's the post office,' trying to defend the image of community life which he wanted to wave at her sarcasms. But she was walking round the room as if she had the same right to it as to a room they had shared for twenty-three years.

She said, 'What's wrong with the light?'

'Nothing. I was asleep, so it was off.'

They were like two children, he thought, who did not like each other and had been put side-by-side at someone else's birthday tea. She switched on the overhead light and grimaced at its shadeless, fly-blown bulb. 'This is ghastly,' she repeated.

'Why don't you light the fire, and I'll come down,' he offered. How strange it was to be talking to her like this — as if nothing had changed; as if he had learned nothing. He was set so far apart — he, Cathal, lurking in his grimy bed; a neophyte in an arcane discipline, robed in white, at the threshold of the chrismarium, knowing only by hearsay the testings to come. He thought: she is outside in the mud of yards and kennels, unaware. He thought: she will live for ever in the yards and die in the kennels.

She said, 'It's all disgusting.' He understood that she meant him, not herself.

'In a way,' he said, suddenly aware that there might be a battle and that he could lose. He watched her, Fair Isle jumper and stitched shoes, breasts, and the slight remains of lipstick not quite worn away. He had thought that she was dying — dying out, but she had only to be present, and the full danger of her came with her like a crown, he saw, of locusts which could devour him and his. Locust Queen, he named her. The God-act of naming . . .

He said loudly, 'It would be quite a help if you went downstairs and lit that fire.' He made a movement suggestive of pushing off the bedclothes, but she gave no sign of being about to leave the room. He realized that she probably could not light the fire — certainly could not chop kindling.

He said, 'O, shit. I'll do it,' and sat up.

When he passed through the room on his way to wash in the bathroom beyond the kitchen, she was indeed chopping kindling. When he returned, dressed and a little shaky, the fire was burning and the table lamp casting an intimate glow over his used crockery.

She said, 'I brought supper with me, but I'll have a cup of tea now. I'll make you one, it would pull you together.'

Cathal moved three lumps of quartz and a piece of turquoise glass he had found in the river, and flapped guiltily at the cushion he found pressed into the back of the chair. He sat himself delicately in the firewood box. He was not going to bring the other armchair in from the kitchen.

She called to him from the kitchen, 'Where's the milk?'

'In the bucket outside the back door.'

Silence, then, 'Ugh! It's off.'

'Can't be, it's this morning's.' Was it? He could not remember. No, this morning had been the post-van and then the trial with the black spot. It must have been yesterday that he had walked to the post office and bought milk. Mrs Post Office hated the way he brought the polythene water bottle and poured all four pints into it outside her shop, even though he always rinsed the milk bottles under the stand-tap and put them neatly in the red crate.

'What's wrong with the fridge?'

'Nothing that I know of.'

'It's not working.'

'I've turned it off.'

'Why?'

'I don't need it.'

'Well, I do, so we can switch it back on, mm?'

This was his chance. Take it, take it without thinking, blindly, bugger the risk. 'No,' he said clearly.

But it was wasted. She ignored his reply.

She passed him a craft mug with one of McKier's teabags floating in it. The surface of the tea had little yellow globules of fat gathering round the edges of the bag. He pressed it symbolically against the rim of the mug — who knew what McKier might have in his teabags — and dropped it into the fire, which spat. The Locust Queen was watching him hungrily.

She was going to stay the night.

He stared at her, the tea half way to his mouth. He could see each individual eyelash and eyebrow. He said rapidly, 'The cows are on cake at this time of year.' She was still watching him from between the eyelashes. 'That's why the milk tastes different.'

'Cake, Cathal?'

'Cattle-cake. Hard feed. Not all grass. Winter.'

'O, farming.'

'For God's sake, Gemma, what are you doing here? Why have you come?' He thought that the aeon before pulling the trigger of the gun in the mouth must be like this. In his mouth, or the Locust Queen's? Would it make any difference? He was a killer in either event.

'It's only ten days to Christmas. I've brought the cards down that you really have to sign.'

She said it so ordinarily that he lost his breath as if he had actually been struck. She had simply not noticed that he was killing her.

In a frenzy he shouted, 'Christmas cards? You brought Christmas cards here? I'm not having Christmas. There is no such thing as Christmas here.' That was what he had agreed with McKier: that there was no Christmas this year. 'Show me the cards. Gemma. Pass them over, let me see them.'

'All right, take it quietly. We can't post them tonight!'

'Show me,' he shouted.

They were not robins — nor angels — but an elegant reproduction of Mappa Mundi with an appeal printed discreetly on the back. They were beautiful. He would like one for himself, really, but they were all written: to Morris with arch thanks for favours unspecified, which Cathal read as 'keeping quiet about Cathal'; to his mother; to the jet-skier who cried into his Glenmorangie; to her mother; to her god-daughter. There was a terrible coldness in his head, a void. He could not understand the words: the 'Happy Christmas' and the greetings in what he supposed was her handwriting. He thought that he must be on the brink of another terrible ordeal: Gemma would turn into McKier and come for him; or into the Tracker, with Cathal's wrist in his teeth as in a man-trap . . .

He raised his head slowly and looked around the room. It was altered, all the shadows in strange places. By using the table lamp, which he never did, she had thrown down the burned stones of his fragile cottage and immured him in a pretty prison, the soft light concealing all the ugly bars and the fists of the goalers. Not a neophyte then: a savage in a Byzantine cage. He glanced quickly at the door — his door, the door that had cried out to him one damp morning of flaying and crucifixion, of a terrible death, and he had been in no mood to listen to its sorrows, had he? Would it stand to for him or for her? (Jesus, why had he not had the compassion to listen to it?) Outside the door was a bitter winter night with all the hill-camps of Britannia Prima as cold and hard as iron, iron shield bosses covering the breasts of the fallen land; and out on to those frozen roads she would fling him and all he called his own.

IT WAS THE LOCUST QUEEN WHO WOULD FILL THE ROOM

Or he might throw her out and lock the door against her, mightn't he? He put his hand down and felt the white stones beside the box where he was sitting. The hardest rock in the known world, quartz. Heavier than skull bones.

She said, false-gently, 'You do look a bit wild-eyed. Have you taken any aspirin?'

He denied aspirin. She said she was glad, because she had brought some wine in case he had none. She would warm it by the fire. He was polite and opened the bottle with the corkscrew she knew was kept in his kitchen drawer. She told him about the presents she had bought for her relatives, his relatives; the parties she had been to; the many, many people who had asked after him and sent him Christmas greetings. She did not tell him any of the questions they had asked her about him, or how she had replied. The quartz warmed in his hand. From time to time she glanced at it and looked away.

She said that her mother, and his, had made other arrangements for Christmas this year. Her mother had booked into a Country House Hotel in Devonshire, and his was having an old friend for midday dinner. He said that that was fine. It was fine, wasn't it? She agreed that it was fine.

It was not that he did not know what she was going to say next; he just was not quite ready for her. He was not absolutely certain yet on whose side Door would stand to. He declared hunger. Fortunately she had brought a spinach quiche, which would do well after 'flu. In order to eat it she went upstairs to comb her hair while it heated in the electric oven. He watched her carry her overnight bag up with her and heard her footsteps in the real bedroom. He sat like a wire mannequin, vibrating at her movements. To quieten his trembling he picked up a second white stone and rapped them together, rap rap rap, as if someone were trying to get out.

After they had finished the first bottle of wine he looked in the carrier bag in the kitchen and found two more.

'Last time I got tight I nearly got run over by a Landrover,' he said humorously. 'What is it you're driving? Not a Landrover?'

'Not funny.'

'No? Why not?'

'I think we should talk before you make jokes at my expense.'

'It wasn't at your expense. Or do you dream about running me over?'

To his amusement she did not reply. Then he realized that it was not funny — it was terrifying.

'What do you dream about, Gemma?'

But she refused to answer, even though he shouted at her. He thought he saw fear in her eyes and wondered if she saw the fear in his head. Whichever of them was the more afraid, he thought, would do the other the greater hurt.

He said, 'You're afraid of me.'

'No. Should I be?'

'Yes. It's time you were. Don't you think so? Don't you think I have gone a little mad, become a bit dangerous? I mean, you never know with madmen, do you? You can't tell how much you may be hurting them, because they aren't the same as the un-mad, so you can't judge. If you twist the wrong bit of them, how do you know? Don't you think I've gone a bit mad? Don't you?'

'I think you've gone a bit drunk or a bit feverish.'

'What's the difference? What do you think takes over in your head when you are feverish that is different from the thing that creeps in when you are mad? I think they might be the same — so it makes no odds if I am mad or sick.'

'You said you had 'flu.'

'O, Gemma! You came down here to talk to someone with a madness — about whether to ignore it, perhaps so no one could ever say that you had kicked me when I was down, or whether to use it as a reason for kicking me. Have you made up your mind yet? Shall I tell you something about it so you will find it easier to decide? What shall I tell you about — the man in the forest who bites me like a pack-dog? The rat inside my arm? The way McKier wants to tramp on my liver, or the big black birdie that flies down the pit-shaft? Imaginative stuff, isn't it? Heady —'

She was shouting back, 'Stop it! Stop it!' And he went rap rap rap with the two quartz stones, rap rap rap rap, to make her heart beat faster. She sprang up and walked around the room, touching things. The things she touched were his: his dead ash leaf on the mantelpiece, his magpie feather on the stairs, his crumpled shirt in the bookcase.

'Don't touch my things' — rap rap rap rap —

'They are not just "your" things. This cottage — and you've turned it into a hovel — is part of a marriage.'

'This cottage, like any marriage, is a lair. And I'm in it, too.'

She laughed. It sounded a little shrill — she, too, had drunk a great deal. 'What a ridiculous thing to say, Cathal. For God's sake, go back to bed and sleep it off.'

Sleep off himself? Go to sleep and wake up in Cash-and-Nooky Land with the cottage door shut behind him, its tongue cut out, and the vast swinging worlds shot out of the sky? Wake up in the grey twilight that the City called darkness? Ideas came in articulate form: words to describe to his un-mad mind the reasons for the pain in his heart. There are no words for extreme pain, only descriptions of it and names for the fear of it. He thought: in a different age, sentenced to the gallows or the wheel or the cross or the stake, this is what I would feel when they told me. When his un-mad mind asked him what, in such a case, he would do, he replied without hesitation:

Kill them before they kill me.

There was a cold lump in his stomach, a cold buzzing around his temples: the Locust Queen setting the swarm on him. He looked at her, pacing through every shadow, every patch of light; stealing the shapes he had made with the firelight or the overhead strip, robbing his place of its own secrets, exiling its occupants; flinging its ruins wide so that instead of a sheltering enclosure on the cold hillside there was nothing but shapeless boulders and burned stones. There was nothing left, after her. Nothing.

He cried out, 'Not yet.' He was on his feet now and moving into the centre of the room putting his very body, his limbs and belly, his testicles and brain-pan, into the middle of the room, into its heart; and from there he would fight for its life. For his own. It was the same thing. Kill her before she killed him. The door would stand for him, he could tell now. Those planks had not endured out there on the hill, on the track to the dinas, for eighteen decades of storm and strain to be felled by the Locust Queen at Cathal's back. Door would stand behind him. The land that had been rock and that was now the walls of the cottage would stand around him. He stood in its heart, part of it, one of its organs, his water its water, his broken ribs in its shelter: one life-form.

He shouted, 'I am at home here,' unable to make verbal logic out of what he knew. This is home. Here I am houseled. There was a wildness in his bloodstream, the strength of honey, and he marvelled at its sweetness, he who was so used to weakness and powerlessness and the despair of his own cowardice. He raised his arms and felt his muscles; felt the warm quartz stones in his fists, and his feet light on the smooth slate floor — a creature in its own element, a salmon at the cataract, a wolf by the road, a man amongst his kind.

He said, 'You can't kill me here. This is the one place where you can't do it. Go away, Gemma, go away. This is a dangerous place.'

She was still at large in the room. Circling it, he thought, as if she wanted to be behind him. He moved as she moved, keeping her in front of him. He had been afraid of her for so long and for so long had never thought himself able to combat her. He could not understand why he had gone on and on, through all the Christmasses and weekends and dreamless, wasted nights, allowing her to eat away at him. Feed on him.

He said, 'You can go. You aren't leaving anything behind. There's only a bit of me left, and you wouldn't want that bit. Why not go before something happens. I won't touch you — I'll stay over here. Go, Gemma, please go now. This is a dangerous place.'

'Are you throwing me out, at this hour of night, to drive to London on my own? Cathal, women don't do that any more — don't you know that? Suppose I punctured or broke down? Anyway, I haven't enough petrol.'

'You really were going to stay the night? Here, with me here?'

She raised her hands, palms out, striking at the air. 'This is not a dangerous place — this is our weekend cottage. I am staying the night and in a separate bedroom, and I am going there now. Please keep out of my way.'

He knew he could not let it happen. He felt his blood quickening.

'Go,' he said thickly. 'For God's sake, don't make this happen.'

'Stay where you are, Cathal. I'm going to the bathroom and then I am going upstairs — for the night. I shall be quite safe — you never bothered to take that ugly great bolt off the bedroom door, did you?'

He heard her words but did not understand them, only knew that she was coming for him as the Tracker had, and McKier, and the bird in the pit-shaft. The muscles in his hands and fingers swelled, tightened like cables under stress. He brought them together and rapped the white quartz, rap rap rap, meaning something, but knowing she would ignore the threat: rap rap rap. The locusts were buzzing more loudly and loosening out from around her into the room — onomatopoeic buzzings grown out of the sounds 'bothered' and 'ugly' — so close to his ears, thrumming on the tiny ear-bones inside his head.

'The voice of the live earth is raised . . .' someone sang: the door or the polished slates underfoot or the boulders of the walls or Cathal who, the white stones rapping, crouched running and ducking in the centre of Castlegate, his chest bent low over his rapid knees. Sweat from the thrumming and the dancing and the pain in his ears and the recently hurt ribs and arm grunted and whined in his throat. He ducked and ran, eyes white rimmed, lips stretched, his teeth bare and sharp . . .

Cathal was leaning over the back of the chair, shaking so violently that its legs rattled on the floor. A car engine roared and a car door slammed. He was gasping, choking for breath, spitting and retching. The car was silent now. There was blood on the floor and on the walls. The door stood open and the table lamp was overturned, the hot bulb making the side of the shade stink like brimstone. As soon as he could control the shaking he must set it upright — the thing would go on fire. The door groaned on its hinges, swung a little and, in the end, closed.

Gently he said to it, 'It's all right. It's all right.'

After a while the shaking subsided, and his breath came more easily. He straightened up but his knees buckled so that he had to twist himself into the chair by gripping its back as if he were injured. Presently the smell from the lamp grew so threatening that he forced himself to stretch out and catch hold of the flex where it ran along the floor. He pulled the plug out of the socket by jerking the flex, and the light went out with a slight pocking sound.

In the fireplace two of the logs were still glowing. He shoved them about with his foot until they broke into flame against each other. Some minutes later he felt balanced enough to lean forward and hold his freezing hands over their heat. Later he was strong enough to pick up two more logs and wedge them next to the flame. In a little while he would stand up, but not yet.

The firelight brightened. He sat and stared at it, feeling its warmth all down his body, leaning his stiff chest towards it, his hurt arm. He thought perhaps the wound had been broken open — it had not pained him like this for days. Eventually he would look and see. There was plenty of insulating tape in the first-aid box. He might even mend the lamp if he had broken it, pulling it out like that —

There was McKier's face at the uncurtained window. There had been a car — he had heard it. Amazing vehicle, with laughing daisies on it! He began to laugh himself, knew it was hysteria, but could not stop. Laughing, he pointed at the door and gestured to McKier to come in.

'You look as if you might like this,' the old man said, shutting the door firmly behind him against the night cold. 'I'm on my way back from the Black Lion, as luck would have it. Have you any mugs — tankards, perhaps, in chased silver? Never mind, we can drink out of the bottle.'

'Why not?' said Cathal, still laughing, holding his hand out for the gin.

12

McKier quoted softly, ' ". . . this Both the yeares, and the dayes deep midnight is . . ." '

He was sitting opposite Cathal, his slippered feet stretched out in front of the polished hearth. He had produced some strangely shaped and lavishly filled mince pies, and the empty plate sat between them on a bundle of the transactions of the Birmingham Archaeological Society. A tureen of mulled wine warmed itself in front of the fire, and the goat lying in a large tallboy drawer, bedded with straw, snored gently behind the sofa. Cathal very much wanted to go to sleep, but McKier was anxious about the goat who was suffering, he said, from shock, her roof having blown in on her earlier that evening in the gale. He kept jumping up to go and look at her and give her saucers of the hot wine, and Cathal had to draw his feet in to let the old man pass. The goat had sunk casually into exactly the sort of abandoned stupor that Cathal was aiming at, and no longer even twitched her delicate lips when McKier bent over her.

Now, in response to Donne, Cathal looked over his shoulder at the window, outside which the storm was still howling. From time to time the noise of the wind rose in pitch and screamed, gouts of dark smoke backed out of the fireplace, and the curtains swayed and bulged in the draughts from the rattling frames. The brass rings tinkled on the brass rod.

'The isle is full of noises,' he remarked with asperity, as something crashed in the yard outside. 'None of them sweet, and all intent on hurt. Will it get quieter when midnight is passed?'

McKier: 'That depends on what the sun has found down there.'

'And with what memories it rises?'

'Undoubtedly.'

Cathal shifted nervously. 'That's a frightening image. Suppose it rises red? What am I to think then?'

'Now, now, we are having an evening with no blood-angst. Have some more wine — we might as well get drunk since we are not going to get anywhere else.'

'McKier, I need to know —'

'I have nothing to tell you. I was not there.'

Cathal leaned forwards, his hands twisting in each other as if looking for someone's to hold. 'Weren't you? Weren't you there in any way at all? McKier, I have to know what happened. There was blood on the walls and on the floor. There was a bandage over my arm, but it was bleeding again — I assumed the blood could have come from there. But it may not have been mine. There was such a lot of it.'

'If anything had happened the police would have come looking for you.'

'Only if she complained or had failed to get back to London. She might not have gone to the police. Almost certainly wouldn't have. You have to think, McKier. That's a hell of a road out of here — she could have gone off it at a dozen places where she wouldn't be found for weeks at this time of year. Or had to pull off up a track — and nearly all those farms are summer pasture or second homes. She could be anywhere. She's supposed to be here, no one would look for her. And I won't know what I did. I won't know if I was . . .' He thought: able, but found it too difficult a word.

'Then, I say it again, ring her up and find out.'

'No!' No, because if she answered —

If she did not answer —

McKier repeated, 'We are not getting anywhere, so we might as well get drunk.' He dipped into the tureen with a great, tarnished ladle and refilled his glass. Anonymous bits plopped as he dropped them in.

Cathal said, 'I've killed her. She's dead. Whether she is or not, I have killed her. I've thought that I may have killed her. It's not only the physical thing that matters, it's the idea. It's recognizing her, naming her and then being able to kill that.'

'Naming?'

'Yes — when I recognized her, I gave her a name. I went for the she with that name.'

'Ah, the God-act. The god gave and the god hath taken away . . . I don't think you need worry about the blood.'

'I have to know.'

'But you do know, don't you? She's gone. What did she leave behind? Empty wine bottles, a comb with some fair hair in it and a packet of Christmas cards. You burned the cards, I disposed of the bottles, and I've found the comb very handy to do the goats' beards. It's an unusual sort. You can't get anything like that in the post office.'

'You make it sound as if we had tidied up after a murder. This is too serious for that. I've killed her.'

'Maybe,' said the priest. 'Or maybe not. Maybe she named you, and the you she named killed her? What then? Who killed her then? Or, Cathal Kerr, did someone else name you? Are you someone else's Cathal, god-made for someone else's purpose and set to task to what — practise? Exercise? If the sunrise is red tomorrow morning, is it bringing up a memory from down there or a dawn?'

'Listen to the wind. It's angry — is it angry? Can it be angry? What are you saying, old, old man — how old are you? I've often wondered.' Then, 'Was it you?'

There was a moment while Cathal understood what he had asked.

'McKier, how long were you outside the window? What did you see? What did you do? Where were you when she came out of the door? What did you do, McKier?'

The wind was wilder now. It had fierce rain on it and flung the rain and gusts of hail clattering against the window, rapping on the glass as if it had so many talons. It drove on iron felloes which sloshed and rumbled in the mud of the yard.

'No. It wasn't me,' McKier said softly, scarcely audible above the tumult outside. A door crashed, very close.

Cathal leaped up, 'You know! You know what happened. Tell me, you bloody man.' He saw a McKier, bloodstained and frenzied, with a great iron weight in his hand, raising it high over Cathal's own head; saw the arm quiver with a huge intensity, and the weight begin to fall; and he looked down into the old man's eyes where he sat by the fire, staring over Cathal's shoulder at the shuddering window.

'You, Cathal Kerr, have a journey to make,' McKier said. His voice was very soft and lilting — *ocha, ocha,* like kelp on a flow tide. He was staring past Cathal, and maybe not at the window. 'Some of us, travellers you might call us, make the journey all the time. Some of us never find the road, or are afraid to travel on it. Some of us wish to and cannot. Those are the unfortunate ones — pity them. Some of us go one way and never return. Some get lost — pity them. It is a dangerous road, and many have died on it. You have set out and have glimpsed the danger. There is no one, Cathal Kerr, who will or can tell you how the road will serve you. You travel alone.'

Cathal knew that the old man was saying something to him which was true, but there was so much noise, so much howling and lashing out there in the dark, that the soft words were hard to hear; and the sense of them was tossed and blasted in so much wind that it seemed about to split from crown to root and come crashing in, destroyed and destroying. He bent over the old man who sat so still, watching with merciless eyes, and shouted to him over the deep screaming of the storm,

'Is it the same for each one?'

'O, no' said McKier, clearly in the firelit room, 'I wouldn't dream of crushing your wife's skull between two quartz rocks.'

Into the absolute silence Cathal whispered, 'Did I?'

'I wasn't there,' said the old man. 'Did you?'

It was the first time that the Tracker had been out of the dinas at midwinter. The flesh part of him, that was full of pig-meat and barley, the king's politics and love of Carac, was afraid of being unleashed out there in the forest at this most particular time. His flesh thought that there were dangers for which he had no name, absences of law and sequence to which his carnality had no response. His skin became cold and rough like river sand, thinking of the sun's long night and the perils it must pass through, down there. When it came up in the morning, to what would its long shadow point? What would it bring with it, that first instant of strike into the year?

The north had its long, pale fingers in his spirit; and because he was so much an animal he felt it as if the white fingers passed right through him and fastened on to his spine. So he moved northwards and upwards into the smell of dangerously open land with no track to follow; eye pupils so large that all the covert-green iris had vanished with the last of the year's last day, and on the wide black lanx of his vision each dark amongst the darks was distinct — was to itself alone, and to the Tracker, singular. A jay watched him darken the dark and become nothing. Foot-prints on the forest floor filled in as the snow flurried and gusted between the tree trunks and fell from tossed branches.

Loping on sinewy legs, sniffing, peering and stopping — nothing but a listening — he moved on until the grey light began to gleam, and the sour smell of naked bare rock drifted in the widening gaps between the pines and birches. The sharp, clear note of a hunting buzzard rang against stone. The edge of the forest drew back behind him, and the north stood in the sky in lines of silver light and clarion white peaks. The snowfield was mazed with tracks. An owl had struck, and a tiny prick of track came to an abrupt end in a toss of thrown snow and deep slashes in the white. Nearby a crow had set down, hopped and taken off again. There had been nothing left for the crow. The Tracker selected one set to follow back to the forest brink, where he sniffed at the pine trunks, chose one, climbed into it and sat hunched against the rough bark, perched, waiting.

The slope rising in front of him was almost bare. The sunless daylight glazed directly at it so that it struck back light and hurt the eyes. There were rooks in the sky now, spinning on the wind, beating up the airlifts and swooping down almost to tree level; searching, seeing from every angle, every slant, where death might have come in the snow — a chilling corpse, or not quite a corpse yet, staining the painful white with a flicker of blood-heat.

There was nothing for the rooks, either. Ice formed on the Tracker's lips. The side of the mountain in front of him was an intricate pattern of planes and angled surfaces, divided by sheer black cliffs where lines of ice and snow ran along clefts and ridges and by grey lacunae where it fell away from him and rose on the other side, glaring and blank. A few stunted and broken growths, smashed hopes of life, slanted like thrown spears away from the wind. Alone, without the forest, they had no hope. He crouched, motionless on his branch.

The cold deepened, and the dark from inside the forest crept out along the mountain before the Tracker left the tree and came out on to the snowfield. The wind was less strong now, the clouds breaking and showing white and pearl undersides — until suddenly they seemed to fling themselves aside so that the whole western sky behind them blazed in tiers and turrets of gold. The Tracker, holding his breath in awe, saw walls and cities, mountain ranges and great plains, seas without margins, rolling and merging, sweeping across each other; bulwarks of pink and saffron, shimmering and shining and streaming shafts of molten bronze and bars of red gold into a blue space so luminous and so distant that the end of the world seemed only a spear-throw away.

The brilliance withdrew. Deep tones of blue and green seeped down from above and left only a fragile blur of sea-green behind the massed bulk of the mountains to the west. A single star stood to the north. His body prayed, swaying with desire. His breath clouded in the cold; and he saw his breath — by which he lived; which was his sign, as it was of all animals — float out from him and pass into the air that had shown the glory. He desired, with a ferocity that twisted the muscles of his mouth, to go with the breaths, to become air, to blaze and turn to gold and be forever in the spirit of the living world; to be breathed in by trees and infants and harebells and the light in running water.

He rose white from the snow. The crescent moon between his tines was so bright that it shone out over all the ground around him, and he raced over it in great leaps, each bound a flight and a joy so great that he had laughter in his deep throat and bliss in his rippling hide. Beside him pure white hounds galloped in pairs, their red ears laid flat against their heads — for they loved him and were running with him, and he felt the wind of their movement and their song of delight. When he opened his eyes they were not there, but for a lingering moment he felt the stag in his blood and heard the singing. Then it, too, was taken, and he rolled over; a shuddering and sick man under a heap of skins, too weak to do more than jerk his calf muscles.

As soon as he moved he was the focus of attention. He felt many men around him, smelled their breath and their flesh close to him. Their voices were loud, and he thought they were shouting; he was afraid they were shouting at him. He could not understand the words. He was tied into the skins and could not move. He was imprisoned among the many bodies which loomed over him, bending in and forming cage bars above him; bending closer and coming in on him to crush him. He screamed and his ears exploded with pain and his lungs burst into flame. They threw him into a vat of icy water and laid him to dry on a bed of firestones, and all the time they shouted and grew. Once they grew so large that he tried to scuttle away between their legs but they

184

trod on his chest and staked him out on the frozen lake with burning arrows through his ribs. He did not know how long it was before he saw that they were men with anxious faces, and women who rubbed snow on his head and breast to take away the fever. He tried to smile, to make them pleased with him, for the feeling of peril was writhing in him like maggots, and his guts turned to water and shamed him.

They told him that they had found him deep in the snow, and that the hounds had dug him out. That they had brought him in as a prisoner, prepared to torture information out of him or kill him, until he had started raving in their own language, or as good as. That Barrectus was deeply concerned about him knowing him for a native man of the forests, and therefore of great value. That the feast was long over, the fires dowsed, but there was plenty of good broth and some beer; and that he would have as much as he needed, and clothes, too, when he could stand up in them. That they had saved his right foot and that he would be well soon. Here, they said, drink this. And this. And later this, too. And eat this, and breathe in these herbs.

They let him sleep after he had tried to creep away from their attention and hide behind the logs heaped by the door. His frostbitten foot was wrapped in sticky bindings, stained black by the dried leaves that heated his skin and kept his blood running and breaking out so that his flesh did not go green. He had slept and slept, waking briefly for broth or hot beer laced with willow juice — it might be at night, or by daylight; sometimes he could see snow falling outside, sometimes weak sunlight.

She was small and wide-faced with blue, horizontal eyes that seemed to be always laughing because the lower lids were straight and not curved like most people's. He loved the eyes, thinking them to be the colour of vetch at midsummer, and would lie staring into them, dreaming of warm nights and the rippling call of nightjars. She was big-breasted and wide-hipped, and her face was freckled like a trout's sides; even the backs of her hands had little brown flecks. He asked her if she had been left out in the rain as a newborn, for it reminded him of rain-showers on a pool. She laughed at him and said her name was Aife and that yes, she loved the rain but as for having been left out in it — he was still talking in his dreams!

He wanted to ask her why she was caring for him. He could not tell if she were young enough to be still living with her mother or old enough to be with a husband, but from her assurance and boldness he thought she was more than a child.

She said, 'You cannot go back to the forest like this, the forest will kill you. You don't want that, do you?' She had such a voice as stars would sing with, he thought.

'Speak again,' he pleaded.

She said, 'The forest will not have the injured in its boundaries. The injured must die. That is the law of the forest.'

He said, 'I have to die in the forest — I am the forest,' and felt a white brilliance in his mind as he spoke. He had never said that before — never thought it in the way that the human body of him thought. But he had known it in the water in his spine, in all the inner parts of him that flowed. The vetch-blue eyes pulled at him, drawing him out of the forest.

'Some day,' she said, so low that it was the evening breeze in honeysuckle, 'but not yet.' Then she laughed again.

He saw that her lips were the colour and fullness of haws, and her clothes all yellow like birch leaves and green like elm leaves. He said, 'You are as beautiful as a wood-land. I would be at home in you.'

'Some day,' she said, 'but not yet.' She reached out and

touched his lips, but he did not understand what they had said to each other.

Barrectus' camp was no more than that. It was a collection of huts and tents and temporary turf structures with massive white boulders at their corners, put up in the curve of the innermost of the two ramparts of an old, deserted hill-fort. Tucked in there, it did find some shelter from the blizzards and bitter winds of that winter, and the nearest bank had a new thorn fence around its crest, very tight and high, with rough wooden platforms to provide watch-posts. The horses and cattle that Barrectus had brought with him from the north were lined along the space between the lower bank and the unkempt, overgrown ditch where water collected, and which was now shoulder deep in snow. The horses were thin and listless and there were no more than forty of them, the pregnant mares with swelling bellies, stick-like legs and backs as high-ridged and lumpy as a wild pig. The women, the Tracker thought, were not much better, and there was a dull likeness between their straggling hair and the unkempt manes of the horses. The cattle seemed to have fared better, but there were no pigs or sheep, and the goats were noisy, bleating painfully and giving little, thin milk.

He stared around him, standing in the shelter of the low tent he had been living in with the nightjar girl. He called her that, at first to himself only, and then to her face; and she had laughed that single-noted, rippling laugh that never failed to make him smile in response. The hardship of the camp was a compelling contrast to the luxury and indolence that the dinas had developed through the strange hushed years since Badon. Barrectus had made no claim to kingship; his fighting men were hard, taut men with huge appetites for laughter and catastrophe, and a desire for battle that was immediate and self-centred. To the Tracker they appeared as so many weapons which any man strong enough might wield. Barrectus held them to him by constantly dropping to them colourful hints of the bloodshed and consequent plunder he expected of them in the coming season and by the lure of his allusions to the gentle pastures of Ynys Môn and the sheltered cwms of Cadwallon's frontiers. On these sly foundations the men would build futures of fame and wealth won by spear and javelin — visions that included trials and testings to the limits of endurance, the supreme expression of battle-ardour, and the achievement of feats so spectacular that poets would feed on them for ten generations. There was beer-talk, too, of severed heads bumping against the horse's shoulders on the long ride back and of wild, ecstatic cattle drives across moonlit mountains.

'I know of you,' Barrectus said, his jay-blue eyes as cold as the ice in a crevasse. 'The sailor, Theodoric, spoke of you. Said you read the minds of men and animals. Do you?'

'I am poor with words.'

'But good with the nose? Good in the base of the spine? Sharp-eared — a wildcat's hearing?'

'Perhaps.' He felt caged in again. The hut was small, the wind blowing the smoke at the benches and not letting it rise into the reeds of the roof. The walls were cluttered with hanging harness and spear shafts and leather armour stinking of duck-grease. He shifted so that he could see out of the door, give himself back the outside. Barrectus sat hunched, a heavy man dangling on a chain of unknowns.

'You know every track in this forest from here to Segontium, to Deva, to Agricola's halls in the west? The trees tell you the way?'

'I know ways — some that are there, some that are no longer there. Some that are never there.'

'A poet?'

The Tracker thought of the laughter his terrible rhymes

caused in the llys and smiled. 'Not a poet. The poet talks to me, he makes the rhymes.'

Barrectus: 'And what do you make?'

'I make . . .' He hesitated. 'I tell the king of the dinas what the trees say. The king makes thoughts. I tell the king what the wolves do, and the king makes plans. I tell the king when the great ash will die, and the king calls his priest. I make nothing.'

'And what will you tell your king this time?'

'What Barrectus says. What he does. How his men smell of battle and his horses of dying. What he asked me.'

'And what will your king do next?'

'That is for the king to do.'

Barrectus sat back, pushed his legs out to the smouldering fire. 'It has been a hard winter here,' he said slowly. 'Cadwallon Longhand is well named. He has a spear in every stag and every boar from here to the sea. He has cattle in every sheltered valley and men on every high place. He stakes me down here with no grazing, no meat, no beer and no fighting. Tell your king about the itch in my fighting-men's palms.'

The Tracker watched a white cloud the shape of a violet leaf drift eastwards across the pale blue sky. Behind such a cloud there would be others, darker, unshaped.

Barrectus said, 'That sailor, Theodoric the Goth, had only one desire: to take my men and Longhand's men in five ships to Leinster. To put an end to King Illan. He was not thinking of battle or spoil or reward or wealth. He was thinking about the sea. He thinks of nothing but the sea. If going to battle is a way of going to sea, then he will go to battle. If not, I think he will put out one evening, follow the sun and never come back. Who knows where the sun goes at night? He has tales of islands out there which sing, and islands made of crystal — and he believes them. One evening he will put out and not even the Bear will be able to stop him.'

At the name of the Bear, the Tracker turned away from the clouds and looked across the dark hut at Barrectus.

'The Bear,' he said, thinking. Then he said, 'To the Goth and to Marcellus the Horse Master, he is the Dux. Dux Bellorum. Leader of Battles. We call him the Bear. Is he the same man — Dux and Bear?'

'Two men?'

The Tracker shifted on his seat. 'No, one man with two faces. Or more. Like . . .' He left the picture in his head unspoken.

'I have never seen him. But I have heard things lately. Longhand has met him — many times, I believe. He must be an old man now. Very old men see things approaching which young men stand too far back to see. If the Bear is really in touch with the gods, then it must be because he is growing towards them.'

'A tree to the light,' the Tracker said.

'Yes, but what light? Old men with faces turned to the gods . . . Suppose he wants to go to them — what sort of Dux Bellorum will he make then? Old bears behave one way, warlords another.'

The Tracker thought of Carac in the fire-pit and the spear flying eighty Roman yards across the river. He thought of Carac leaping into the howl of battle, life-fight for a man who desired to die. An old man. He said, 'He is Dux Bellorum still. What the Bear does, the Bear knows. Bears are dangerous, always. If it were not so, we would have heard. The Goth would know. Marcellus would know —'

'Marcellus the horse thief? He found nothing worth his taking here.'

The Tracker said, 'He took all the best from my king.'

'These battles are won and lost by the horses. Think of Badon, what he did with the horses there.'

There was a silence. The silence that always came after the name of Badon.

* * *

His Winter Nightjar was in the tent when he came in. In the dim light he could see only the gleam of her eyes and the pale hint of her throat. He said, 'I am well. My blood runs and my head sings songs to me again.'

She said, 'You are going away.' It was not a question. He had not known he was going until she said it. It was why his head was singing songs.

She said, 'You are going back to the forest. It is your love. I have washed the forest off you with pure snow and smiled with you as no animal smiles. I have warmed you warmer than a beaver's fur, and fed you better than the hazeltree. It was not enough.'

He saw in his heart the sweep of the ash boughs, the great trunk of the oak. He saw a hind in the frost by a stream, a stoat belly-up in a shaft of sunlight. He saw a man with whom he had fought, shoulder to shoulder, and a rowan in full berry where a pine had fallen. He saw light between an alder and a holly and a great ash tree beyond. He saw his love, his belonging. He said nothing.

She said, 'Give me a gift, a token. I have spent many nights with you and I have nothing.' Her voice no longer rippled, there was a call in it which carried. He heard it like a kite mewing, a call that could be heard over vast distances. It made him uneasy and he turned away from her to the door, as he always did, to see the outside — to keep the outside in him.

She said, 'I have given you red gold and black cows — o, yes, in my dreams I have driven a herd of cattle to a field where they stood up to the knees in meadow flowers, and I left them there for you. I brought a gold thumb-ring worked with wire as fine as a hare's sinew, inset with garnet and bluestone and green enamel, and I put it on a black and white stone shaped like a badger's back and left it there for you.'

Still he said nothing, staring at the white strips of cloud high on the back of the sky, riding the wind.

She said, on her feet now and holding out her hands to him, putting her hands on his arms and so close that he could feel the heat of her body: 'In my dream you came to the field and the stone and each time you smiled. I thought you would take the gifts — didn't you?'

He said, 'I did not dream this dream.'

She said, 'I brought a pure white mare. She had a flowing mane like spray over the waterfall, and eyes like polished jet, and she was big bellied.' She gripped his arms and her voice rose into a singing cry. 'I left her by the stone so that you would come and take her and she would know her way back to me wherever you asked her to set off from.' She was shaking his arms now, crying out like a tree torn in a hurricane, shaking him, herself trembling and stamping on the earth floor. 'She had a bridle of scarlet silk and buckles of wrought red gold with boars' heads.'

He said, 'It is a beautiful gift. I have no horse — I have never owned a horse, I will dream of your spray-white mare,' thinking to calm her.

She shouted, 'When you need her you will find her by the rock like a badger. Use her.' She swung away from him, and her weeping was harsh and unpractised. She did not weep much, he thought.

She sat on the bench where he had lain for how many days and nights? After a while he turned away from outside and came and stood over her; put a hand on her hair. 'I will bring you a token — a gift,' he said, 'When the first of the camp's cattle drops a bull calf, go to the stone like a badger in your dream, and I will have left a gift for you.' He felt a pity for her that hurt him like a poison berry in the gut. He wanted her voice to stop weeping and ripple like a nightjar again. He wanted her hands on him to feel like a hound's gentling or a tame blackbird lighting on his wrist, not like the chains in which they drove the slaves from their homes.

'Will you?' she whispered. 'Will you? I will be there.

When you hear the first calf's little moo-ing at dawn, think of me. I will be by the rock.'

'In your dream,' he said, stepping back, taking his hand off her hair because his hand was heavy and had warmth and strength in it; and also because her hair was soft and his hand wanted to stroke it, even a little. When he turned and looked out of the door the sky was grey as if charcoal from the smith's fires had blown over it. He said, 'I will dream of you in the spring, Winter Nightjar,' and was gone out of sight by the time she reached the door to catch him to her breast.

Far out on the hill, when the day was dying away in the west, he heard a keening in the sky and could not tell if it were a homing hawk or a mourning woman.

He did not want to return to the dinas. He did not want to be inside the fortifications, locked in with Fiác's angry, life-scorning god to roof him over; with the king twisting and turning among the heartwood images, prowling the omens with an antique drag-net; with Carac burning up in a sacral fire. There was a malaise, an ill smell attached to his idea of the dinas, although he had no knowledge of any cause for it. He had come out of the high snowfields, out of the sight of Eryri and the beauty behind the sunset, with the great stag's leaping bliss deep in the marrow of his bones and the sound of a winter nightjar behind his hearing. He had come through the forest as through his own self, moving amongst the trees and the shadows along tracks that were there and not there as through the states and conditions amongst which, on another plane, he moved: the animal habit; the plant habit; that in him which was also in the soil and the rain and the rock-face of Cadair Idris. He had journeyed from Barrectus' camp on both a homecoming and an adventure through the trees of the forests and the rides of his mind. But now there was a sour, cold stench on the draughts blowing down from the dinas. He knew the smell; he had learned it early in the winter. It was the metallic smell of the Goth.

So he stood against the Central Tree, the snow not so deep around its roots, sheltered as they were on this lee side of the trunk. On the other side the wind had piled it up in a great sloping buttress, icebound into the indented bark, but here it was soft and no more than ankle deep, so that he could feel the twisted root stock and the wiry stalks of new growth under his sound foot. He stood very still so that he should not crush or deform the infant tree.

If time were integral and not linear, he and Cathal would have come together then under the Central Tree in the late afternoon of a day at the beginning of the twelve hundred and sixty-fourth year after the founding of Rome (or the nineteen hundred and ninety-third after the birth of Fiác's Christ Saviour): two men under a tree in the colourless light of early January, come there for a gathering, a reining-in and collecting of elements of themselves and of serial events in time, which were beginning to break loose and disperse along dark tracks. They stood in silence, one with his spine pressed against the tree and his hands laid on its bark behind him, the other with his forehead resting against it and his arms on either side of his head, fingers in the bark's grooves as if they were handholds. A light wind stirred in the dry boughs above them. There were dark clouds massing in the sky, and the rush of water from the river made an absolute of their quiet.

Because this evening the sun would set a few seconds later than it had last night, and because tonight would be a few seconds shorter than last night, there was that in the cells of the tree which would not die just now. There would be spring. The two men stood against the tree for so long that their body heat melted the snow clinging in the bark and thawed the ice in the topsoil where their feet rested. Such minute micro-climatic changes at a time of extreme crises in the life cycle of a plant can make the difference between life and death. Unknowing, the two men who had come to receive, gave. As long as they stood still, they gave.

The daylight was going out. Still they stood without moving. The clouds rolled heavily from the north, and their shapes faded into a lightless dark that settled over the hills and seeped down into the forests and woods, took out the far corners of fields and the bends in paths. The cold deepened. There would be night. Their warmth was no longer sufficient to keep the frost from the ash tree.

When for the tree the time of their giving was over, they straightened themselves and turned away from it into the cold and the coming night. For an instant they walked on the same path and in the dusk it could not be seen if there was one man or two. Then Cathal went down towards the cottage, and the Tracker turned up to the dinas.

13

Cathal found his way down the path quite easily. When he reached the gateway on to the road he turned, leaned against it and looked back up the track. In the dim reversed gleam off the thin snow, which still lay in uneven patches and small drifts carved into crescents and curves by the wind, he could see the path trailing up between the black trees until it bent dimly between them and vanished. It hung in the frost like a lure or a symbol.

He turned from the gate and looked along the road. There was no traffic on it at this time of a winter's evening. Like the track, it was patched with snow through which tyre marks and footprints showed up glassily in the dusk. He knew at once that it was the Bright Road, where he had perched as a bird and watched young Maccudeccetus laugh at the golden leaves clinging to his shoulders, and along which the soundless chariots had sped; that the narrow wheel marks in the low drifts which stretched across it opposite gaps in the field wall could have been made by their iron felloes as well as by a bicycle.

He stepped across and bent down, peering at the deep grooves in the snow. One pair certainly had a tread, but it was dark and he could not see the other clearly enough . . . He straightened up, and in front of him the Bright Road travelled along the side of the valley above the river. The road where his cottage stood was also there, interposed and contingent; both were under his feet and both were in his head.

On an impulse he knelt down, the better to put his hands on the road surface as he had put them on the bark of the Central Tree. The road was hard and bitterly cold, with minute flecks of solid ice embedded between the gravel and the tarmacadam where it was clear, hard as stone where the frozen snow still lay. His hands gained nothing from the contact.

He ran them over the frozen road surface as if it were a woman's breast, so gently. So gently, again and again. The cold and stillness of it were terrible. If he put his lips to it, kissed it, would it live? How could he quicken it, if not with desire? He let himself sink upon the road and slide down over it, laying himself full length along it, his forehead pressing on it as he had pressed against the bark of the ash tree. 'Home' was in the power in his forearms; in the grip of his fingers on the ice, reaching through to the buried paving; in the force in his thighs.

He lay there for what seemed a long time. No, he would not revivify the Bright Road by love. The depth of his sigh brought the cold so deep into his lungs that it ached there. He sat up slowly and then rose to his feet, chilled and rejected. There was no surprise in this. There was only one way. The black circle on his ceiling allowed no indulgence,

no easy passage through the senses. He must go back to the
the cold, the slate floor, the consuming circle, the journey.
But first —

He turned away from Castlegate and walked on along the
dark valley floor, the river pounding in its dark bed below
the road.

'McKier,' he shouted, beating on the door, 'McKier, I need
to talk to you.' The only light showing in Hengardd was a
dim and flickering line showing round the side of a blind
over an upstairs window, thin as the reflection on a blade.
It cut out into the yard and glittered in fleeting spasms on
the dirty snow shovelled into heaps against the outhouses.
From the sheds a disturbed rattling and the fluster of
feathers answered his call. The silly car was in its place by
the barn, so the old man must be in. Cathal beat again, but
there was no answer. He felt anger moving up in his throat.
He wanted McKier now. He needed to know what McKier
had seen when he came to the cottage on the night of
Gemma's visit.

The little light gleamed like a candle flame, swayed,
diminished, flared again. But the blank windows on the
ground floor had nothing to reflect, and were utterly still.
There was no smell of wood-smoke, only of animals and
dead weeds and cold mud. Hengardd was empty.

He shouted again, 'McKier, I want you. McKier.' But not
even a goat answered, not a breath in the ivy. It was as if
the place did not want him there, had shut itself up and
retreated out of his world. Not empty, he thought: absent.
Deliberately absent. Tonight McKier would not be here for
him. The flamelight in the upstairs window was not a
welcome, only a sign that Hengardd stood and would stand
as long as the old man required it. It shed no light for
itinerants or the sick.

Cathal turned away from the door and faced the night

and the road alone. As he passed the narrow gap between the barn and the old stable, he heard a strange, high-pitched singing — monotonous, on one sustained note. It came from beyond the gap, where the ancient garden lay heartbroken in the grip of winter. He knew it was McKier, in there in the dark among the relicts and the closed plant-forms. The thin, aged voice held the long, long note. No sound in the yard, no movement in the creepers or the interstices of the wall.

The note faded, ceased. So still was the night that Cathal could feel the beat of the river between the icicled rocks far up the valley. So silent was the yard, so concentrated the quiet that he held his breath as he crept over the stiff, unkempt grass and out through the stone gateposts, Imp.Caes. uncaring in the dark. Behind him, high and frail as starlight, McKier sang again in the Garden of Livia.

The wolves were out. He could hear them calling across the snowfield. The moon was elfin in its first quarter and shed little light. The road was frozen hard, spines of packed snow standing in treacherous ridges between the cracked stones of the derelict Roman paving. The brambles, saplings, thorn bushes and gorse at its wide verges humped in sinuous banks, one drifted against another, so that they seemed like a new barrier thrown up between the forest edge and the inflexible roadway. Iced-up slots and tracks flitted across it, full of shadows and knife-sharp at the rims. On either side the trees stood rigid; not a flake drifted from the weighted boughs, and not a twig stirred, nor any creature breathed warmth into the dead air. Only the calls of hungry wolves, echoing from ice-sheet to crag high up in the mountains, ran and met and ran on again across the silence.

The Tracker moved up the river, where the ice hung in spear blades from the rocks, and the spray sifted black and brilliant as a polished mirror over the drowned limbs of alders. The deep roar of the water in the narrow cleft ran through his thighs and his skull bones in the tunnels of the otter. High on the snowfield, the scent of flesh ran wet and sweet along his lips.

There was a coming. Far out along the road, far off along the sound-roads above the road, there was a coming. A fleck of snow dislodged and filtered down from the pine tree. The coming became a feeling in the ground, less than a breeze, extra to the waterfall downstream. A thousand footsteps away the movement became sound below the sound-roads, and the wolves fell silent. The wolf in the Tracker moved closer with the pack. He felt one of them come down through the forest over to his left, wide of the immobile does. The road was bare, a swathe of empty sub-light.

Then the coming clarified: thin leaves of silver spun from the height of the canopy; the soft thump of hooves and the sound of each individual hoof-beat; the clink of metal. A mule brayed. The pack were here now, down by the roadside, couched behind the gorse and the hazel saplings in their bank of snow. Their rank, carnivorous stink lay dead in the frost. The mule brayed again, and her hoof-beats skithered and quickened. There were horses with her, and men whose leather creaked, and whose weapons bumped and swung. His thighs bunched. The soft wolf-panting around him stilled. The leap was coiled ready in them, in the loins and the stiff neck tendons; and in him, deep between the hips and at the base of the skull.

Two riders, three horses, two mules: hot, red meat and quivering lights. The last mule, the trailer, *is the one . . . Tomorrow, fed by her, we will spring from rock to rock, higher — further. It is her gift —*

The loosening
the spring
the immaculate dimension —

'No!' he was shouting, 'No!' — baying, howling.

Wild, in full tongue at the front of the pack; the huge power of wolf-muscle knocking against him. The mule screaming, a horse down on the ice. The Goth sword-mad and enormous on the snow-lit street. Hooves wheeling and striking, clumsy baggage reeling, reins flying loose . . . And they were gone, and there were only the struggling horses and the Goth and his man grabbing and cursing and catching; and the Tracker, aside, panting against a shattered drift.

When he had finished cursing the Goth said drily, 'Somebody's god was looking sideways tonight. Yours or ours?'

The Tracker made a flick with his hands. He had no words for this. Greed for the taste of new, pulsing meat was still on his gums. He spat, spat and spat on to the churned snow.

Taceas.

After a while he said, 'I heard your coming,' which was a lie. He rode into the dinas on the Goth's third horse, saying nothing more.

The Tracker squatted near the door between the empty hall and the inner chamber. The king of the dinas stood against the wall. It was dark, the only light being the reflected gleam that filtered through the doorway from the main hall. He stood very tall and thin, his breastbone with its few white hairs showing where the front fold of his cloak had slipped. His thin face was taut, and his eyes glowed green under their grey brows. He was gripping the tall wand he carried as a sign to the dinas that his mana was active, and twisting its ferrule into the floor, swaying it to and fro, as he listened to the Goth.

The Goth said, 'The Dux sees danger in everything. The whole Saxon settlement from the Dyke to the eastern sea is unstable. Cato of Dumnonia will not be able to hold them if

200

the Dux is fighting up here. That is the spear-talk. Those are the battlegrounds, the horse-needs, the swords. But that is not all. The Irish are ranging the seas of the west, the Saxons of the east. The sea routes could flow as red as the Dubglas, and the movements of hosts and armies — men, slaves, war-bands, trade, everything — be drowned in a bloody tide if the seaways are not held for the Dux.' He spoke harshly — the cracked sound of a man for a forbidden love; the sound of a gannet gale-swept over burned and wasted land.

The king said gently in the half-dark, 'You will go back to sea? Your Dux will let you keep his seas for him?'

The Goth shook his head, as if afraid that any love-talk would weaken him, coax him away from some trial in which he was to fail but had, nonetheless, to undertake. 'Later. There is something to be done before that.'

The king said, 'It is Marcellus the Horse Master who would have come if it were only a matter of spear-talk. Or a much lesser man. But you came — why you, Goth? What expensive thing is it you have come for this time?'

It was quiet in the chamber. Close and very quiet. Not even the ripples of the cool water in which the king's mind stood disturbed the silence.

Then the Goth said, watching the stillness of the king's wand,

'A god.'

The Goth said, not looking at the king but at the motionless wand, 'It is in the Dux's mind that the people are in need of a sign from the gods, a signal that Badon is not over; a talisman of their own that is of all of them and for all of them, and that is not out of Rome — for the people are no longer Roman, however the few like Marcellus may think. It is in the Dux's mind to bring back, from the fathers' fathers, a sign from their gods that will go with him as the standards went with the legions in Magnus Maximus' time. A visible, unmistakable, touchable god-sign to the Kind from the Kind's own gods.'

'Might it even be,' said the king, 'that it is the Dux himself who is in need of the unmistakable sign?'

'Might it even be,' said the king, after a long pause, 'that the red cloak which he has worn for his new "empire" and your victories for so long — your sign at Badon, blazing down that hill among the horses — is stiff with dried blood? Is it too red, Goth?'

'You pay for blood with blood. What else but blood divides us from death? Dead men don't bleed.'

'For what god-sign does the Bear ask the gods?'

'For the return of a god-sword for the use of the Kind. If the gods give the Bear the use of their sword —'

'There are no more god-swords in this world.'

'Not in this world —'

It was cold now in the chamber. The walls, steeped with tales and rememberings, sweated little chill drops from the dreams of the fathers which beaded on the painted shields and trickled down the red paint of the father's signs, staining as they dripped.

The Goth went on, 'It is in the mind of the Dux that the need of the Kind for a blood-sword is so great that he will kill for it. He would kill us all for it. I must fetch it for him. And I am more afraid of this than I have ever been of anything. Give me help.'

'He would ravage Annwn for it? The Bear?'

'Not ravage — just claim and bring home, as a father a lost child. He says.'

'There is no such sword as this.'

'Ask the Tracker. Ask him who dives in water like a salmon, sees from crags like a hungry kite. The Tracker knows where the god-swords are.'

The king: 'Is this true?'

The Tracker: 'It is true.'

The king said, looming tall in the half-light, 'It will kill us, Goth. All of us.'

There was silence again. Again the king broke it. 'It will not come here. It will not visit the dinas.'

'No.'

To the Tracker it appeared as if the Goth was already broken.

The king said, 'I will go into the forest with my poet. When I come out, we will talk of this again.' To the Tracker he said, 'You will see to it that no man, beast, bird or serpent hears what my poet will say to me, or I to him.' He moved as if to touch the Tracker with the wand but passed by him out of the hall without contact.

Taceas.

Circle upon circle . . . The black water over the tall white fall. Circle upon circle . . . The raven above the whitened trees. No rest here or here or here — *ocha*. Circle after circle . . . The fox, the tiny shrew, the pig, the squirrel. Round and round the circuit of the canopy . . . The roebuck looking for rest. Circle upon circle around the nemeton, where the king listened to his poet.

The Tracker moved in the snow, right-handed, in and out of the great trees and between the whippy stems of young growth, breathing on them and rubbing his palms and armpits on their trunks. Hollies and the occasional yew stood heavy in the pale afternoon, and these he shook so that the snow slithered and tumbled into unnatural heaps which he trampled and stained yellow with urine. Badger and fox — *Taceas* — tawny owl, wren, kestrel and chaffinch — *Taceas*. He passed the wild cherries, red as rawhide. Only the rowans he did not touch, leaving them to his left on the radius of the king's circle. Grass snake and adder, sleep dreamless under the stone. Red deer and wild cattle thieved here in lean years or overpopulated years. Mice, moles, shrews . . . A polecat raised her kitts under the bole of this hazel. Chaffinch, wren, partridge on the ground — *Taceas*. Moving downhill to the bank of the river booming in the rocks, rimed and jagged with green icicles . . . A muted memory of the Winter Nightjar's hair ran across his hand but was ephemeral; and he ran on among the rocks, the upper planes malign with virgin snow, crystalline and sharp, the underbellies black. *Taceas*. Shreds of fern and liverwort stirred in the cold susurration of the river; water-rat and otter.

Uphill now, past the cave under the crag. Grey foxes snarled at his passing; stones ousted them. He squatted and defecated at the entrance to the cleft, so that they would not return tonight. The king's secret, he ran on; the king's watch. Late afternoon mellowed gold between birch and ash. Heather under the snow up here; chough and lapwing, capercaille and red grouse; the red deer and the wolves across the crags to the east — *Taceas*. No hunting here tonight. Kite and buzzard, merlin and hungry gulls come in from the desolation of the sea-cliffs — *Taceas* tonight. Down now, straight into the golden haze where spirits of queens and memories of emperors sift and glide like visions between gilded pillars and ivory pillars — and there, like a rent in the king's silence, the man he had been waiting for.

'Taceas,' he said, his hand to his lips.

Cathal Kerr came out of the holly-grove towards the Tracker — unsteady, drawn by the eyes. Eye to eye they stood for a moment in the space between a young oak and an aged pine. When the pine fell, the oak would shade over the forest floor and the pine's fruit would starve of light. A doomed place, this — it would not come again. Cathal stood in a mandorla of gold, struck from behind by a molten shaft of sunset; and then in a mandorla of blood, rippling around his outline as if he were drowned upright in a full river after some final battle at the ford.

It was what the Tracker expected. He held out his hand. There was silence in the forest — the king's silence, that the Tracker had made. He stood as still as a blank milestone. Across an immense distance of seasons Cathal, too, reached out. Their hands reached for each other as the sun went out, the mandorla went away, and Cathal was gone. The king's solitude was complete.

Sunset and night and sunrise: listening, fasting, watching, listening. The king's poet is the centre of the circle, and all around him the forest is in trance — not a live thing stirring, not a heart beating. The Tracker is the king's silence, is the king's secret on the points of his nerves. The Tracker is the king's mana in a line drawn in a perfect circle around the king's listening to his poet. Loping like a grey beast; the king's beast.

Sunset and night and sunrise and morning, the king's beast circled the king and his poet. And when at noon they came out of the forest, the Tracker followed them like a wraith of many forms along the road to the great watch-gate of the dinas, where Fiác the holy man clung to the top of his ladder, his small bell clanking like the call of a lost bird of passage.

This time Cathal did not run from the wood in terror, but came slowly down the track. The sunset dyeing the sky across the river sank into a deep rose into which the purple ran from above and which faded away into an ætherial sea-green which he thought of as spiritual. He stopped. The hills on the far side of the valley seemed so close that he could see every bend of the single track road that twisted up between the stone walls; every thorn tree, every sheep, every change in the hue of the winter-blasted grass stood out as if a surreal lens were focused upon it. The snow had nearly all melted back from the open fields; the trees dripped, and the track ran with loose water, little cuts and springs and streams carolling and bouncing in the dark brown floor of the wood, sudden white flecks which might be bright quartz or a broken icicle caught in their sides. The bitterness had gone from the air. A woodpigeon murmured, and there was a star in the green sky — one, very bright, which did not sparkle but shone steadily like a lit symbol. In the part of the wood where he thought he had seen the shadow of a man beside an oak tree, the snow had still been thick and there had been no sense of thaw. He thought that he must have been on the north shoulder of the hill where the sun never shone from autumn to spring. He thought this but did not really believe it. The shadow of the man, or almost a man, had been the same shadow as that with which he had wrestled and he had said the same word. He had, Cathal believed, held out his hand as if to touch him and as, in return, he had reached out, a cloud, or something, had darkened the wood, and when the light brightened again there had been nothing to see, nothing to hear or touch except the trees and the unquick snow.

As Cathal stood watching, the vivid clarity of the hill opposite faded, and the track darkened. The single star lit other, flickering little lights in the heavens, and all the purple and rose drained away into deep indigo. Only a faint glow of green illumined the west — and it was in this weird light that he again caught sight of a man-shaped shadow in the trees to his right . . .

FIND THE WORD — but his brain was frozen.
Who are you? — but his tongue was rigid.

The man-like shadow had a huge hump — a grotesque out of mediaeval legend, a fantastik. It slipped among the trees, and a twig snapped sharply under it. Straining on leashes, three small animals, one hairy like a griffon, the others smooth like fairy bratchets, tugged and panted harshly against their collars in front of him. They were moving fast, weaving and twisting down the hill in front of Cathal — who suddenly jumped forwards, shouting,

'Gethin! Gethin — are you Gethin?'

The dogs snarled and screamed in rage; and the man raised a hand in a strange gesture and was gone.

Cathal ran into the trees, brash and hummocks and briars like barbed wire tangling his legs and arms. 'Gethin!' he shouted again, but there was no answer. Apart from the clatter of the disturbed pigeon there was silence in the wood.

He turned back to the track and hurried down it, his heartbeats choking, and a cold blur behind his eyes. At the side of the road he stopped and stared up and down the empty tarmac. The moon, early in her first quarter, shed a luminescence over the last streaks and hummocks of the snow. There was no one on the road. There was absolutely nothing on the road.

He turned towards the cottage, still hurrying, not looking behind him. As he reached the gate he heard the sharp yapping of terriers, and the dog-pack was there under the ash tree. On the doorstep there was a rabbit, freshly killed.

He did not walk fast these days. Now it took him nearly an hour to cover the two miles to Hengardd. He carried the rabbit in a plastic bag, and with every step the dead thing bumped slightly against his leg. Its deadness disconcerted him — its potential meatiness allied with the deadness and the sweetness of its damp ears and huge eyes; the now-stiff legs which poked against the side of the bag in rigid peaks. The thought of the chickeny stew which the old priest would make of it with the vegetables from his terrifying garden and which one or both of them would eat, brought saliva to his lips and nausea to his stomach at the same time. He wondered why its fur had stayed so damp-looking.

The wall of Hengardd had turned dark in the rain. Black, almost. He had not truly appreciated how like a fortress it was. How on the road side there were no windows; how the chimney-stack was jaggedly shaped like castellations. That the wall was too high to see over. A tumulus of ancient manure with rusted oilcans and tyres that had seen a massacre protruded from the winter-black nettles. The silence was tough, unbroken by the rapping of drips from the trees — *rap rap rap* — a sound as deep in his bowels as yesterday's bread.

'McKier,' he shouted, 'Come out of there, McKier. I have something dead for you, priest! Come out and get it.' Reaching the gate, he heaved it open on its rotten hinges and strode into the yard where the yellow-eyed goat stared at him from her tether, and water spilled from the broken gutters.

The old man was standing by the disused cowshed opposite the back door to the house. He was exactly in front of Cathal when he marched triumphantly into the yard, the Safeway's plastic bag swinging from his dying arm. The old man was smiling — about to laugh. The daisies on the silly car were already laughing.

McKier said, 'Whose dead thing, Cathal Kerr? This is a present, not a symbol?'

Cathal saw the laughter and saw that it was directed at him. Rage rushed along his arms and up his spine into his head. 'How in hell should I know? It was on my doorstep last night. I saw Gethin in the wood with his dogs and a sack on his back and I assumed it was from him. I assumed it was to eat. I did not assume it was a symbol.'

'Why come all the way here, with a dead animal, to rant at me?'

'Because you and I still have things to trade, Priest McKier.'

'What is it you came to offer me that I do not already have?' The old man still seemed to be smiling, but it was not quite a smile. 'I asked you whether you go where you go in the dark, or whether you are fetched. You have not answered me yet. I said I would come back for the answer. Did you come to bring it to me?'

'You aren't going to frighten me off, priest.'

The cold eyes were flint-hard on him again. 'You frighten yourself, Cathal Kerr. I do nothing, say little, instruct not at all. How could I frighten you?'

The old man had moved, and was staring through the dark slype, between the dripping sheds towards the dead January garden. He said: 'The Bright Road runs through there. The mediaeval road runs along it to the house side, and then turns downhill towards the river. The original Roman road ran straight on. The central path across the garden is lying on top of it.' He was speaking without expression. 'If you scuff up the gravel you will see the paving. All the traffic on the roads comes through my garden. You called it the Garden of Livia — but the Garden of Livia is a fiction, a fresco on a wall, an artefact. It is an illusion of the division of the times —'

Cathal shouted, 'You want to steal my visions and turn them green-rotten. You pervert and distort and thieve, and leave me hurt, night after night, visit after visit. But however mighty a colossus you may grow at night, with your steel toecaps and your sling-stone eyes, you want something from me. Because it isn't you that walks the Bright Road, McKier. It's me, me . . . And you want me to tell you how it's done, don't you? Because you don't know. I know — I do it, or it is done to me. And you are left behind, left out.'

Mckier's voice sounded removed, as if he spoke out of another place or time. He said, 'I need no one. I am no one.'

'Enough of this, priest. I came for you, not for a no one. I came here to deal with you — not to give you something, but to find you. The one you say isn't there, right? That's the one I'm after.'

The old man repeated, 'Do you hear me? I am no one. Do you understand that? Can you understand it? I, McKier, am no one. I don't need you. I never asked you to come here. You came to Castlegate and you came to me. There is the gate — you have even left it open so that you can leave without difficulty.'

And if there were no home to go to?

Cathal said, 'Don't tell me to go home.'

The drizzle was still drifting steadily through the yard, the gutter dripping into its puddle and the wet guinea-fowl treading their pernickety way to the shelter of the leaking barn. Water pattered from the ivy leaves on top of the wall to those below and ran along the bars of the gate to gather at some ordained spot before splashing into the mud of the car tracks.

He waited, but the old man stood silent, still staring between the sheds into the garden, as inaccessible as the unbroken stone face of the house. Cathal put the dead rabbit, in its bright plastic bag, on the ground at his feet. For a moment it stayed upright and then, very slowly, tipped over towards him.

As he turned in horror for the gate it seemed to him that McKier was calling after him, 'When the raven comes up from underneath you, get on her back and ride her . . .'

THE BOOK OF THE RAVEN

He glutted black ravens upon the fortress wall
Although he was not Arthur . . .

Aneirin, Y Gododdin

The tactical pattern of Arthur's battles is one of open warfare, in which
fortified places played little part and river-crossings were all important. Most if not all of his troops would have been mounted, and would
have fought from horseback with sword, lance and javelin, approaching the enemy in a series of rushes rather than in a coordinated cavalry
charge.

Leslie Alcock, Arthur's Britain

[In his lament for the dead prince, Llywelyn's bard] compares the
mingled cries of that stricken land with those which, once before, long
ago, had been heard, after a battle, at Camlann.

As all the world knows it was at this battle that Arthur met his death,
and within the context of Welsh tradition Camlann equates with
disaster.

David Jones, The Myth of Arthur

14

The dream of the ford had been dreamed, and the land covered over in the purest white. The ravens, deep-winter hungry, were gathering in the heights above Camlann. And the king's poet had revealed one of the last of the remembered Forbidden Things to the king and so had taken him aside from his physicality and rendered him invalid as a whole man — had crippled him with taboo and the danger of his mana.

The Oldest of Men, understanding this, moved his low stool away from the king in the inner chamber of the hall and placed it beside Echw. There he would sit now, whittling delicately at the roe-deer bone from which the Tracker had asked him to carve a comb for the Winter Nightjar. The teeth of the comb were thin and fine as hoar frost on the yew, the back beautified with little triplets of circles, with a tiny dot in their centres, which seemed to the Tracker to be the raindrops of spring, the daisies of summer, the light snowflakes of winter.

In the corrals the hip bones of the cattle stood out, gnarled and worn, behind staring ribs; their dark, lacustrine eyes were glazed over and set deep in hollow sockets. The cows in calf shambled uneasily across the churned and shotten mud and snow. One in particular, an old cow with scars on her knees and broken hooves, swayed as she moved, her belly gross and unevenly distended with an early calf. If she dropped it too soon, both she and the calf would die in this weather.

Up on the wall-walk Fiác howled penitentially. He looked to Easter, his feast, at which he hoped to baptize the entire dinas, exorcize the Kind, throw down the images, fell the oak trees to build a church, speak with winged spirits and die wonderfully with the Bear in neophyte's robes, chrism'd and victorious. Once he ran against Carac's spear (but was pulled off before the iron tip had broken through to his gut) to prove to Carac that his love for the Bear's soul was as sacrificial as Carac's for the Bear's spirit. He cut A and Ω into the sheet-ice that covered the west face of the inner rampart, and *chi-rho*s in the ice on all the drinking pots. Fever flamed over his waxy cheekbones, and chronic dysentery had him constantly at a stumbling run from his chosen prayer-stations or down his perilous ladder. Once, when Echw had drunk too much, he admitted in a whisper that Fiác was extraordinarily clever with a shield rim, and would have made quite a useful fighting-man if he were not mad. He was even prepared to give him one chance in a battle, so long as there were no Baptized on the enemy side; but Fiác was not to be told, it would send him hysterical. In this way Echw, like the Oldest of Men, was declaring his leadership of the host and claiming the next kingship.

When the comb was finished the Oldest of Men brought it to the Tracker where he sat by a stick fire, staring at the horses. He had selected four for the journey that had to be made: a heavy old dun for the Goth, a young grey with a reputation for sure-footedness for himself, a gentle roan mare for the king of the dinas and a shaggy brown pack-carrier for the slave who would accompany them. The fifth horse he had not chosen. There was no animal in the corrals of the dinas which corresponded with the description the king's poet had given him.

The Oldest of Men put the comb gently in his lap. The Tracker turned it over in his hands in wonder. The Oldest of Men had had the smith line the grooves and outline each circle with red gold, and he himself had painted in green and red inside the gold. The bone was gleaming white where he had polished it and the bright metal and the new paint glowed and shone in the flicker from the flames and the weird, pale light off the snow. It was a thing of extreme delicacy and great beauty. The Tracker wrapped it gently in moss and put it inside his sheep-wool tunic in a little

213

leather bag. He knew that when the time came, he would find beside the black and white stone shaped like a badger's back a white horse as exquisite and pure as the ancestral Horse in the hills down by the Dyke; such a horse as that of which the king's poet had spoken.

Two nights later, in the bitterest hour before dawn, the aged cow dropped her bull calf, and their helpless lowing woke the Tracker, who was in time to touch them both before they died in the iron frost.

The lake lay on a slant across a line from sunrise to sunset, the great mountain a throne for giants on its northern side. It filled the valley so that there was no land except a dank crescent of shallow reeds and marsh at the head, where the river seeped in and a strip of phragmites and juncus, willow scrub and mire outlining the south shore where the sun was held back by the mountain for most of the daylight hours. At the end of the lake the river spilled angrily out, throwing débris and spray over dark rocks.

A king, a fighting-man and a wild man stood together on the narrow path that slipped through the willow roots and sedges on the south shore. The water of the lake was partially frozen, so that the surface was dusted with lying snow blown over ice, but further out it was dark as pitch, unreflecting, stirred by the rough draught of dawn.

The faces of the three men were white with cold, bloodless and stiff. There was ice around the king's mouth and in the beard of the Goth. Their leggings were clotted with snow and stained black from the mud of the lake's margin. Their long plaids flapped drearily in the chill air, bulky and unevenly wound around them without brooches to keep them in place. There was no metal of any sort worn or carried by any of them. The cold moaned in the reeds. A small group of black moorhens struggled with the ice to reach open water. The men stood at the very edge of the ice, where the snow hummocks of the reeds flattened out between the contorted roots of the willows into the strangely mottled surface of the lake. Here grey and white and dark grey met and merged where the lake had thawed and re-frozen so that the ice was of different thicknesses. The lake and the mountains were still; only the dismal half-whistle of the breeze cutting across frozen stalks encased in ice circled the silence. It was a terrible place and a terrible time.

The king of the dinas stood on one leg on the edge of the ice, his grey hair trailing across his face under the hood of his wrappings, his eyes heavy-lidded, half closed. At one with his mind, being his mind, he was fully awake in the world in a way he had not been since before Badon; but because the king had a way of moving from one world to another, it was not always obvious in which world, or when, he was awake. The Tracker had long been accus-tomed to seeing the king's mind stand on one leg in still water and he stood quietly near him.

The king's stillness was absolute. The Goth, hunched in a great wrap with a worn lion-skin inside it tied around his shoulders, leaned against the trunk of a naked crack-willow, biting his lower lip. From time to time he would glance at the king, waiting for the king to arrive at the temporal point when he would initate the action of which the Goth was so afraid. But the king was not waiting. He was being. When he had fully become, he would enter into the Goth's world. This the Tracker understood, in as much as he was able to understand anything — for as the king's state depended on knowledge, so the Tracker's resulted from the absence of it; and he stood near the king as one of the stunted willows and as the reeds in their sheaths of translucent ice.

Still the king stood on one leg at the edge of the black lake.

*   *   *

Then the king stirred. The movement was so slight that it might have been no more than a breath of snow on a bird's wing, but in the Tracker's stasis it ran as traumatic as a crevasse breaking open. The Goth flickered a look across the lake, to the king, at the Tracker. The moorhens had gone. The dark clouds which had been lying on the shoulders of the great mountain were stealing down its sides, swaying across the ridges and hollows of its structure, reaching into its clefts and swinging over its secret routes. The Tracker moved into the extremities of his perception, slowly, a hollowing out of his pelt. The spine of the salmon is as supple as flowing water — give its strength; the eyes of the tawny owl are as far-sighted as the full moon — give the light . . .

The king bent and unwrapped his leggings. His bare, old man's legs were blue and white, thin like a tall bird's. He moved slowly out on to the ice, stiffly, the long wand held tight against his breast. He had gone some distance before he came to a standstill. The first cruel little flakes of the next snowfall sidled across the ice behind him, the wind sighed in the reeds. Out on the ice the king turned slowly around, staring. He moved in one direction, stopped and turned. Then, further out, he stopped again to turn and stare — to wait for the flutter of snow to lift, a cloud to pass on; a peak, a notch in the horizon to show between the clouds and the fast little flakes. Briefly he stood still, and then his voice rang out like a thin horn call across the waste.

The Tracker went to him unclothed, moving wide of the king's own footmarks, circling around on untrodden ice. When he was quite near to him the king laid the wand on the ice and moved away. The king's mana lay alone on the smooth grey surface. The Tracker, no more now than a thin skin of acute sensation, drew himself towards the wand with his eyes so intensely that the wand moved, sinuous as a serpent, black on white. When he reached for it the serpent raised its head in love and the Tracker drew it to him, cradling it in his arms. Give the cold blood, the unblinking eye . . . He set the point of the wand against the ice by his feet, the ferrule against his breastbone, and leaned hard upon it. He walked with it that way in a ring, grinding it into the ice with his own heart and the king's mana. When the circle was joined he drove the wand deep into the groove he had made — here, there — until a plate of ice cracked out, tilted and creaked against its own rim. The cold blood, the sharp fin... He pushed the roundel of ice so that it sank briefly, and he thrust it aside under the surface. The black water was exposed at his feet. A few flakes of new snow settled on his hair, but on his body they dissolved instantly, for he was smeared all over with goose-fat. The lungs of the beaver, the speed of the otter, subtlety of the salmon . . . The black water lapped at the rim of the hole. Nearby the heron stood on one leg on the ice, his head buried against his chest. Lungs of the beaver, breathe — and breathe . . . And plunge.

The black water gripped him as if it would sheathe him in an unborn fish's scales, cold beyond life. The darkness wavered and glowed green and amber. He strove downwards, surge after surge of the supple spine. Weed and light meandering; slimy gravel, murky boulders across which something metal slid and drifted away; aqueous, filtered colours streaming over his shoulders and driving, urgent legs. Give — give . . . The light coming sidewise, membranous; miniscule detritus whirling and somersaulting; gigs of sand; fingernails of the drowned as opaque as shell at the tips of pale phalanges; and the fish darting to the right. Near the end, now — the heart bursting into flame, the breastbone crackling, the eyes gelling over as if freezing, the brain darkening, the water darkening. And here — in heaps, cluttered and piled on the stones . . . Mallets of Sucellos beating in the ear drums: *á death, á death* . . . Lungs of the beaver, eyes of the salmon —

There: unmistakable, in a bolt of light streaming like a
spear shaft through the freezing murk. Grab, wrench free of
the slime and ooze. A chain drifting downwards, a group of
terrets, a nave-hoop and a dagger falling open sidewise and
resettling, slow as a drowning feather. Eyes of the salmon,
see nothing — NOTHING — but the light shaft. Dragging
the weight, pushing it upwards, point first, at the bright
circle. Eyeballs mazed over now, ears smashed open. Give —

He broke through the round hole unevenly, the sharp ice
tearing a strip of flesh from his back, and the sword in front
of him landed clattering and spinning on the frozen surface,
colliding with the king's wand. They rang out — a high,
thin alarum that shivered in the flight feathers of the
mallard and sang in the claws of the kestrel, the thin blood
of the heron.

Beaver, salmon and otter returned to the dark and the
disturbed, spoiled hoard. The Tracker could not breathe,
could not hold on to the cracking edge of the ice hole. He
had no blood in his arms, no power to pull his weighty,
greased body from the water. Blood ran from his back,
seeping into the ice, melting the edge of the hole — a
scarlet, steaming orifice; and the Tracker struggled on its
brink, a speared salmon too heavy for the spear shaft. The
freezing water took his hips, his thighs, his calves, his feet
and dissolved them into itself. The ice cracked like a whip.

Because he was a fighting-man and a man of ships and
water, and because he was more afraid of what the Tracker
had done than of his own death by drowning, the Goth
reached him in time and dragged him on to the splitting ice,
pulling him like a corpse across the surface, trailing a hot,
red smear through the snow that was coming down now,
spiralling over the unequally frozen lake. The flakes thickened, were bigger. They blanked out the mountains, then
the northern shore, then the red marks on the ice. The Goth
breathed hard, warm, reeking mouth odours and stomach
odours — all flesh and living, and stinking, sweaty leather

— that wrapped around the naked Tracker and rubbed his pelt so that it returned gradually to him. The Goth knelt by him, binding his feet and legs into his leggings, rolling him in the great plaid, scrubbing his face, hair and neck with the cloth, hugging it around his head with rough, rapid movements as urgent as flight. He knelt among the sedge hummocks, his back to the lake, and over his shoulder the Tracker could see only the dizzy snow and the careering flakes racing out of the dim whiteness.

The pains came from nowhere known to him before. They racked him with molten iron in the muscles, burning oil in the veins, and hurled him about, writhing and screaming in the Goth's arms, threshing among the willow roots and the deadly ice-sheaths on the reeds. Coot and moorhen beat invisibly through the air at the raucous noise; frozen stalks and twigs snapped and cracked like a horseman's whip. The Goth shouted at him, at the Bear and the king and the snow and the enthroned giant and strange other beings with whom he was familiar and at enmity. When the agony drifted away, surging and retreating like waves on an ebb tide, the Tracker lay gasping, air in his lungs, his pelt whole, his rolling eyes steadied and fixed on the Goth.

There was only the Goth, there in the blizzard. The world had gone away. Otter, salmon, beaver, stickleback, all gone. Mountain and forest, gone. The darkness of the dense white was broken only by the great bulk of the Goth; his breathing the only sound in a silent cell — the isolation of guilt made manifest. The Tracker and the Goth looked deep into each other's eyes and each looked away.

Later, the Tracker said, 'The king?'

The Goth shrugged helplessly. His dark, bereaved face turned aside, his eyes staring blankly at the spinning wall of snow.

He said, 'The ice was too thin in places . . .' And then, 'He had the sword . . .'

He gave the Tracker some strong, Gaulish wine from a

leather bottle. It gave the Tracker the illusion of strength and made him weep. It was a terrible time and a terrible place.

The Goth urged the Tracker to his feet; and together, but never meeting each other's eyes, they began the long haul along the whispering lakeside and up into the pass at its head where they had left the slave, blindfold, with the horses. One behind the other they staggered and slipped and trudged up the road, wrapped secretively in winds of white, lonely beyond any means of contact.

The sound of the wind across the sharp edges of a recent fall of scree tightened on to a single, high note and held it. The scree was slightly ahead of them and to the left, just beyond a massive outcrop whose white outline reared up in the blowing dusk like a fortress wall. The wind sang on and then dropped its note into a keening like that of a lover for the dead — human or other or of some different time, it would be the same sound, the same note. The Goth and the Tracker accepted the music as they had accepted the guilt and the loss and the loneliness; and it was only when they were right under the fortress, which had not been there in the morning, that they saw that it was the king of the dinas who was singing, and that he held the sword to his breast with one hand and the wand in the other, and that his mana was about him.

He came down the rough shoulder behind the outcrop on his thin, bare legs, ice and snow frozen on to his features so that he seemed to be wearing a white mask through which his eyes burned green. He had the sword by the hilt as if he would use it against them, but turned it and held it point up as the Tracker had brought it through the ice. In his old, frozen hands it quivered like a live thing.

He said to the Goth, 'Take it. I want nothing of this.'

The despoiling of the lake hoard breached the flimsy

boundary which kept the worlds apart. It had never been strong, especially up here in the mountains, but now it lay broken open like a weak palisade after the rape of a fort. As long as the thing was in the king's hand, and the king had his mana upon him, the spoiling remained unconsummated. But at the moment when he held it out to the Goth, and the Goth took it in his secular hands, it passed from one state to another, and the definitive act was committed.

The snow whirled on the north wind as if it were pouring through the gap in the worlds' boundaries — pouring a whiteness, the colour of the other world; the symbol that heralded its advent and signified its presence. Silent itself, it streamed through with a dim roaring in the whitened rocks, a crying out and a multiplicity of notes as if horns were blowing for some unspeakable battle and keening for its outcome. The wind which flayed the Goth's naked hands and wrapped around the hilt of the god-sword was at the same time the wind which tore down from Eryri, and out of the breach in the walls of Caer Siddi. When he turned away from the king to carry the thing up the track to where the horses had been tethered, he staggered and reeled in the force of the winds at his back as one who was being driven out and for a few steps appeared almost to run from them.

It was the Goth who lashed the thing to the saddle of the pure white mare to which the Tracker had brought them. They had found her shivering by the great boulder with the badger-like quartz stripe, as he had known they would, ragged brown sheepskins tied over her flanks and withers to keep her warm. The Tracker had put his face into the skins and smelled the smell of the Winter Nightjar, and when he left the golden comb in the little bag on the great stone he had lifted it to his lips and kissed it, knowing that she was close by and would see him. Nonetheless, he had not looked back when he led the mare away.

It was the Goth who rode in front now, leading her through the drifts and the screaming and the onset of darkness. It was the Goth who brought all the horses into the high bawn on the far side of the pass where they spent that appalling night, and the Goth who slept with the thing clasped in his arms, his head on the hand-grip, while the king lay with his burning green eyes unclosed and his back turned, staring at the darkness. For the Tracker it was a night he could never afterwards remember; a night suspended in absences where all the conditions he inhabited were withdrawn from him, so that he would have said that that night had never been and been grateful.

It took them three days to reach the dinas. The king never spoke again. Only the Goth muttered an occasional order; now and again the slave asked for directions. It was apparent what had to be done, what dry fish eaten, what summer hut crawled into at night. In one of these the Tracker found a clump of nettles still partly alive, and the king's frostbitten feet were rubbed and bound in the blackish leaves. The white mare was given the warmest place each night, and snow was melted for her to drink. The Tracker found parts of the undersides of the reed thatch which were sprouting a pale, eerie green in a dark corner, and fed them to her. The other horses pawed snow from exposed areas where the snow had been blown thin, and the Tracker and the slave beat tangles of briar and bramble so that they could pick at the exposed dead leaves and the hanks of dark grasses beneath. There was no good in any of it. Their eyes grew lustreless and their flanks hollow. They shivered continuously. On the third night the slave suggested that he should lie against the white mare to press the warmth of his body into hers; but being only a man he had even less heat in him than she had, and the Tracker pulled him away. Still the king said nothing.

They reached the dinas in the evening of the third day. It lay in the snow across the summit of the hill, a drift among drifts. The ramparts were whitened out, the ditches blurred into curving hollows, and the great gate as stark and icebound as a rock crag on the mountain. There and not there. Visible only to certain men in certain states of mind. As the white mare, with the thing lashed to her gaunt and trembling side, began the long pull up from the street by the river, the dinas showed itself and obscured itself between the snow-laden branches of the forest edge; trees misshapen by the snow, grown strange and unfamiliar — as it were, different trees from another time. The Tracker had seen the dinas fade and waver on many occasions when he came in from the other conditions in which he existed in the forest, and always he had seen it as the spirit state of the dinas in a part of the dinas' pattern which had not yet been knotted. Now he came in behind the pure white mare and knew that in the coming of the thing which she carried, that knot was being made.

It had stopped snowing that morning, although the sky was still a grim, lightless grey. As they came out from the changed trees the dinas stood out above them, white beyond expression, as perfect as any unliving thing: Caer Siddi, translated upon the shape of the dinas.

They all saw it. And then they all saw it not to be so now that Carac is running out, and Echw and the fighting-men behind him. There are standards and battle-horns mounting the rampart walk, and smoke gusting balefully from an oven, a fire, a forge. The horses are calling to each other, and the cattle and fowl and hounds set up an outcry, a greeting and an ovation that the king is coming in.

But the king is not coming in yet. Exhausted, famished and sleep-starved, his breath rattling with phlegm in his chest, his hands blue on the reins, he rode his horse in front of the pure white mare and stopped her on the track. The Goth looked at him out of deep, brooding eyes, and they did not speak. Behind the king the fighting-men and young men and the king's grandchildren and the hierarchy slowed and stopped. The Goth slid off his horse and gave the reins to the slave. He stood in the centre of the track. The king's poet came out from among the hierarchy, his face white at the lips. He stared at the thing lashed to the pure white mare's side and at the Goth. Then he turned to the shovelled path around the outside of the dinas wall and led the mare into it as into a white tunnel out of the world. The Goth walked after him as if he had taken on the king's age.

The king wheeled his horse about, held the wand high like a spear before the battle, and rode into his dinas, green eyes steady, shocking with power and wisdom — *och, och, och*; Carac, favoured at last, running beside him with shield and sword.

15

The thing had been kept in the nemeton in the forest where the king had spent the night of learning with his poet. The shrine had been hastily purified to receive it and now was covered with snow and the purest white. Since the ground was hard frozen and the snow as deep as ever, a temporary enclosure had been made, digging out a narrow fosse through the drifts. It was not expected that the thing would be abroad for long; it was to be taken on the pure white mare south-east to the Bear as soon as the Goth had prepared it to go about.

The presence of the thing so close to the dinas was deeply troubling to the hierarchy, since the king of the dinas, to whom everyone looked for guidance, was still silent. He had not spoken since he handed the thing to the Goth, saying that he wanted nothing of it. The slave, who knew some of what had passed up there in the mountains, was given the best of the hierarchy's food, as custom suggested, and then strangled, his body taken and thrown in the river some way downstream where the current slowed and the water was deep and quiet. The idea seemed to have come from the king's poet, who let it be known that he had knowledge beyond what was expected of him. The dinas was very poor in slaves, and the unconvinced murmured about expensive gestures; but no one was prepared to take the risk of defiling it. So as many of the rituals were followed as could be put together from hearsay and faulty memories. The king remained aloof, fasting through the days when the slave was feasted, and he never thereafter recovered his appetite.

It seemed to the Tracker that the king's entrance into the dinas, when he had ridden tall and high like a victorious battle-lord, his mana strong and his green eyes bright in his ghastly face, was the last thing he was ever able to do; that the preventing of the thing from coming into the dinas was his final act for the dinas, and that he was doomed from the moment he completed it. He had consummated some act and was finished. The Tracker waited for him to die. Whatever the king had achieved during the long years when he had led the dinas had not been martial. He fought few battles and allowed the defences to decay; but he had re-established the meaning of the nemeton for the dinas, rebuilding the shrine, re-erecting the displaced images, clearing the undergrowth from the groves and the enclosure and being there himself more often than in the llys.

As long as the thing was in the nemeton, the king would not go there. The king's poet stayed with it much of the time, and the Goth never left it except for reasons of nature; then Carac would stand outside the shrine until he returned. The Goth's part in this was difficult for the Tracker to understand and he wondered whether the Bear had been unwilling to demand sacrilege of a man of his own race, to put him into such peril. Only a man who believed as the Bear did, and the king did, could be asked to commit it. The Goth, being of a different race but having similar beliefs — vaguely knowing, indeed, a few of the same stories — and being given in a

225

different way to different forms of the deities, was perhaps safer. That the Goth did feel safe with the thing was evident. It became his lover, the transubstantiation of his spirit. He slept with it, woke with it. He polished it and sharpened it; he picked the last of the mud and dry slime from the incised patterns on its hilt with a woman's needle, turning it over and over on his knee as if it were his favourite love-child. He transformed the shrine into a miniature workshop for the thing's restoration, his patient, sailor's hands moving over its surface with a precision and a gentleness that he never bestowed on a horse's rein. Carac stayed as near to him as he could, but never touched the thing, just watched the Goth's hands with burning, hollow eyes that had a red flicker in them. Beyond the enclosure, outside the nemeton, the Tracker prowled, day and night, until he would have said that every creature and every leaf shared in the presence of the thing in the forest.

On the eve of Imbolc, Fiác, who had grown as skinny as a barley stalk, coughed continuously and spat blood into the snow, found Carac in one of his happinesses in the hall, clutching his ritual shield and singing. Carac told him that he had been talking to a winged, white spirit, a sort of eagle of excellence who had swooped out of a cave and settled on a post beside him. Fiác, who had come to upbraid Carac, fell suddenly silent and began to quiver from head to foot. Carac went into a long description of the fierce beauty of the white eagle, the jewels and precious metals and mighty fortresses that the eagle possessed and the exquisite colours that shone and rang like music around him. At that Fiác had burst into screams of wild laughter, tearing at his breast with his long, dirty nails so that he bled openly on to the floor. He grabbed a handful of the slices of Carac's mushrooms, stuffed them into his mouth, and chewed like a hungry bull calf. Carac had then fallen asleep but Fiác had run mad, tearing off his clothes and rushing out into the murk of the dinas and the bitter north wind, his eyes radiant, crying, 'Christ-Saviour', 'John' and 'Allelujah', so that all the rooks in the forest went up in a panic of hoarse cawing, and the goats broke their tethers. The dinas was accustomed to Fiác's Allelujah spasms and did not at first react, but after a while it became obvious that this was no commonplace event, and everyone turned out to watch.

Fiác banged into doorposts and water-towers and the outside hearths, burning himself and cutting himself and bruising himself. After a while Echw sent some of the youths after him, finding the exhibition disgusting and fearing that Fiác would kill himself right at the beginning of Imbolc. The youths thought it wonderful sport, almost as good as a hunt, and pursued Fiác, baying and barking; and then one of them let the hounds loose.

It was the Goth's man who cut off what was left of Fiác's right arm, as he had done for other men after battle. The women of the dinas sewed up the calf of his leg, his buttock and the hole in his belly. They could do nothing about his tongue.

The Tracker, deep in the forest on the far side of the nemeton from the dinas, heard the sounds of his mother's death, felt something white split in his head and a rush of blood around his gums. He stopped, so still that even his heart paused. Then it started again with a sick thud — but within, it seemed, a different body. He put out a hand that both was and was not his hand and gripped the thin trunk of a young holly tree. His mother's fathers had been holly trees in the times of the trees; he was a holly tree; he was also, and not, the wolf under it, the bird in its boughs, the man gripping it and the leaden sky over it. This, the Tracker knew, was not shape-changing as he recognized it; this was the all-becoming; the all-consuming and all-consumed. He walked away from the tree towards the nemeton with a stride that he had never owned before.

227

Outside the shrine the Goth was rubbing the thing very gently with a hare's scut. When he saw the Tracker come through the trees to him he rose to his feet and put the little bunch of fur down on the bench. The Tracker walked towards the thing as if there were only he and it in all the worlds. The Goth held it out to him, and for a brief moment the Tracker put his hands on the god-hilt and took the whole weight of it in its entirety. Just for an instant, just for the single beat of his heart, the indrawing of this one breath, he held the heaviness of the whole world. It was enough. He looked into the eyes of the Goth and saw there how the weight had broken the man, how he would never dance again, nor leap on a horse, nor spring into a summer stream. He was now nothing more than a frame to support the thing when it went about.

The Tracker said, 'He will kill us all,' as the king had done — and the king was dying.

After a moment he said, 'What of Carac?'

The Goth: 'He will be a hero. He will come with me when I bring this thing to the Bear, and the Bear will have him in his own guard for the thing's sake. And Carac will go down with the Bear, as we all shall. Your feast is beginning. It is not my feast, and I will leave at dawn. I shall have only Carac and my own man with me — the dinas will not know. It is five days' hard ride, and we will do it in five. The wind will be behind me, and my god rides the wind.' He spoke in hard, practical terms, even of his god.

The hairs rose on the Tracker's back. The Goth's Lord would ride south to the Dyke during Imbolc.

The Goth placed the thing carefully in the shrine, and came out into the square enclosure amongst its heaped-up banks of snow.

He said, 'This is the beginning,' but he did not say what was beginning. He asked for Carac to stand in the enclosure, for he himself had things to do. With his weapons, he added.

The Tracker ran towards the llys. He saw the hounds, coupled and leashed, and how some of them had dried blood on their breasts and forelegs. And he saw the future in the storm clouds to the north, building up hugely in iron grey fortifications, banks of time heaped upon each other before a gathering wind, sweeping up the day and hurtling it closer to the dinas and to what must come to the dinas. The next year was hurrying towards the dinas as if the pace of the moon in the night skies had quickened, and the future had foreshortened, bunched itself up like a great bird of prey stooping to the strike. He saw that the day, and the clouds that were rearing up to strike the day down and devour it, were carrying the Leinster oared boats on their shoulders and that, massing in their barrows and tumuli, the painted Picts, rank upon rank, swept together, charged, re-formed and ran towards the dinas in swirling columns that sounded in the leafless branches of the forest like a great sea breaking against the foot of the rampart.

All over the open ground of the dinas and in all its dwellings, the Kind were now jostling and moving and preparing. Nothing was yet finished, everything was to be. A pregnant woman had not yet given birth — the nine days' pangs were crushed in her, and she cried out; but it was not quite time for the next generation. There were things which had to have happened, and they had not happened yet: water which was just coming to the boil in a cooking pot as the Tracker swerved past the fire; a yellow-dun horse raising its head to neigh, the sound not yet made; a half formed spear ferrule in the smith's tongs, hammer raised to beat out the metal; the king still alive; the sun still out.

Across the mountains the Winter Nightjar raised a golden comb to her tangled hair, and the storm clouds darkened.

The Tracker came into the hall with a bound. Carac lay sprawled on the floor, his painted shield magnificent across his body. A dead warrior as yet undead, who must be woken in order to die.

'Wake yourself, Carac, it is time . . .' But he did not know for what it was time. 'It is time,' he shouted. 'It is beginning.' His mouth was filled with bitter spew and unable to make words, whether curses or love-songs or lies, that would save Carac. The Bear would carry Carac on his shoulders in the battle, as he would carry all the sins since Badon; and the weight would bring all of them down.

He cried out, — 'He was wrong' — seeing, as the king had always seen, how the charge down that hill had swept the Bear and all his works to the foot of the dinas; and how the noise of it was howling even now among the dwellings of his lovers.

He had already lost Carac . . . The Tracker said again, 'It is beginning.' And Carac turned to him and smiled with the sweet gladness he had had as a child.

The Tracker said, 'The Bear will have you,' remembering Carac's agony in the fire-pit by the river; and Carac nodded, pushing out a hand warm with sleep from under his cloak. He put it against the Tracker's, palm to palm, fingers to fingers, and for a light moment the hands stood together. Outside, the wind tore down from Eryri, thudded and moaned against the walls of the llys, seethed among the high stack-gables of the thatch, reached in along the floor of the hall, searching, seeking, finding. The hands drew slowly apart, and the Tracker stood aside while Carac rose, shook himself down and began to gather his weapons from their places on the wall. With them he took the spear that he had cast across the river. He held it out to the Tracker, who touched its point with delicate courtesy.

He said, because it was all there was to say, 'It is time to go.'

Carac said, 'Bury my grandfather. Love my sons,' and was gone out into the north wind that swept so coldly between the dwellings of the Kind.

For a while the Tracker stood alone in the hall, staring at the doorway, which was empty. It hurt him in his heart that it was empty. Then it began to hurt him very deep in his body, in the parts of him that he drew away from when he went out into the forest. It was so long since he had felt hurt in those parts of him that it brought tears to his eyes; and through the tears he saw Carac again in the doorway in a wavering, rainbowed double-image, so that Carac was all painted in the colours of the ritual shield and in red, and his double was red. Then the tears washed the images away, and there was nothing left.

In the inner chamber the king of the dinas was dying. The Tracker went in to him and put his head on the old man's knee and let the pain rest on the king, along with the sins and the time and the time which would come after; which is the wage due to kings.

Cathal had found two old oilcans in the dump behind Castlegate, and these he had brought to the front of the cottage. He put an old plank from a broken cupboard across them and made a bench in the sun. On this he was sitting, staring into the valley at the rough line of willow scrub and reeds that marked the line of the river and listening to the full music of its spate. The snow had all vanished, even from north facing corners of the fields, shadowed deeply where the stone walls met; and pale, aqueous sunshine washed the hillside with a warm light. To Cathal it was spring. In the ragged disorder of the dump he had come across innumerable tips of strong, dark little spears which he took to be snowdrops wakening, and for a moment he had looked forward with delight to the morning when he would open the back door to take the milk from the bucket of cold water and find them all in flower. He found it strange in himself that he should think so fondly of such a delicate season and longed for the primrose sunlight to last so that he could continue to feel this way — or at least for the assurance that it would return. In the wood behind the cottage a pigeon was cooing, the murmurous sound nostalgic of content and idleness; and he wondered if such a season would ever come to him again.

The long months since he had come to Castlegate had changed him greatly. He knew that by looking into the bathroom mirror when he shaved. There was grey in his hair, and his face had become much older and much thinner. For so long now he had taken it for granted that each movement in the annual cycle was, for him, its last, that now he was made uneasy by the concept of another autumn, another winter . . . The perpetual cold, the perpetual dark, the pain of stiff wounds, the continual fear of the dark, of the almost things and the things of the dark? Could this dread that presented winter to his mind as an impossibility mean that he was ready, now, for the end of the cycle? That he did not have it in him to live?

He looked at a long, pastel-painted room filled with spring sunshine and maybe vases of narcissi and thought that it was in such surroundings that his mind would probably have to spend the rest of his life: carefully bland and mildly analgesic. Perhaps there would be great picture windows; but there would be dove-coloured venetian blinds closed over them, behind which tinted glass would soften all harsh, natural colours — sky-blue, sunset-gold, grass-green. All sounds of baying, croaking, cawing or wind in bare branches would be muted, and quiet carpets and soft upholstery would shield the body from sensation. In such a prison, he thought, his tears would be warm and never sting his bitten lips.

A forever of gentle weeping in that calm? Instead of this he was going to stay here, hidden in the valley, and ride the raven, penetrate the Central Tree until the event was over — for him. And it was that image of himself dragged out from Castlegate before the experience was consummated that made him shave and comb his hair before he went to do his shopping from Mrs. Bowen at the post office; swear casually with the Second Farmer; wave at the post-van . . .

He was not mad. Far from it — he was on the edge of wisdom. He was among the outliers of his own metaphysic. Cathal and Cathal Kerr had reached the point of separation, and Cathal, as he alone knew him, was committed to the journey into the forest, or whatever the forest stood for. Cathal Kerr would have to deal with the other matters on his own. So uncover the cist among the slates of the floor and get in there with the spirit; take it home, take it to its kind. Not lonely now — all of us together — the Kind . . .

He saw this now as unremarkably obvious, but not something which he ought to write on the back of an envelope, lest the coroner added 'schizophrenia' to the list of things that Cathal had died of. He still had an urge to die accurately.

When he stood up from his makeshift bench he had the usual moment's giddiness in which a sudden darkness, cold and disorientation made him afraid that he was falling. He never had fallen, so his mind was not afraid of it; but his physicality was, and he thought that his physicality was also probably very afraid of dying — that at the last moment it would probably let him down and exhibit a terror which was not his. In that event also he would die inaccurately. Unguardedly, he put his hand on the door — an unconscious, physical action to reassure the physicality; but the wood of the door refused this interpretation of the event and screamed at him,

'You have axed me, flayed me, nailed my parts to a frame — have you not done enough without ignoring me?' and 'Murderer, murderer, lift your leg and piss on me — it's better than forgetting my crucifixion.'

'It's all right,' he said soothingly, 'it's all right, I know,' as he would have done to a distressed child; and the door grew quiet under his hand as if he had a special way with it. All that was wrong with the door was lack of acknowledgement — not unlike dying inaccurately, he thought. He wondered briefly if the whole of Britannia Prima was crowded with howling, jostling wood daemons, screaming silently into silence of the manner of their interment — internment — both. If he alone heard them, then the anguish and the noise would break his head open. If he did open his ears to all the wood killed in Britannia Prima, and it did break his head open, then the wood would have its revenge.

He knew that his lips were giving the door planks a little smile of encouragement as he passed through into the dim room of the cottage.

He made his passage through the first stages of his practice without undue difficulty or trauma.

'Alle-*lu*-jah, Alle-*lu*-jah' sang the corpses in the tunnel as he reached them, this time hurrying past — but not skilfully, for the uneven paving stones under the black pools were heaved and tilted by the activities of generations of past badgers and the collapse of a Flavian mine gallery over which the tunnel ran. So Cathal lurched from side to side against hidden lintels and crumbling brick-courses, putting out a hand to steady himself against the dripping origin of slime and disturbing the leg bones of the skeleton-bundles. There were so many of them down here, packed in tight against each other, skull to skull — *ocha* — clavicle to clavicle, femur to femur, tilting and leaning and no longer distinct. Vortigern, supremo, with black worms crawling from the fissures in his skull like tongues, each one piping, '*Eu, nimet saxas!*' like a hundred little winds in split wood. Patrick, St., tipped sideways by the penetrating tap root of some great tree, now lay twisted so that Cathal saw that it

234

had been an elemental staff that had propped him up, and that it now lay among his vertebrae, the crooked end fallen out into the tunnel and the sacerdotus' skull twisted sideways so that the eye sockets were staring upwards into a dark humming with a deep groaning and powerful words of prayer in an unknown language. *Ocha* . . . Never before had Cathal heard the bones speak or the water drip or Ambrosius calling, 'What is in the foundations of this place?' over and over again while the last stains of the purple dye seeped out from his winding sheet and dissolved in the chill, black puddles around his ankle bones and were washed out, gone . . . Allelujah.

Wading into a pool of crimson: blood, undried. Gildas will deal with it, when the time comes. But it is not blood, it is Imperial dye — it is the end of Ambrosius, who could not see far enough because he has no eyes, now that the time has come when he is needed for his Sight. Visionless Emrys, who let the worms vanish away into the lake before the shewing was over, or perhaps was afraid to let all be revealed.

'Is that what you did, Emrys?' he shouted at the blind man, 'Fucked off and let them believe you'd told the whole truth?'

'What is in the foundations of this place?'

'I know!' he cried out, 'I know what is in the foundations, O Latter Day Caesar, .IMP.CAES.'s *knee* bones fastened to the *thigh* bones/And the *thigh* bone is fastened to the *hip* bones — of who, Bundle? All jumbled up together, is it, your ear bits and Aelle's ulna and my sacrum in a little leather bag?'

The violence of his shouting brought a trickle of small stones and periglacial gravel through the natural cleavage in the slate which rattled on to Patrick, St.'s pate, disturbing it so that it turned to Cathal and whispered, 'You have departed from this world to go to Paradise. *Deo gratias.*'

'No,' he shouted. Prop up the falling roof with Hengist's

spear shaft, Germanus' crozier, timber frames from Wroxeter and Cadbury . . . Patrick, St. was not having him yet. He was not ready, he was unready. It was not his time. So run, run —

'Alle-*lu*-jah!' sang the darkness behind him, glossy with black lines which whirled in a great funnel, catching up with Cathal and taking him sweeping, upside down, flying and banking; roared with him to the lip of the great shaft; screamed in its confines and left him there in the bright silence which flowed up from it, sweet as thyme-honey, gentle as ewe's milk.

Cathal stood at the edge of the pit-shaft, shaking with exhaustion, sweat pouring all over him and dripping with minute raps on to the stone ledge where he clung. All around him the dulcet air hummed as if with bees dancing, and perhaps at the bottom of the shaft there was not the sky, with his miserable planet drifting away into extinction, but a bed of peonies and gillyflowers? The sound of the bees was in his ears and then inside his skull, and the drilling pain of their foraging antennae thrilled among the squamous coils of his brain. As they flew round his head before crawling in through his nose and lips he could see that they were not bees but locusts, big and little locusts and gemmas; and his mouth was full of them, so that he could not scream out his horror or his agony. He cast himself, head rolling and jerking, from side to side of the shelf at the verge of the tunnel until his hand slipped and he was again in space, riding on the pain through waves of sweat and urine and saliva which poured from the holes the locusts and gemmas had made in him. The pit-shaft stretched up out of sight above him and down out of sight below him, filled with gold and scarlet liquid pounding in the tunnel which was a blow-hole in the world; and its green-rotten stench made him retch and gag. Locusts, bees and gemmas gushed from his throat in a harsh, scaly crowd that cut into the sides of his tongue. Peering down over his cheekbones he could see them rush out in dense swarms and enmesh themselves, drowning in him as he suffocated in them with every spasm of vomit and thrust of the tunnel's peristalsis. Clenched in the rhythmic squeeze and surge of the blow-hole, his arms were pinioned and his legs caught; blood was rushing up his neck, pounding into his head, blacking out his eyes and his ears; and still he could not scream.

The beating changed subtly, became dryer and crackly and brought a hot wind that surged past him. The bees, gemmas and locusts had gone, but he could still see them, scrabbling away, rattling on dry, yellowed stalks, broken-winged or upside down, spinning and buzzing and being drawn away as the flood dried, and the storm wind pumped closer and fiercer. Now he could scream — now he was free, kicking and flying again. And the glinting, topaz eye of the raven was coming up from underneath . . .

'When the raven comes up underneath you, ride her,' McKier had said. Cathal could feel her coming up, feel her wings crash and flail as she came up, up the red and green and yellow tunnel, twisting it into a violent, intricate route with her wings. He felt the green strand thrown across the red and watched, straining to see because of the danger to him if she should disrupt the sequence and make a hole in the interlace; but he was only half able to follow because of the tossing and the rhythm. Sometimes he was looking up into the dark, and lost sight of the moment when the green was flung under the yellow, and the red fell straight down between them to buck to the left and cross on the outside. The beak of the raven was up under him now, closing on him, the strands dragging in her feathers. As she flapped and rose, the point of the beak within strike of his crotch, he screamed with such violence and terror that his legs spasmed close and backwards, and he saw that he had struck her on the side of the head.

'Och! Och!' she screeched — a coarse, grating cry that

croaked up the cleft of his buttocks and up his back and shoulder; sharp as iron, curved like a gaff. As she passed, the red strand was dragged across his right arm; and he grabbed it, clung to it, knuckles cracking bone from socket, wrists tearing — but he had a hold of his colour.

Every barbicel on her black vanes was a lurching foothold or handhold for him. Harnessed into the red strand, he stretched for the barbule above, hauled his vast, cold weight up behind him and scrabbled with his left foot for the next foothold. The green smashed him in the face and nearly dragged him out of the great feather back into the blow-hole, where desolate hootings and hornings swept up and down and around the raven's wings as she beat upwards through them. But she wheeled over in her flight, tilting her back so that the green was whipped out from under him and streamed away to the right. He heaved himself one more barb higher and closer to the strong, blood-filled rachis where he could rest for a moment. Fraction by fraction he climbed up — barbicels and barbules to lock the slipping feet in; barb after barb to knot the fingers in; rachis after vane after rachis, feather after feather. Light (which must have been day) came and then set, and in the dark of the night it was harder to climb, and colder; but dawn came when he was close to her back, and by afternoon, when the sun came out, he was riding on her, the red like reins in his hands, and wind of her flight tossing in his hair.

The wind was from the north-west, and she was flying straight into it. He shouted at her to turn, and pulled on the scarlet rein, twisting it round his wrist and yanking at it with all the strength left to him; but he was weak and she took no notice but flapped dismally on so that the sun would set over his left shoulder. This was so terrible to him that he began to cry like a child, tugging and choking and pulling. She flew slowly on as if he were not there. Far below, the fields were overgrown and gross with thorn and bracken, the walls broken down. Wild animals scattered from carcasses as the raven's shadow passed over them. The air was so cold that his hands turned blue; the nails were lapis lazuli and verdigris and had no feeling, and his feet were stiff as icicles and slippery in her black feathers. He would fall, screaming — but she flew on towards the cleft in the mountains where the snow streamed from the peak like a veil, and the pines tossed black and violent on the lower slopes.

She was diving towards them. Cathal's knees dug into her sinewy neck as he slithered along her, tilting down, about to cascade forwards into the crooked glen, crying and clutching at the patterned cloth in which she was harnessed. She thrust her feet forwards and bunched for the strike.

His illness was terrible. It was death coming. He lay on the floor, his throat raw and swollen with thirst, his eyes closing, the lids huge and resinous, glueing the lashes to each other. Heat burned and swept up and down his trunk, bitter cold gripped his extremities. His gut was void and hollow, and his torn muscles empurpled with sprains. The ceiling and the corner of the table swayed to and fro and up and down, and the floor lifted and surged so that he might have been in a ship. He prayed to them to keep still and let him rest, but his joints were on fire, and his left hand was rapping on the polished slate; so he prayed to the table to fall on it and pin it down so that he could rest. He had been good to Wood, so good to Wood. Understood Wood's anguish, stroked it, soothed it, developed a special way with it. It had stood by him before — the Door standing at his back when he had gone for the Locust Queen. It had been there when he had killed her, as he now knew he had, for in the pit-shaft they had not taken capital letters, the locusts and gemmas.

Please come and fall on my arm and stop it — rap rap rap on the floor, rappity rrr . . . This was dying.

It would be dark out there. It was nearly dark in here, bits of amber light clipping through the gum over his eyelids. A dead fly could be caught in amber and live for ever, mummified in the warm gold. Perhaps hung between a woman's breasts, and warmed by her, softly, an afternoon sun fallen asleep in her bosom.

It was in fact the door which saved Cathal's life that day. It had swung open, and the sun had been able to shine straight in through it. For an hour and a half it had shone steadily over all his body, and there had been just enough heat in it, there where he lay out of the draught against the table, to warm him and relax him enough to sleep for a few minutes at a time. When he finally woke the sun had moved on, but he had enough strength to roll over and begin to form a little plan about reaching some water.

16

The first horn of Imbolc called. Horses shivered, stamped, bridle-pieces clinking. The second horn joined the first; a deeper, harsher sound, vibrating in the soil under the snow. They called, boomed, fell silent. Bronze strap-ends clattered against leather; hide creaked; hooves shuffled and skithered. The sound grew and multiplied into a hundred notes as every mineral plane in its reach threw it back in echo: a hundred horns across the land, dimming and blowing and sounding and resounding from the stone face of the ramparts to the rocks beyond the snowfields; from the shield bosses of the hosts to the overhanging cliffs above the cataract. It flung the birds of the forest and the birds of the high wilderness into the sky as if by force. It passed into the men and the horses gathered on the exercise field below the dinas and it made the same sound in all of them, man or slave or horse or hollow in metal. It set up the same vibration in them as it set up in the ground under their feet. It filled their sinuses and fossae and rippled in the liquids of their tooth sockets and in their spinal cords, running from one to another, from man to horse to bronze to iron to man.

One after another the front rank of each host began to beat their shields with the shafts of their spears. At first they made a hard clattering, rapping like a myriad anvils, and then steadied into a beat. The horses flung their heads up, sidled, and one or two of them backed away, kicking nervously. Old horses left in the corrals neighed and galloped restlessly up and down the fencing, remembering. The leashed and coupled hounds barked and then bayed, singing and howling above the pitch of the war-horns and the thunder of the shield-beating; frenzied and nerve-ridden, slavering. Echw let it go on and on to the limit of control. Give the hot blood — give . . .

At the moment when the lowering sun touched the pine trees on the west flank of the far hill, the king's cart came out of the gate of the dinas and slowly down the trampled snow track to the exercise field. It was drawn by the two golden horses that the king loved, yoked side by side in the Irish fashion, the long pole between them tipped with bronze and their bit-rings and the terrets on the shaft pricked out with red enamel, shining and gleaming in the coloured rays of the sun going down through the tumultuous clouds. The cart was painted blue, black and green in the patterns of the king's kin, the wheeling triskele with boar's head terminals in triple roundels. Against the snow it was brilliant: a magpie's back, a dragonfly vehicle; and out behind it the long train of the king's cloak floated between the rear shafts and whispered on the white ground the length of a horse's stride.

The cart had been arranged so that the king was supported against a heap of black and white badger skins, but seemed upright, the staff in his hand, silver ceremonial plaques tinkling and clinking from the shaft. As he came on to the field the fighting-men shouted, and the horns blared, and the beat of the shields broke rhythm and drummed like thunder in the mountains. His gaunt face was concealed behind the gilded eye-ridges and rich nose-piece of his helmet; the incised decoration on the cheek-protectors caught the light so that his emaciation was disguised, and only the green eyes, smouldering behind the metal mask, were the eyes of the king, their father, in the form of the king, their song. His charioteer, on foot beside the horses, kept his hand on the leading reins quivering and mobile so that the golden horses fussed at the bits, arched their crests and agitated slightly — not enough to shake the king, but enough to display their spirit. The gorgeous cart wheeled at the end of the field and strutted past the front lines, the king's right shoulder to the hosts, the heavy torc around his neck thudding against his thin collar-bones. Behind him, strapped to the wicker body of the cart, two wooden images rode at his back.

Group by group, family by family by family, they keened for him, for themselves and for the dinas in its evening light.

Behind the king — at a distance, to emphasize the king's separation from mortality — Carac, in full display, rode upon his iron grey horse: the king's favoured grandson, the king's body-man, the king's arm. His long blue cloak with its richly embroidered border was fastened at the shoulder with a great, white-metal brooch, the heavy terminals bulky with ringed necks and punched, offset squares that caught the light, the hinge-grip rounded like pale, powerful knuckles. His head was bare, his reddish hair combed back in fine strands and tied into a long horsetail, the darker brows and moustache staining his brightness. He held the reins in one hand, in the other the long throwing spear with its wicked iron head. Seeing it, the Tracker hissed through his teeth, knowing it from the worn and blunted ferrule to be the spear that Carac had thrown across the river on the day of his frenzy.

The king's driver brought the painted cart to a halt, facing the hosts, and Carac drew up beside him to his right hand. This was the dinas' affair, as the fertility of the dinas rested on the festival that would begin the next night. This was an inturned, enclosed event, to do only with the king of the dinas and his pattern, and made up only of the strands which were a part of that pattern. The deep eyes of the images stared at the hosts, and the hosts stared at the king and fell silent.

Into the silence the Goth came quietly, cradling in his arms, as if it were a beloved child, the thing from the lake hoard. He was mounted on the pure white mare, his red, Romish cloak spread out across her back. Her mane was combed until it shone like silver waves of the sea; her hooves were gleaming with lustrous oil, her forelock twisted into a sparkling curl, and her shoulders and haunches as smooth and shining as virgin ice. He was dressed in all his wealth and all his pride to do the thing honour, but he wore it gently like a lover; as he passed near Carac the younger man flared like a hero, and the Goth, for all his magnificence, seemed merely a servant to the idea of the thing he carried. He wove his way deliberately between Carac and the hosts, and from all the throats breathing out there on the snow-bound field there came a deep, yearning sigh.

Moving sunwise, and very slowly, the Goth carried the thing in a great, sweeping circle around the hosts. Behind the face-mask of his iron and gilded helmet, his dark eyes glittered as if through the purest water. Under the red cloak he wore a full cuirass of chain-mail, the links stained and bent about the waist and over the right breast — mail that had seen battle, that had stopped spears. His tunic was scarlet with a gold border, his boots of black pig-leather, his belt and harness fastened with heavy silver buckles, the strap-ends finished with silver trellis work. High on his shoulder a great gold and glass brooch shaped like a soaring eagle, beak upturned and wings hunched — a power sign, a blood sign — glowed like deep wine or internal blood. His sword swung sheathed behind his right leg, the hilt of wrapped silver plates, the multiple grooves spun as fine as linen round the grip, worn nearly smooth with use, the top and the guard simple, thick discs of rilled silver. The scabbard was heavy and elaborate, chape and mouth mounted with ropes of beaten gold. Behind him his man jogged on foot, carrying the great round shield with its high, protruberant boss and iron rim, and a clutch of spears. The alien, Frankish throwing axe, looted long ago, glistened with fresh oil in his belt, and his cloak was fastened with round gold chip-carved brooches taken from the dead below Badon.

The thing the Goth carried was wrapped in white silk, wound round and around and secured with a bronze cloak-pin the length of a girl's forearm. Only its shape indicated what it was, its length from whence it had once come. He carried it with his right hand around the hidden hilt, the blade resting across his body and on his left arm. So, slowly, he moved around the hosts, and the fighting-men turned where they stood, their eyes fixed on the thing he carried. He passed the sons of Holly, with their green cloaks crossed with dark lines; the sons of Oak in brown and red, and the yellow, zigzagged stripes of the sons of the Hazel. Around the outside of the field, in thick, silent groups, the women and children and the old men of the families watched from around the wild fires, roaring and sparking in the wind, long plaids wrapped close about them.

Carac was the first to bound out into the space between the fighting-men and the watching crowd. At the movement a roar went up from the host. Carac's blue eyes glittered as if lightning struck behind them; great globes of shining sweat gleamed on his forehead and throat; the silver brooch flared on his shoulder, and the blue cloak swirled in an arc of colour, vivid as a kingfisher and a craftsman's dream. Holding the spear high over his head, Carac wheeled the grey horse round, parading him, agitating and distressing him so that a thick creamy lather sprang out under the reins and Carac's boots, and white circles ringed his eyes.

With a clatter and a thudding of hooves the groupings of the host broke up, and there was a rush of fighting-men, nervous horses, men running and shouting, spears held high and shields banging. They closed up behind Carac, and Echw rode between the crowd of them and the quiet Goth with the thing cradled across his breast. Echw shouted, facing the noise and the surge of the host, angry and proud at their violent emotion and the stink of their hard-trained bodies. He watched them as a craftsman might stare at a masterpiece — Is it finished? Is it perfect? Is it ready? He watched them jostling and shoving, straining to come closer to the wonderful thing, to give to it, to give for it; to give everything. Their women called out and sang and shouted names and love-words and charms. The children screamed, some cried in fright; the king's poet broke into a high song, and the war-horns and the tall carnyx blared the harsh, maddening note that brought the red gleam into the hosts' eyes. The king's fighting-men, Echw's army. He pushed against them, even against Carac, shoving the dun horse's hindquarters into them, letting him squeal and kick; leaning out with his spear shaft and jabbing at the foremost, muttering curses which were his sort of praise; holding a space for the Goth.

The Goth, his work done, rode the pure white mare slowly from the field and back into the snow-banked track that ran round the foot of the dinas. For a moment the hosts tried to follow him, but Echw and Carac blocked their way, and Echw urged them back on to the field, riding against their passion, hard and unforgiving. The Smith rode up and joined in beside Carac. When they had finally turned the hosts, and Echw and the Smith were riding behind them, goading them, driving them back, Carac spun the grey horse away from them and galloped up the narrow white passage after the Goth.

'Bury my grandfather. Love my sons,' he had said. The Tracker, bumped and jostled by the fighting-men around him, watched the blue cloak disappear round the curve of the dinas.

It was evening now. The king of the dinas left the field in his cart, his face hidden, his eyes as dull as moss faded by frost. The clouds had turned black and covered the sky. The wind howled across the dead, winter fields between the naked trees, night in its claws. It was dark now all along the Bright Road from Annwn to Camlann.

It was late in February, a high, blue day with the rooks noisy up on the wind currents and the snowdrops fluttering under the walls and trees. A conventional spring day. In sheltered spots the willows were fattening, the skins of the white, silky buds to come reddening and beginning to split. There was a dearth of eggs in the post office, and the parsnips were woody and wrinkled. In the kitchen at Castlegate three potatoes on the bottom shelf had sprouted pink and green shoots which had writhed between the shoe-polish and the ant-powder towards the light from the window, which was bright and dusty in the sunshine.

Cathal Kerr, weak and still bruised from his experience with the raven, was sitting at the kitchen table to take advantage of the sunshine. Through the window behind the sink he could see the last of the snowdrops in the old rubbish dump, and the wood beyond stretching steeply up to the hill-fort. He had a pad of lined paper in front of him and a pen in his hand, but he had written nothing. He was staring out of the window, his sleeves pushed up to the elbows so that the sun could warm his skin. He had been surprised and rather angry to see how thin his arms had become — that there were definite hollows between the two bones and the lines of muscle.

He felt very tired, and had spent the slow days of his recovery deciding to go no further with his journey. This morning he had scraped the black circle off the ceiling. The paint underneath had shown itself up cleaner than the surrounding area, so he had rubbed it with his fingers until it had become grubby and merged with the smoke-staining around it. He had stood for a long time with the paper circle in his hand, not knowing what to do with it. It was only a piece of paper cut off a grocery wrapper, but at the same time it had a sanctity, or a power — a mana — which made it feel like a form of blasphemy or sacrilege to crumple it up and let refuse reduce it to nothing. The idea frightened him, and he resisted the impulse to see it malevolent at the bottom of a plastic bin. He thought he might burn it when he lit the fire, on the principle that one burned unwanted Bibles rather than expose them to mis-use, and that flame was purifying. In the meantime he had left it on the mantelpiece in the sitting room out of the sun, so that it would not fade or wrinkle.

Never look out through a door and peer at the rage outside? Never look up at a window and see the eye of the raven or the eye of McKier or the eye of the Tracker peering in?

How lonely would he be?

He rose suddenly to his feet and tottered unsteadily around the room, previewing his suffering with rising panic. He would never ride the raven again — not now that she was stooping for the kill: only find a way to be there for her when she came down out of the sky for him. Would that be more terrible than dying of the palsy?

He tried to imagine death by palsy, accurately, as he had never done before. Realistically: the speechlessness as in nightmare where the voice-box is clogged with terror; the watching faces coming closer, distorted as in a fish-eye lens; the jerking, uncontrollable limbs (and orifices); the conscious mind and the ear hearing the commentary on his dying — right into the silence . . .

He was still on his feet and had reached the wall. He spun round, found it hard to balance, and put a contused hand out to the back of the chair. He had not, would not, fall. He could not, would not, die of the palsy. It was obscene to think that he would let himself die of the palsy — that he would hide himself away here all this time, kill the gemma and then go crawling for the very death that he had fled from. Horrible to think of his body in others' hands, and he alive to witness it. No vocabulary for this, only dreadful sounds like a dog retching . . .

He would not die of the palsy. He had not in any way resolved the question: '*Who is the Tracker?*' but had now finished with asking it. It made no difference who the Tracker was, in what condition he lived, in what aspect. It was enough that there was a strand in his pattern which interweaved with his own; that they had wrestled together, shoulder-pommel to shoulder-pommel, up on the ramparts. It was the Tracker for whom Cathal would be so lonely. It was the Tracker he had come to Castlegate for, or who had come there for him. Because of the Tracker he would not die here in the sunlit kitchen of the cottage, or behind the tinted glass of a pastel-painted room. He had heard the sound of horns blowing in the forest. He would die on the downhill in the crooked glen.

He was in love.

He had never been in love before, and had not recognized love when it had come to him.

He sat in the sun at the kitchen table, smiling gently. 'Death by Love' would do very nicely on the label tied to his toe.

It was two more weeks before Cathal had the strength to walk along the valley to Hengardd. He had been relieved that McKier had not visited him, and at the same time unsettled, for he had at times been certain that there were aspects of McKier which existed in the same way as Mrs Post Office existed, or the postman, or the farmers. Today there was no one on the road, and the road was in every visible way that which the Council maintained and had little to do with the First Cohort Sunici. The gay, windy weather had continued, the wind cold but the sunlight bright enough on the south slopes to bring a vernal silver fuzz to the willows, which he fancied must feel soft like his own maturing beard. It had set the thrushes singing. He walked slowly, holding the sleeves of his jersey down over his cold hands. His hands had been cold ever since he had twisted them in the red skein about the raven's neck in that bitter sky, so he had made holes for his thumbs in his jersey seams to hold the sleeves down like mittens. He stopped every quarter of a mile or so to rest, sitting on a flat piece of wall or a blank slab of stone in the bank, always in the beneficent sun. He smiled at the warmth of its touch on his scalp, exposed now that he had lost so much hair. Here there would be primroses; here small, wild daffodils and scented thorn blossom and scurrying, coloured finches dropping nest material. He felt tired and oddly paternal, imagining the spring flowers, the lambs, chickens in the farmyards and the long cool evenings. Relieved, though, that he would not have to take part in it himself. He no longer had the energy for expectation — it had been necessary to take a length of dirty orange bailer string from a gateway to hold his trousers up.

He thought of his search for the flowering blackthorn at mid-winter. There were buds now on these twisted black trees, so gnarled and weather-struck and cruel. *That the thorn flower, And that the world pass away* . . . So many worlds — a world for every life, perhaps, animal and vegetative, blossoms and thorns; and the indestructible patterns of molecules which could not ever pass away.

'DEATH IS NOT FOR ALL OF US,' McKier had said . . .

The sky turned white. Around every stone in the wall a mandorla of blue and violet light shimmered like water; every thorn branch was outlined with green and gold, and the roadside ditches wavered like a brass riband in the breeze. His hand, his left hand, when he held it out, was beautiful. The nails were delicate as cowrie shells in sea water, the skin like peach and silk with misty, translucent edges through which the bright road glittered with mica and pyrites, and showers of bridal diamonds drifted as slowly as snow from the tips of fiery buds.

'*Ocha*,' he said aloud, and drew his exquisite hand across his face, wiping it all out. '*Ocha, ocha* . . .' The grief-word. 'Time to move on.'

He found McKier sitting on a canvas camp-stool on the border of a mosaic floor in the middle of the yard at Hengardd, which was cordoned off from the road by an orange and white plastic police tape. Heaps of stone and jagged plaster, piles of brick and boarding and broken funiture, fragments of glass and splintered frames surrounded him. The yard stank of limewash and soot and rotten wood, and the college scarf was white with dust. High above him the vacant gable of the roof gaped like a black and broken jaw. Where the end wall of the house had collapsed out into the yard, the interiors of the rooms sagged naked and indecent, all their privy places exposed to the high, bright day which had brought the violets into flower under the wall. As Cathal stood, shocked, in the gateway, trying to understand what he was seeing, a joist in the upper floor cracked and broke, and a shabby upright chair lurched out of the half-room and smashed on the fallen lintel of the back door.

McKier looked up at Cathal. 'What do you want now?' he said.

Tiredness was creeping through Cathal's limbs and into his back and neck. He would have to lie down; the walk had been too long for him. But the wall had fallen out of Hengardd, the yard was full of demolition rubble, and there was nowhere even to sit properly. He wondered if the Garden of Livia was still there — but the Bright Road passed through it with all its traffic, and there was nowhere there to rest. Perhaps the goat-shed . . .

He said, 'I am tired, McKier. Can you help me?'

'No. I can't help you. It was always your idea that I could, not mine, remember?'

'I need to lie down.'

'Have a gin.'

'McKier — I think I am going to die now. Here, in front of you. And I hate gin. I have always hated gin.'

But McKier, groping under the canvas stool, brought out a bottle. From under the flaps of his old coat he produced a thick, turquoise drinking cone which he half filled and passed to Cathal, indicating that he himself could drink straight from the bottle.

Cathal tried to raise the great weight of the little glass in his bruised fingers.

'Here's to next time,' he said, thinking that it was quite funny, since he was dying. He made a queer sound, but could not hear if it was a little laugh or a sob.

McKier's eyes were very close to his own, peering in, it seemed. Looking for something. His mouth was moving, and Cathal thought he said, heard him say, 'Now tell me who I am.'

With a great effort Cathal managed to hold the forefinger of his daft left hand to his lips. He smiled.

'Taceas,' he said.

There has never been a night so dark. Never has the ground been so solid, or the air so dense. Here we wait. The grass is tussocky, its blades coarse. Some drops of rain fall, slow and heavy. Just below, in the dark, the river runs over stones.

We wait. Up on the hill they, too, are waiting. Barrectus, who has turned for profit, as it was known he would; Illan's men — up there in the dark.

This time it is they who will charge downhill.

Rolled in plaids, heaped around, waiting in the dark, there are many men here at Camlann. Somewhere, here, a hand to reach out and touch in the dark, palm to palm. Kind.

The dark goes on. There is no movement in this dark place in this night; cold and still waiting.

Waiting.

There has never been a night so dark. Come closer, come. It will soon be dawn.

They moved forward towards the bright Irish chariots, side by side in the press of the hosts, shoulder-pommel to shoulder-pommel in the morning of Camlann. When the iron spear held unsteadily by young Maccudeccetus went in between his fourth and fifth ribs on the left side, he raised his palsied arm to put his hand on the trunk of the Central Tree. Drips of rain ran in the rills of the bark, curved, twisted, dropped on to lichen and old scars. Not like tears, more like time going on. Just running down the bark of the tree in unstraight courses.

GLOSSARY OF
NAMES, TERMS AND PLACES

Anglicized spellings of Celtic names are listed here in the form used in the text, but may vary in other books.

Ambrosius (Ambrosius Aurelianus): a mid-late fifth-century British war-leader, the son of a possible late Roman 'pretender' Emperor. Known to the Welsh as Emrys. The ninth-century writer Nennius tells how Ambrosius saw the red dragon of Wales and the white dragon of the Saxons fighting in a pool below the foundations of Vortigern's fortress (q.v.). A post-Roman defended settlement, Dinas Emrys, in Caernarfonshire, was found to contain a water cistern uncannily reminiscent of this tale; popularized by Geoffrey of Monmouth in the first half of the twelfth century.

Annwn (various spellings): Welsh Celtic Otherworld, adjacent to this one and at times emerging into it. Associated with youth and beauty, plenty and wealth, longevity and bliss. A parallel reality abominated by Christian missionaries and demoted by them into a sort of Hades.

Barrectus: named on a probably fifth-century memorial stone, now lost, from Tomen-y-mur, Caernarfonshire. John Morris suggests that Barrectus might have been brought down from the north of England in response to the Irish invasions of North Wales (*The Age of Arthur*, Phillimore, 1977).

The Bear: 'Arth' (meaning 'bear' in Welsh) is frequently part of a place name (e.g. Arthog, Penarth). Gildas (q.v.) refers to a 'stronghold of the Bear', and by a (slightly strained?) argument some scholars have interpreted this as a nickname or totemic name for Arthur.

Cadwallon Longhand (Catwallaun Lauhir): died 534. In power in area of approximately modern Gwynedd. Good evidence suggests that he defeated Serigi, son-in-law of King Illan (q.v). M. Millar, in her *Saints of Gwynedd*, (Boydell Press, 1979), dates this as possibly as late as the 520s.

Caer Siddi: an expression of some aspects of the Otherworld, associated with warriors, an island fortress, and calamitous results if despoiled.

Cato of Dumnonia: viewed by John Morris in *The Age of Arthur* as a significant ally of Arthur's in the wars against the Saxons. In June 1998, a sixth-century inscribed slate excavated at Tintagel (Cornwall), in Dumnonia, attributes the inception of some structure there to an ARTOGNOU, seen as a possible form of the name ARTHUR — which, if so, would support Morris's theory.

chi-rho: monogram based on the letters CH R in the Greek alphabet, originally a secret sign for 'Christ' but still in use as a symbol.

Coit Celydon (Cat Coed Celyddon): one of the battles attributed by the ninth century to Arthur. Linguistic evidence places it in South Scotland — the Caledonian Wood.

Constantius (II): Roman Emperor, 337-361.

Cunedda: a British warlord from the area around Edinburgh. The date of his transplantation/migration is a matter of debate. He and his 'sons' have a dominant rôle in Welsh tradition.

dinas: fortified, often hill-top, stronghold; usually of a local king or warlord and his immediate kin and associates, from fifth century onwards: frequently wealthy. Means 'city' in modern Welsh.

Dubglas: Literally: 'blue-black' — i.e Blackwater. Several battles attributed to Arthur by ninth century were fought over this river. Many theories as to its location have been suggested, none of which is provable.

Dyfnwal of Clyde: flourished circa 500, viewed by Morris as a significant ally in Arthur's Northern wars.

Germanus, St.: Bishop of Auxerre, 418–circa 448. Led the British to victory against Picts and Saxons when on a visit to refute Pelagian heresy, which stated that the human will is capable of good without the intervention of divine grace, in Britain. Traditionally the cry of 'Allelujah!' so horrified the opposition that they scattered with no resistance. The incident is associated with the plain of Llangollen in Powys.

Gildas, St.: sixth-century author of *De Excidio Britanniae* (*The Ruin of Britain*), which includes a long-winded, vociferous diatribe against the contemporary mid sixth-century western kings and the delinquencies into which they have fallen in the peace following the battle of Badon. The exact date of composition is arguable, but Gildas seems to state that it was 44 years after Badon.

Hengist: war-leader of the Saxon band invited by Vortigern (q.v.) and given part of Kent. The subsequent revolt of these Saxons is traditionally taken as the inception of the Anglo-Saxon conquest of Britain.

Illan: died 527. Uí Dúlainge king of Leinster, said to have made several expeditions against Ynys Môn (Anglesey) and to have been father-in-law to Serygei (Serach). Finally expelled by Cadwallon (q.v.). The date of the final expulsion is possibly as late as 520. For the purposes of this novel I have been using the early dates for Arthur's activities, as set out by Professor Leslie Alcock in *Arthur's Britain* (University of Wales Press, 1971). Here he suggests 490 for Badon and 511 for Camlann.

Kanovium: Roman fort on River Conwy, Caernarfonshire.

Kind: a social grouping usually based on blood-ties, something loosely between a clan and an extended family.

llys: hall, sometimes aisled with opposing doors in side walls and subsidiary rooms at one end: central to the social and economic functioning of the warrior society.

Maccudeccetus: Irish pagan name taken from a memorial stone of first half of the sixth century in Penrhosllugwy church, Ynys Môn.

Mac Erca (Muirchertach Macc Ercae): died 536. King of Tara, made Illan king in Leinster.

Mana: a strong spiritual power which can be harnassed for good or evil purposes.

Nemeton: a sacred clearing in a wood which may itself be sacred. Celtic; Iron Age to early Middle Ages.

Och — Ocha: used in numerous forms in Celtic languages to express both battle-rage and intense grief.

Patrick, St.: origins and dates highly contentious. He was probably a pupil of Germanus (q.v.), and died before 500. Amongst his letters is an excoriating attack on Coroticus of Clyde, ruler before Dyfnwal.

Samhain: Celtic feast of the changing of the year, celebrated on the night of our November 1. Pastoral aspect: the bringing in of the herds to home pastures. Spiritual aspect: time of greatest danger of intrusions of the Otherworld, manifested in sorcery and shape-changing.

Segontium: Roman fort, modern Caernarfon.

Siege of Badon: Arthur's most renowned victory. Site contentious. Date debatable. Here, I am following Alcock in placing it circa 490.

Tribruit: River battle attributed to Arthur by the ninth century. No evidence to suggest its locality.

Vortigern: fifth-century British leader of Romano-British extraction. Welcomed Saxon settlement in Kent and used Saxons as allies against forays by Picts. The political implications of his title (it does not seem to be a proper name) are unclear. His actions led eventually to the destruction of Britain and the emergence of England.

Ynys Môn: modern and older Welsh name for Anglesey.

SOURCES AND ACKNOWLEDGEMENTS

I am very grateful to the following for their permission to use the quotations at the front of each Book, for which they hold the copyright:

to Faber & Faber for lines from *Epoch and Artist*, David Jones, 1959;

to Mrs D. Williams for lines from *The Burning Tree*, translated by Gwyn Williams, 1956;

to David Higham Associates for the lines from Charles Williams' poem 'The Calling of Taliessin' from, *The Region of the Summer Stars*, Oxford University Press, 1944;

to the Trustees of the David Jones Estate for the lines from the poem 'The Tutelar of the Place', *Agenda*, Special Issue, vol. 5 Nos. 1–3, 1967; and for the passage from 'The Myth of Arthur', *Epoch and Artist*, Faber & Faber, 1959;

to Thomas Kinsella for the lines from his translation, *The Táin*, Oxford University Press in association with Dolmen Press, Dublin, 1969;

to Phillimore & Co., for lines from *The Age of Arthur* by John Morris, Phillimore edition, 1977;

to Thames & Hudson for lines from *By South Cadbury is that Camelot . . .* by Leslie Alcock, 1972;

to the University of Wales Press, for lines from *Arthur's Britain*, by Leslie Alcock, 1971.

'The Spoils of Annwfn' translated by Kenneth Hurlston Jackson in *Arthurian Literature in the Middle Ages: A collaborative history*. Edited by R. S. Loomis, Clarendon Press, Oxford, 1959.

The wording of the passage from Chapter 56 of Nennius' *Historia Brittonum* is reminiscent of many well-known translations but not an exact quotation of any of them; likewise the phrase from *Y Gododdin* was taken down during a lecture given by C. S. Lewis in 1959 and does not precisely match any published translation which I have since seen. The quotation from *The Mabinogion* is from the old, much-loved translation made by Lady Charlotte Guest in 1849.

Every effort has been made to reach the copyright holders of the material quoted in *On the Bright Road* and obtain their permission for its use. In the case of any oversight, please contact the publishers directly so that the correct acknowledgement can be made in subsequent editions of this book.